"Do you have an extra room, by any chance?" Damien asked.

Molly laid down a spoon and looked at him with such hope. "You'll stay here? With me?" Her relief was nearly palpable.

"I have an idea," he said, using his most businesslike tone. "How do you think Jensen would react to your having a live-in lover?"

Her beautiful mouth dropped open, and her eyes widened with shock. Then she laughed, that full-bodied, head-thrown-back laughter he remembered from when he'd first met her. His own smile widened in response to it. Even her child giggled and patted its sticky hands together.

How would it be if Molly touched him with a bit of that caring she showed so easily to her family? She must have some to spare. It needn't be anything permanent. Love certainly wasn't necessary, or even something he wanted from her. That would be a little too deep for comfort. He wished only for a taste of how it would feel to know someone cared.

Dear Reader,

It's the beginning of a new year, and Intimate Moments is ready to kick things off with six more fabulously exciting novels. Readers have been clamoring for Linda Turner to create each new installment of her wonderful miniseries THOSE MARRYING McBRIDES! In *Never Been Kissed* she honors those wishes with the deeply satisfying tale of virginal nurse Janey McBride and Dr. Reilly Jones, who's just the man to teach her how wonderful love can be when you share it with the right man.

A YEAR OF LOVING DANGEROUSLY continues to keep readers on the edge of their seats with *The Spy Who Loved Him*, bestselling author Merline Lovelace's foray into the dangerous jungles of Central America, where the loving is as steamy as the air. And you won't want to miss *My Secret Valentine*, the enthralling conclusion to our in-line 36 HOURS spin-off. As always, Marilyn Pappano delivers a page-turner you won't be able to resist. Ruth Langan begins a new trilogy, THE SULLIVAN SISTERS, with *Awakening Alex*, sure to be another bestseller. Lyn Stone's second book for the line, *Live-In Lover*, is sure to make you her fan. Finally, welcome brand-new New Zealand sensation Frances Housden. In *The Man for Maggie* she makes a memorable debut, one that will have you crossing your fingers that her next book will be out soon.

Enjoy! And come back next month, when the excitement continues here in Silhouette Intimate Moments.

Yours,

Leslie J. Wainger
Executive Senior Editor

Please address questions and book requests to:
Silhouette Reader Service
U.S.: 3010 Walden Ave., P.O. Box 1325, Buffalo, NY 14269
Canadian: P.O. Box 609, Fort Erie, Ont. L2A 5X3

Live-In Lover
LYN STONE

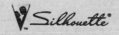

INTIMATE MOMENTS™

Published by Silhouette Books

America's Publisher of Contemporary Romance

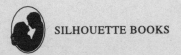 **SILHOUETTE BOOKS**

ISBN 0-373-27125-5

LIVE-IN LOVER

This edition published by arrangement with Harlequin Books S.A.

® and TM are trademarks of Harlequin Books S.A., used under license. Trademarks indicated with ® are registered in the United States Patent and Trademark Office, the Canadian Trade Marks Office and in other countries.

Visit Silhouette at www.eHarlequin.com

Printed in U.S.A.

LYN STONE

loves creating pictures with words. Paints, too. Her love affair with writing and art began in the third grade, when she won a school-wide prize for her colorful poster for book week. She spent the prize money on books, one of which was *Little Women.*

She rewrote the ending so that Jo marries her childhood sweetheart. That's because Lyn had a childhood sweetheart herself and wanted to marry him when she grew up. She did. And now she is living her "happily-ever-after" in north Alabama with the same guy. She and Allen have traveled the world, had two children, four grandchildren and experienced some wild adventures along the way.

Whether writing romantic historicals or contemporary fiction, Lyn insists on including elements of humor, mystery and danger. Perhaps because that other book she purchased all those years ago was a Nancy Drew story.

In appreciation for pep talks and the lively exchange of ideas, this book is dedicated to fellow adventure lovers Debra Webb, Dianne Hamilton, Martha Kreiger, Mary Bauer and Rhonda Nelson.

Chapter 1

Damien Perry popped the cap off his bottle of Guinness, shook his head and laughed, a mirthless sound, as most of his laughs were these days. Sad commentary when a man had to check where a message came from to determine who he was supposed to be.

His thumb traced the postmark on the unopened envelope that lay on the bunk beside him. *Nashville, Tennessee.* Ah, yes, his role as an assassin.

He'd spent almost a decade now assuming other accents and identities, and the job was getting old. The Bureau loaned him out to other agencies for joint operations as if he were a piece of office equipment.

He had considered resigning. Government pay was atrocious, even with the hefty allowance for designer clothes on assignments such as his last one. The investments he'd made with his inheritance would insure he never had to work again.

But what would he do if he quit? Hang out a shingle and use his law degree?

Damien scoffed and took a good, long swig off his stout. He kicked off his deck shoes and got comfortable, determined to enjoy this leisure even if it killed him. If he didn't gear down between jobs, he'd burn out for certain.

The plain white envelope lay there as if daring him to rip it open, so he did. No letter inside, just a small rectangle of beige linen card stock.

He smiled for real when he read the name on it. *Marian Olivia Jensen.* He only knew one Jensen from Nashville. It had to be her. What on earth could Molly want from him? He flipped the card over and read the handwritten message on the back. *Please call. I need your help. This is urgent. M.J.*

He lay back on the narrow bunk in the cabin of the *Anna Louise* and held the card aloft to examine it further. The line beneath her name bore the words "Freelance Graphics." Below that a post office box, phone and fax numbers.

How had she gotten the address of the post office box where he occasionally docked? Few knew of it.

The Bureau had used the Florida address a couple of times to contact him since he had been working the boat thefts up and down the lower east coast.

Now that the DEA had rounded up the smugglers who had been appropriating private craft for their runs, Damien was taking six weeks' leave on his rented sloop to wind down.

When he'd gone into the small post office branch to cancel the box this morning, the mail clerk had given him the envelope.

Michael Duvek, the regional director in Memphis, must have given Molly Jensen the address. Other than her brother, Duvek was the only person they really knew in common.

But Damien hardly knew her at all. They had met only twice while he was in the hospital in Memphis after that

Nashville fiasco. The acquaintance was memorable for him, despite its brevity. A bright ray of sun on one of his darkest days there six months ago.

She had been visiting her brother, Ford Devereaux, the agent he had shared the semiprivate room with after they'd both been wounded. Absently, he ran a finger over the puckered red scar on his right side, just below his ribs.

Strange that she should remember him. Damien had just come from surgery and recovery and was barely conscious when Devereaux introduced his sister. What a smile to wake up to. Unforgettable.

The next time she had visited, they had gone down the hall together for coffee—no fun task in his barely ambulatory condition—to give Devereaux and his fiancée a little privacy.

So that was the extent of their acquaintance, his and Molly Jensen's, a drugged-out how-do-you-do, terrible coffee, and a quarter hour of conversation.

But Damien could never forget a woman like Devereaux's sister, no matter how short the association. Just thinking about her made him smile with remembered pleasure.

She was tall, a few inches shy of six feet. Lithe and graceful, but too energetic for a model. She'd moved more like an athlete. Perfect skin, auburn hair that shone like polished copper and a laugh that made her green eyes sparkle like gems. Such expressive eyes, he remembered.

Damien recalled how much he had wanted to touch her. Not sexually, exactly, though the idea certainly had merit. But just to see whether her joie de vivre was tangible, maybe even contagious. It had been.

As luck would have it, she had touched him first, just an arm beneath his to lend support. He'd been infinitely glad to be alive in that moment.

He looked at the card one more time and got up, sliding his bare feet into his shoes. What would she need him for so urgently? Though this certainly stirred his curiosity, answering her summons might not be a wise move.

She hadn't mentioned a husband, but she was most likely married. He knew she had a very young child because she had whipped out pictures and bragged that day.

A baby girl who was not especially photogenic. A smile tugged at his lips. In the photos it had worn one of those ruffled garter-looking things around its bald head and a fancy dress to match. He clearly remembered the poor thing only had two teeth shining in that wide grin.

Now why had he wasted brain cells storing inconsequential details such as that?

Damien didn't care much for children. At least, he didn't think he did. As it happened, he'd never had the opportunity to know any close at hand. Judging solely on what others had said about them, they were messy little creatures, noisy and wildly unpredictable.

No, it definitely would not be smart to reply to this message of Molly Jensen's, given that she was married and a mother and he had felt a definite attraction. Forbidden fruit always tempted him and Damien had learned the hard way to steer a wide course around it.

This time he wouldn't. He wanted to see her again. If she happened to be off limits, so be it. Nothing said he had to pursue her.

Ignoring his better judgment, Damien slipped on a shirt and headed out to the phone booth by the marina. She'd stirred his curiosity. He would find out just why she thought she *did* need him.

The skills he possessed might be in demand in some quarters of the world, but surely not in that of a wholesome young wife and mother like Molly Jensen.

Molly wrapped her arms tighter around the sleeping toddler and pressed her lips against the silky curls on her crown. ''Oh, Syd, what's Mama gonna do?''

The phone rang for the fourth time and the answering machine kicked on. She listened to her own voice on the recorded message and waited for the beep. Molly dreaded hearing the laugh, that menacing, deep-throated chuckle. She had endured three of these calls already since noon. Their frequency was increasing.

If she answered, he might talk to her, offering more of those snide, oily questions of concern for her and Sydney that only she recognized as threats. That would be worse than these wordless messages, yet just knowing who it was on the line in no way lessened the terror.

"Hello, Mrs. Jensen," a deep voice said. "Damien Perry here. I received your card. If you would like—"

She snatched up the receiver. "Wait! Don't hang up! Hold on a minute, I have to put the baby down."

She ran to the playpen, carefully laid the sleeping toddler next to her teddy bear, and hurried back. "Sorry. I would have answered right away, but I thought… Well, never mind that now. Are you here? In Nashville?"

"No, I'm not. I'm just responding to your—"

"How soon can you come? You can, can't you? I mean, I'm at my wit's end here, and I thought since you were a good friend of Ford's and he's not in country, and Mr. Duvek couldn't—"

"Calm down, Mrs. Jensen. You're speaking too rapidly for me to understand you. Are you in trouble?"

"It's *Ms.* not Mrs. No, it's *Molly* to you, but that's not important. I really need your help—and right away if you can come. Please! It's a matter of life and death."

"Whose death?" he demanded, his words curt.

"Mine," she said, swallowing hard to stifle a moan. "And maybe Sydney's, too."

"Sydney?"

"My baby. Remember? Please, will you come? I honestly don't have anyone else I can turn to. It's too much to ask, I know, but I can pay you for this. Whatever you charge, I can pay you. Maybe not all at once, but we can work something out."

"Wait. Before you go any further, tell me exactly what it is that you want me to do."

"Help me make him stop. I can't stand this anymore. He's called three times today and—"

"Do you know who it is?" he interrupted.

"Yes!" she exclaimed, shuddering. "My ex-husband."

"Molly, listen to me," the voice ordered. "Calm down. I want you to make certain all of your doors and windows are locked, and after that—"

"They *are* locked!"

"Fine. Now, have you informed the police? You'll need an Order of Protection."

"I have one, and I've called until I'm blue in the face, and even went down to the station and talked to them. They won't *do* anything because I can't prove it's him. They can't unless *he* does something and I can prove it. That could be too late. Are you coming or not?"

A long silence followed before he said, "Yes. I'll be there tomorrow."

"Thank God," she whispered, clutching the phone to her chest with both hands. "Oh, thank you." Soon now. Soon it would be over and she and Syd would be safe.

A small measure of her terror had lifted just hearing Damien Perry's voice. That deep, velvety I-will-handle-it tone soothed something within Molly, made her able to close her eyes and breathe more deeply. It renewed her hope, a severely eroded commodity these past three weeks.

Not that she liked the idea of calling on a man to solve her problems, but she had exhausted all her own resources. The police must think she was crazy, calling them about threats that, when repeated, seemed totally harmless. The best they could do was enforce a restraining order, which in itself was as useful as a boat full of holes. Even if the police hauled him in, Jack could be out on bond the same day.

She fastened her attention on Sydney, who still slept in the playpen in the corner by the television. Her precious baby, her Syd, the person she loved most in the world. The threat encompassed her, too, just because she was Molly's weak spot.

How could she ever make people believe a man would threaten his own daughter? They had barely believed him capable of hurting his wife, and most people blamed *her* for that. Everyone but the judge.

The female judge who heard the case was the only one who had bought the truth about him. Thank God she had. But Molly was still the only one in the world who knew exactly what Jack Jensen was capable of.

Molly remembered how he'd approached her last month, the Sunday after they'd released him from jail. He had publicly begged her forgiveness and pleaded for a reconciliation. Right outside in the churchyard after services. Jack couldn't have picked a place with a larger audience of people who knew them, and she knew that the choice was deliberate on his part.

She hadn't been nice in refusing him. He wanted her back, all right, and she knew why. To make her life a living hell. Again.

He had called the next day, more insistent, his tone more threatening than the actual words he used. "A woman shouldn't live alone, Molly," he'd said. "You know, all kinds of things might happen. Just you and your baby, all by yourselves in that great big house. It's scary to think about, isn't it? But I want you to think about it. Think hard."

She shuddered, recalling the way Jack had laughed that grate-on-the-nerves chuckle that made her skin crawl.

Now when he called he never said anything, probably because he knew the court protection order was supposed to bar any communication. But he had found a way.

Jack was a master of intimidation. He had used fear to hold her once before, but Molly was determined not to cave in again.

Some days he parked outside, just sitting in his car, as though daring her to go out. When she did, he followed her until he caught her in a situation where he could apologize again, in front of her mother and several of their friends.

Jack had acted like a heartbroken husband who couldn't bear to live without her. But Molly knew what he really wanted.

She could read his intentions in his dark, narrowed eyes, hear it in the promises that must sound tempting to anyone who didn't know him as she did. Jack wanted *revenge.*

At first, he might have planned to take it privately, but she hadn't been stupid enough to go back to him, thank God. Now that she'd made it clear she wouldn't do that, he'd obviously decided on another method of retaliation. He would terrorize her until he grew tired of it, and who knew what he would do after that? Since the frequency of his calls was escalating, she feared she was about to find out.

Given his doubts about Sydney's paternity, Molly feared as much for the baby as she did for herself. Maybe she should have insisted on giving him proof with a DNA test, but after Syd's birth, she hadn't wanted him to believe that he was the father. No way would she share her baby with that maniac. When Sydney was born, Molly was already in the process of divorcing him and he had been in lockup.

She curled into a ball on the end of the sofa near the loaded pistol. With all her might, she fought the exhaustion that threatened to close her eyes. A nap seemed too risky, as had sleep the night before.

"Hurry and come, Damien," she pleaded with the man she had decided to trust. "Please."

In spite of her efforts, Molly knew she had fallen asleep when the doorbell woke her. Sunlight spilled through the windows. She'd slept all night. Cursing herself for her lapse, she grabbed the gun.

Sydney stirred and would be waking soon for her breakfast. Molly prayed she would sleep a little longer. The doorbell chimed again before she reached it. Molly looked through the peephole.

With a huge sigh of relief, she slipped the chain off, unlocked the dead bolt and pulled the door open. "Thank goodness, I was afraid you'd change your mind. Come in, please."

She stepped back to let him move past her, then hurriedly closed the door and fastened the locks. Suddenly she felt safer than she had in weeks.

"Allow me," he said evenly, taking the pistol from her hand, "before you shoot one of us." He clicked on the safety and slipped it into his jacket pocket.

Then he smiled wryly, just a slight stretch of the lips, the corners barely turning up. "Hello again, by the way."

"Hi, yourself," Molly replied, her gaze riveted on his mouth. She forced herself to blink and look away, embarrassed by her reaction to him. He was still a heart-stopper, even more so than the last time they'd met.

She shrugged and held up her hands, empty now of the weapon and feeling useless. "I almost didn't recognize you with your clothes on." She laughed at herself. "I mean...that hospital gown, you know... So, I see you're well now. Aren't you? Well?"

"Quite recovered, thank you," he replied, and inclined

his head. The smile was no wider, but his eyes warmed with humor.

Lord, his voice soothed like melted chocolate, she thought. Smooth, rich English chocolate, if there was such a thing. Just a faint accent that did funny things to her stomach.

He surely did *look* well. Fantastic, in fact. Molly tried to be less obvious in her scrutiny, but it was hard. The man was a hunk, no denying it. Shoulders like a fullback and a face that would wring sighs out of a zealous nun.

If she didn't watch herself here, she'd be wallowing in a deep case of hero worship. Well, he *was* a hero. Hadn't he come to save her and Syd? Just like that, he'd come to the rescue without even knowing all the details. A guy just didn't get much more heroic than that, in her opinion.

Her right hand started up to brush that sun-streaked wave off his tanned forehead. She stopped just in time, inwardly cursing her eagerness to touch. He hadn't retreated. Hadn't moved or even blinked. He just watched her with an intensity that nearly mesmerized.

Lord, didn't he have the bluest eyes she had ever seen? Azure. Her favorite color.

She yanked her attention off his face and stared past him toward the kitchen. If she didn't curb this adolescent behavior of hers, he would never take her seriously.

"I was about to fix breakfast. You want some?" She asked.

"Just coffee if you have it. Or tea would be fine."

"Tea? For breakfast? Oh, you mean *hot*..."

He smiled again, this time full-out, and Molly thought her heart might stop for good, once it quit bonging around in her chest like a Super Ball. She'd forgotten those perfect teeth. And the dimples. Good grief, no wonder she was babbling like an idiot.

"Whatever you're having will be fine," he said.

A loud, piercing wail erupted. Molly turned and dashed down the hallway into the den to get Sydney before she woke up the entire neighborhood.

"Okay, babe, hang in there. Juice coming up. Dry pants first." Molly ripped the night diaper's tapes loose and began changing her.

"Is it hurt?" he asked above Syd's noisy fretting.

"What?" Molly asked, confused. *It?* "Syd? Oh, no, she's fine. Just wet and hungry."

She pressed down the last tape on the diaper and hefted Syd out of the playpen. Shifting her handily onto one hip, Molly headed to the kitchen. "Come on."

Quickly she plopped the baby in the high chair, washed her hands and poured a sippy-cup full of apple juice. "Like shutting off a siren, isn't it?" she asked with a laugh as Syd gulped the juice.

His mouth quirked slightly to one side as he watched.

Molly dropped several vanilla wafers onto the highchair tray. "Sit down," she invited. "I'll put on the coffee."

She took the basket of yesterday's blueberry muffins out of the microwave, uncovered them, and set them on the table. "You want eggs and bacon? I think I have some in the fridge."

"No, thank you," he said politely, clasping his hands together on the tabletop. "Shall we get down to business, Ms. Jensen?"

"Sure. And please call me Molly. I mean, as long as you and Ford are such good friends—"

He looked ready to argue, and Molly didn't think it was about the first name issue. She supposed he thought asking for this kind of help was too much, even for the sister of a friend and fellow agent. And it was, of course. She had known that up front.

"Look, maybe I was wrong to call you. I've really no

right to involve you in this mess even if you are Ford's buddy."

Even as she let him off the hook with her words, she begged him with her eyes to consider helping her. *Come on, Damien, please!*

He considered what she'd said—and most likely her silent message, too—quietly, and at some length while Molly waited breathlessly for him to assure her he would help.

"You say you think your life is in danger?" he asked calmly.

Molly cleared her throat and looked away from him so she could think straight. "Yes, I do. I believe my ex-husband is insane."

"And you believe him capable of violence?" he asked.

She raised her chin and faced him, mimicking his cool regard. "Yes, Damien, he certainly is capable of that."

He nodded slightly and thought for another minute. Molly liked the way he considered the angles before making a decision. She wished she had that trait.

"Then we had better prevent that, hadn't we?" he said.

"You *are* going to help us?" Before she could stop herself, Molly had reached out and grasped his hands. His large, wonderful, capable hands.

Only one eyebrow raised. "I would be delighted."

He would be delighted. She had to smile at that.

Damien Perry just took her breath away. She loved to hear him talk. If only the subject matter were a little less macabre, she would just sit back and enjoy the daylights out of it.

But she hadn't called him in on this because he sounded cute or because his fantastic looks made the backs of her knees sweat. She needed a man who could handle the situation. She had no doubt that when Damien Perry said he would—delighted or not—he surely *would*.

Suddenly she realized she was still holding his hands between hers and released him. "Oh, sorry," she mumbled.

"Quite all right," he said, flexing his fingers as though she had squeezed them too hard.

Molly rose, her movements deliberate and careful as she poured two cups of steaming coffee, placed them on the table and took her seat. She peeled the paper cup from a muffin, reached over and placed it on the tray of the high chair.

Sydney promptly christened it with apple juice, leaned over and bit off the soggy top.

"Have a muffin. I'll fill you in on what's happened so far."

His aristocratic nose wrinkled the tiniest bit when Sydney grinned at him, her mouth full of purple mush. "Thank you, no. I believe I'll pass on the muffin."

Molly shrugged. Maybe it wasn't fair to bring a friend of her brother's in on this. But Damien Perry had struck her from their very first meeting as a man who could take care of business. Even wounded as he'd been at the time, he had projected an aura of strength and capability that impressed her.

She flatly rejected the thought that there might be another reason his name came to mind when she needed help.

So what if he was handsome as sin itself? Was it a crime to admire his good looks? She was human, wasn't she? And an artist, too. One who appreciated beauty in all its forms. That's all she felt for this man, admiration and appreciation.

All right, maybe she'd felt a little infatuation for him initially, but surely that was normal. Every woman he met must feel that. As soon as she got used to him, it would go away.

Damien was a man of the world and, she suspected, a loner. And that was fine with Molly. That signaled safety. She was definitely not looking for another man in her life when she couldn't even dodge the mistake she'd made the first time.

All she wanted was Damien's help. Then he could go on his merry way and she could enjoy a couple of secret fantasies about him now and then. No harm in that.

''Tell me about it,'' he suggested softly.

Molly jerked her head up and stared into those azure eyes. She almost blurted out exactly what she was thinking, then caught herself. ''Oh, you mean about Jack.''

He nodded, an all-too-knowing look in his eyes. ''Of course. What else?''

Chapter 2

Damien wondered exactly what Molly Jensen saw when she looked at him and why he seemed to disconcert her so much. It couldn't be his job. Her brother was also an agent, so that would hold little awe for her.

He supposed it could be attraction on her part, because it certainly was on his. If that was the case, acting on it would suit him just fine, but he knew it was out of the question. Women like Molly didn't engage in casual sex and brief affairs. They were nurturers at heart, earth-mother types, wife material. Not for him.

She began explaining in a matter-of-fact way how she came to know the man she had married, how he had browbeat her for months until they'd endured a showdown that had ended it all.

During Molly's recital of events, Damien watched with some interest as she gave her daughter more food.

The child had disgusting habits, Damien thought as he sipped his coffee. For all he knew, maybe all children did.

So far, this one had done nothing to endear itself to him. He supposed he could claim admiration for the high decibel level it could reach. It could feed itself, which surprised him.

Somehow he had expected it would still be bald and practically toothless. But this one had grown considerably since Molly had taken those photos of it. It had hair now, curlier and a much lighter red than Molly's. The wide eyes had a greenish tint, but not so green as hers. Bluer, he noted.

They dressed exactly alike, mother and daughter, in dark green sweats with bright red hearts stitched on the left breast. She fascinated him, this odd little Molly Jensen clone, almost as much as her beautiful mother did.

"So, what do you think?" Molly asked.

"Hmm?"

"Oh, that's what I like in a man. Attention. Were you even listening?"

"Of course. Your ex made the calls, you've gotten the protection order…and…?"

"The police won't arrest him unless he *does* something to me. Something they can nail down, anyway. By that time it could be too late. I sent him to jail, Damien, and I'm afraid he's going to kill me for it. And he might kill Sydney, too. He hates that she exists."

Damien gave her his undivided attention. Whether she had real cause or not, Molly Jensen was convinced their lives were in danger. He still thought she was probably blowing things out of proportion and overreacting to the harassment.

No doubt her ex was bitter about spending a night or two behind bars. The cops had likely hauled him in for disturbing the peace and to give him a chance to cool off after the argument she'd mentioned. Now he was playing on

Molly's fear to get back at her for it. Once Damien scared the life out of him, he'd back off quickly enough.

"Is there any way to make him stop?" she asked quietly.

Too quietly, he thought. She sounded like a child herself at the moment. A very frightened child who had no idea what to do next. Her deep green eyes looked to him for answers and her bottom lip quivered slightly.

Damien felt something turn over in his chest at the sight. At the moment, he wanted to strangle Jack Jensen with his bare hands for putting that look on her face.

He could do that, but he wouldn't, of course. Was it possible that she *thought* he would? He had no idea what her brother had told her about their brief encounter.

Six months ago he had gone undercover as an assassin for hire to apprehend right-wingers who wanted rid of a senator visiting in Nashville. One of the Bureau's informants had blown that scheme out of the water while Damien was recuperating from a gunshot. Good thing, since Damien's cover had evaporated with the shooting and resulting publicity. Once he'd recovered, he had gone down to Florida on his next assignment.

Molly might think that his badge made him immune to prosecution, that it would allow him to act as judge, jury and executioner. He'd have to set her straight on that. Intimidating Jensen into behaving himself was about the best he could offer in this situation.

"We'll think of something," he assured her. He would have a talk with the police, then throw a scare into Jensen. That should take care of it.

Those long, graceful fingers of hers worried her trembling lip a second or two before she spoke. "It...it's not as though I did anything to deserve all this, you know?"

Damien almost reached for her then, but clenched his fists instead. "No, no, of course you didn't! The thought never entered my mind."

With a sigh she crossed her arms and faced him again. "I'm not imagining this, really," Molly told him. "He nearly succeeded the last time he tried to kill me."

"He what?" Damien demanded, straightening in his chair.

"Tried to kill me," she said with a shiver. "And he meant business. You should have seen his eyes."

Damien noted the way her fingers dug into the fabric of her sleeves where she grasped her upper arms. She paid no attention to the child who was rhythmically banging her palms on the tray of the high chair.

"Find a paper and pen. Begin at the beginning and tell me everything, in minute detail," Damien ordered curtly. "I want dates, times, names of anyone who was involved."

Molly pulled a magnetic notepad and pen off the refrigerator, ripped off her grocery list, tossed the leaf in the trash bin and sat down. She pushed the ballpoint and small tablet across the table to him.

"Well, you see, we had this fight," she said, avoiding eye contact as though the fact embarrassed her. He watched her absently rub the side of her head with two fingers. "Jack did two years in County for assaulting me. He swore I set him up but I had a great lawyer and a *very* sympathetic judge. She gave him the maximum sentence. When he got out, he called and said he wanted to get back together. I said no." She uttered a mirthless little half laugh. "Actually, I phrased it a little more harshly than that."

Damien tensed. *Two years?* What the hell had Jensen done to her? "How badly were you hurt?"

Molly smiled and made a fist, massaging the backs of her knuckles with the other hand. "I gave *almost* as good as I got. Landed a good one on his jaw. Amazing what you can do when you're cornered." She shook her fist as though it still ached from the blow she had delivered.

"He hit you," Damien growled.

"Mmm-hmm. And choked me. After I broke away and slugged him back, he got in the parting shot." She shrugged. "I fell backward and hit my head. Bled quite a bit and had a...concussion. Guess I looked pretty bad."

Damien clamped down the sudden, murderous fury that shook him and struggled to remain objective. Molly was no frail victim. She was tall, strong, and courageous as hell. But she was still a woman. And, judging by the age of the child, she must have been pregnant at the time of the attack.

Damien decided he had better not dwell on the incident or he'd come totally unhinged. He cleared his throat and concentrated on taking notes.

"After you refused to reconcile, has he done anything overt to make you think he might resort to violence again?"

Molly looked down and flexed her long-fingered hands with their short, unpolished nails. "Oh, yeah. After I had a date."

"A date," Damien repeated, writing it down. "Which date and with whom?"

"My first and only since the divorce. The date took place a week ago. I went to a concert with Joe Malia, a guy who worked at the museum where I was a receptionist."

Damien looked up at her. "I thought you were in graphic arts."

"I freelance. Brochures, logos, illustrations for ads and such. My day job was part-time at the state museum downtown. I got fired yesterday. Jack's responsible. Or rather, his father is. The man has connections on the board."

Damien understood that Molly would probably attribute everything bad that happened to her to her ex-husband and his family. A natural assumption, and he wouldn't argue it just yet. It might be true.

"You used past tense for the man you dated. Was Malia fired, as well?"

Molly looked directly at him then, her eyes darkened

with sadness and roiling anger. "Joe died two days after we went out together. Hit-and-run."

Damien almost broke the pen. "Murder, you think?"

"Well, Jack called me the next day and warned me nicely to be extra careful crossing the street."

When Damien said nothing, she swallowed hard and went on. "Look, Jack was always insanely jealous, but I swear he had no reason to be. He wouldn't believe that, though, and accused me of having someone else's baby. That's what the fight was about, the one that he was jailed for."

The *one* he was jailed for? That indicated it was not an isolated occurrence.

Damien stared down at the notepad, hoping she couldn't detect his rage. All she needed was another irate male around her. He had to remain calm about this and get all the facts.

"I see," he said finally, though he didn't see at all. How could she have stayed with the man after the first episode of violence? He had never understood it. Why would any woman do that, especially this one?

Damien could understand a man being jealous of Molly, but he doubted Jensen had gone after Malia with a *car*. The hit-and-run was most likely an accident and Jensen had merely used it to frighten Molly when he heard Malia was dead.

Using a vehicle to murder someone left too much to chance. No one with any sense used that method. Then again, Jensen certainly could be homicidal without being sensible.

The baby broke the silence. Her dainty hands continued to pound the layer of purple pudding she had concocted out of the muffin and juice mixture.

Slowly, Molly got up and began to clean up the mess as though it was a morning ritual. "I really need to get Syd and my mother out of town as soon as possible. Only I can't think of where they could go that Jack couldn't find them. He knows everybody we know. Well, except you, of course.''

"That would be wise. I'll handle it," Damien said.

Arranging for a safe place would be relatively easy. Getting Molly to go and then stay with them might pose a problem.

"Thanks," she said quietly with a look of profound gratitude, and reached out to squeeze his hand.

The brief touch, just like the others, triggered something unfamiliar inside him. Not lust. Desire was already a given and had been since she had opened the door this morning. Maybe even before that, if he were honest with himself. There had been a stirring of it when he'd received her message in Florida and remembered her from their first meeting. This other not-lust thing, however, he didn't want to examine too closely.

He silently observed while she microwaved a bowl of instant oatmeal with cinnamon and sat again, this time to feed her daughter properly with a spoon.

"My mea," the child announced, sticking her finger in the bowl and addressing Damien directly for the first time.

"Yes, I see," Damien answered, unsure how to converse with anyone that age but glad for the momentary diversion.

"Seeee!" she parroted, spewing fine bits of the oatmeal through her teeth and onto his favorite jacket.

"Stop that, Sydney!" Molly ordered firmly. "Don't spit on the nice man."

She shot him an apologetic look. "Sorry, Syd's only nineteen months, but I think she's hitting the Terrible Twos a little early."

Damien watched the small lips quiver. *Poor little thing. She hadn't meant to spit.*

"It's all right, really," he said, hoping to avoid another

test of his tolerance for high-pitched sound. "She did stop when you said she should." He smiled at the child to reassure her he wasn't angry.

Molly nodded. "Yep. Syd's brilliant."

"Mmm," Damien murmured noncommittally. It seemed a typically mother-like thing for her to say.

Damien had never thought much about motherhood and all it entailed, likely because he couldn't remember the woman who had given birth to him. His uncle, a widower in his fifties, had adopted him when Damien was orphaned at age three.

A succession of housekeepers had provided only glimpses of what a mother around the house must be like.

Damien suddenly felt a tremendous lack, where before there had been only a blank space inside him he hadn't realized existed.

He couldn't chance that what had happened to him might happen to this child. Losing a parent must be the worst event possible for a little one.

Unless, of course, it was a parent like Jensen. He had to keep Molly safe so she could continue to give all she was giving to her child.

"You'll go with your mother and daughter, of course," he informed her.

She shook her head firmly. "Can't do that. Jack would just wait until I came home and start all this again. I think we'd better get this settled while you're around to help me, don't you?"

She had a point, he admitted reluctantly. Molly was right about one thing, the police would not intervene unless her ex-husband did something they construed as dangerous.

Maybe he should allow her to stay here. Together, they might draw Jensen out, make him lose his cool in front of witnesses and threaten her publicly. Even if that was not enough to get the local cops to arrest him, Damien might be able to frighten him severely enough so that he'd give up his plan for revenge and leave Molly alone.

It was a long shot and probably not a permanent fix. The success of it would depend directly on Jack Jensen's sanity. Unfortunately, there were few alternatives.

"Do you have an extra room by any chance?" he asked.

She laid the spoon down and looked at him with such hope, he felt guilty that he had ever considered not helping her even if his hesitation had lasted only seconds.

"You'll stay here? With me?" Her relief was nearly palpable. "You're terrific, you know that? I am so grateful, Damien. Ford will be, too."

As if anyone could drag him away, Damien thought with a wry twist of his lips. Regardless of the reason for it, that brother of hers might not be all that thrilled with the idea of a virtual stranger bunking in with his sister. From the way they had acted in the hospital, Damien knew Molly and Ford must be quite close.

How would it be if Molly touched him with a bit of that caring she showed so easily to her daughter and her brother? She must have some to spare. It needn't be anything permanent, or anywhere near the depth of what she felt for her family.

Love certainly wasn't necessary, or even something he wanted from her. That would be a little too deep for comfort. He only wished for a taste of how it would feel to know someone cared a bit, that was all.

"I have an idea," he said, using his most business-like tone. "How do you think Jensen would react to your having a live-in lover?"

Her beautiful mouth dropped open and her eyes widened with shock. Then she laughed. Ah, that full-bodied, head-thrown-back laughter he remembered from when he'd first met her. His own smile widened in response to it. Even the child giggled and patted its sticky hands together.

Was it so ridiculous, his suggestion?

"Jack would go berserk, if he's not there already," she said with a droll expression. "Not that he still cares about me, even in a twisted way. But he sure wouldn't want me to find anybody else. After him. He always said…" Her voice trailed off and her expression darkened. "No, I don't want what happened to Joe to happen to you, Damien. We'd better scratch that plan."

"We have to draw him out somehow and I believe this will work. I can take care of myself, Molly. And I'll take care of you, as well. Trust me?"

She worried her bottom lip with her teeth for a moment, then nodded.

He stood and held out his hand to her. Molly hesitated only a moment and then shook it to set their deal. To his surprise, she held on.

"Me!" the baby demanded, reaching for him. Hesitantly, Damien extended his left index finger. The small oatmeal-coated hand closed around it, wagging in parody of a handshake.

For a moment Damien stood there speechless, a part of something for which he had no frame of reference. But it felt incredibly good.

Then he cleared his throat, disentangled himself and rested his hands on his hips. "Fine, then. Why don't you pack some things for the child while I make some arrangements by phone? Then we'll collect your mother and—"

"We'll have to wait until she comes home from work at six," Molly interrupted.

He nodded. "Better to make the move at night, anyway."

She turned away then and crossed her arms over her chest. "I'll miss Syd." Damien watched her supple fingers knead her upper arms. A self-comforting gesture, he supposed.

Before he knew what he was doing, Damien had placed his hand on her shoulder to add what he could to that comfort. "Everything will work out, Molly," he assured her. "I'll see to it."

Her sudden smile was a thing to behold. "*We'll* see to it together," she said. Then she patted his hand and moved out from under his grasp to retrieve the child from her high chair.

"Go stow your gear in the guest room, *lover*," she quipped with a brave chuckle that sounded forced. "I have to wonder if anybody in the world's going to buy this hoax."

Again, she laughed, ruefully this time, as she shifted the baby to one hip. "You...and me together? An unlikely match, for sure." She shook her head, rolled her beautiful eyes heavenward and sighed as though the whole idea seemed incredibly bizarre to her.

Damien wasn't laughing. "Oh, they'll buy it," he said softly, seriously. Then to himself, "I'd buy it if I could afford it."

The hours crawled by as they waited for six o'clock. Molly tried to make the time comfortable for Damien, while he seemed determined to make her even more nervous that she already was.

Instead of watching television to while away the time, he watched her. Everything she did, from unloading the dishwasher to folding clothes, he apparently found fascinating.

Syd got the same treatment. She might as well have been an alien from another planet under close observation by a scientist. Damien kept his distance, but rarely let either of them out of his sight for long.

The few breaks they'd had from all that attention were trips to the bathroom and once when he excused himself to make a fairly lengthy phone call to arrange a safe place for her mother and Sydney.

He also checked her security. She already knew it was little better than adequate. There were no fancy cameras or laser beams installed, but there would be an alarm at the police station if anyone broke in.

She'd known she couldn't depend on simple door and window locks and so had bought an inexpensive alarm system. Under the circumstances, she would have gone without groceries to finance that.

And speaking of groceries, it was time to buy some if she planned to feed a full-grown man. He'd been a sport about eating the peanut butter sandwiches and macaroni and cheese for lunch, but that wouldn't satisfy a guy his size for long.

She plopped down onto the sofa beside him and plumped up the pillow next to her. "What shall I buy to cook while you're here? Any preferences?"

"We'll eat out," he said decisively.

"Not every meal, surely!" she exclaimed. "That's way too expensive."

"I'll take care of it. We need to be visible as a couple if we want Jensen to find out about us."

She punched the pillow. "Oh, Jack will find out, all right. Don't worry about that. I wouldn't be surprised if he already knows I have a man in the house."

"If he really was responsible for Joe Malia's death, then we should expect him to react to this fairly soon. Probably within the next few days."

With effort, Molly tamped down her fear enough to sound matter-of-fact. "I almost hope he will, just as soon as I get Syd and Mama somewhere safe. This waiting for the other shoe to drop is making me crazy."

"I can well imagine," he said.

She sighed. "I'd sure like to get this straightened out

before Ford gets home. I'm afraid he'll go after Jack and get himself in trouble.''

"How long will he be away?" Damien asked.

Molly wondered if they ever discussed their cases with each other when they weren't working together. "A month, maybe more. He's on that detail as liaison with your European counterparts.''

"Ah, the car smuggling ring?" he asked.

"That's it. Mary's there in Bonn with him. They said they'll be going on to Switzerland for a vacation after he's finished working.''

"Well, they should enjoy that," he said, looking distinctly uncomfortable.

"I'm surprised they didn't send you, too," Molly commented. "After all, I expect you're more familiar with that part of the world than Ford is.''

Damien smiled and fiddled with the stack of magazines on her coffee table. "I was busy with another matter. We take whatever lands in our laps. That's the way it goes. Not often do we have much choice.''

Molly touched his arm, willing him to look at her. "Damien, I feel like I've jumped the gun, asking you to do this. I appreciate your coming when I called, but you do have a choice here if you want to back out. Ford wouldn't hold it against you. He'd understand and so will I. Your work is dangerous enough, but this could be downright deadly.'' She shuddered, just thinking about what had happened to Joe.

He looked her straight in the eyes and his were full of concern. "Nothing is more important to me right now than ensuring your safety, Molly. Ford being your brother has nothing to do with it.''

That surprised a little laugh out of her. "Then why? Why *are* you doing it?"

Damien looked away and shrugged. ''You said you needed me. That's reason enough.''

It wasn't, of course.

Unbelievable as it seemed, she suddenly wondered if Damien might want to become involved on a very personal level with her. She had to admit, Damien Perry was a very tempting man. However, at this point in her life, she couldn't even afford to think about anything like that happening.

It was one thing to weave fantasies about a guy like him, quite another to take those imaginings seriously.

Yet how could she make that clear to him right up front without talking about it? She couldn't very well do that when the yearning she thought she saw in him might only be a projection of her own. Wouldn't that be the most embarrassing blunder in the world, if he hadn't even considered…?

Molly prayed this was only her imagination working overtime.

Chapter 3

You can't kill her now. Jack Jensen argued with himself as he forced his foot to remain on the accelerator of his dark blue Mercedes Benz. Reluctantly, he cruised by the house again.

He would just love to slam on the brakes, tear up that walkway, kick in the front door and strangle the bitch right now. The jerk she had in there with her, too.

But he had to be careful. So far, he had been. No way was he spending another hour behind bars because of that tramp. He could wait. Play it just right. He backed into the driveway of a vacant house just down the street where his car would be concealed by the shrubbery.

Shadows hid him as he got out and made his way back to the driveway where the bastard had parked his car. He could risk doing this much now, just in case they decided to take off together somewhere. Nobody was getting away from Jack Jensen.

He quickly set his device under the bumper and hurried

back to his own car, needing a little something sweet to keep him alert and on top of things.

All he had to do now was wait until the boyfriend left and Molly went to bed, he thought with a quick sniff.

It wasn't as if he hadn't known she had another man around somewhere, now was it? Molly always had a man. She'd suckered him into proposing by being stingy with that body of hers. And looking innocent as a kid.

Damn, she'd made him feel stupid, but he wasn't stupid anymore. He sniffed again and smiled at the thought.

The phone calls were a start, but he was ready to escalate now. The hit-and-run that killed Joe Malia had been a godsend. Jack couldn't have planned that better if he had arranged it himself.

He relished the sheer horror in her voice every time she'd answered the phone after that had happened. But it was no longer enough. No, he had big plans for Molly.

Jack fingered one of the keys hanging from the ignition, grinding his teeth and watching the house.

"C'mon, babe, why don't you send him home and go to bed? Turn out those lights and give me some dark time. A half hour's all Jackie needs to plant your little surprise. Just a tiny something to make you think about me."

The oak mantel clock struck ten. Molly had called her mother earlier and explained the plan. The problem now was to explain to her mom why she wouldn't be staying with them herself.

"It's time to go," Damien said as he stood. He glanced from his thin gold watch to the playpen where Sydney talked to and wrestled with her teddy bear. "Does she need to, uh…"

"Go potty?" Molly said, laughing at his refusal to repeat the kiddie lingo she knew he'd heard her use with Syd. "No, she's fine." Sydney hadn't quite learned what was expected of her yet, but was very vocal about her bathroom training nonetheless. "She's suited up for bed and goes out like a light when you crank up the car. Great traveler."

"That's good," he said, lifting the large suitcase and over-size tote that Molly had readied. He headed for the back door that led out through the garage.

Molly flipped on the outside lights and followed, carrying Sydney and the teddy bear. She looked longingly at the new steel-gray Lexus sitting in the driveway.

"We'd better take my van," she suggested.

"You can trust me to drive," he said coolly.

Molly clicked her tongue impatiently. "I do. I was thinking about the car seat."

"Oh. Well, those things are portable, aren't they? I'll change it over."

The very idea of watching that exercise in frustration appealed to Molly in a very devilish way. Riding in something other than her boxy rattletrap appealed even more. "Okay. Have at it."

Molly took pity when, a good quarter of an hour later, he backed out of the car to catch his wind from all that under-the-breath cursing. She whisked Syd off the fender where she'd perched her and held her out. "Hold her for a minute and I'll fix it. It is tricky."

He grasped Syd under her arms and held her out from him as though Molly had handed him a full-grown rattlesnake. Molly hid a laugh as she crawled into the back seat and began wrestling with the seat belt that he had twisted through the wrong holes.

When she emerged, her breath stilled at what she saw. Damien held Sydney close, her face tucked into the curve of his neck. He leaned against the side of the car with his eyes shut and his bottom lip caught between his teeth. One large hand applied gentle, irregular pats to Syd's back.

This was the first time he had held Sydney and the man looked transported. She hated to interrupt.

"Want me to take her?" Molly asked softly.

His eyes flew open and he appeared confused. Reluctant, too, which amazed her. "I believe she's nodded off," he whispered, making no move to give her up.

Molly laughed and reached to take her. "She'll go right back to sleep, I promise."

"You're a very good mother, aren't you?" Damien commented thoughtfully as he carefully handed Syd over.

"Don't know how good, but I am dedicated," Molly answered, snuggling Sydney against her and kissing the side of her face. "And I mean to make sure she's safe from Jack. No way am I going to let him hurt her."

He grasped Molly's arm gently and turned her to face him. "Do you really think he might hurt her just to get back at you?"

"That's about the size of it," she admitted. "As far as Jack's concerned, she's just an extension of me and an embarrassment to him."

"Be honest with me, Molly. Are you certain she *is* Jensen's daughter?"

She looked him straight in the eye, angry that he would ask, but also understanding why he had to do so. "Absolutely. Jack's the only man I ever had. And, believe me, one was quite enough."

There. That should crush any intentions he might have of starting anything between them. If she had read him right. If not, he'd probably think she was a total idiot.

Damien nodded. Whether that meant he believed her about Jack being Syd's father, or that he accepted her word she was through with men, Molly didn't know. Both, she hoped.

Molly put Syd in her car seat and tried to ignore the flutter in her stomach Damien had caused, the same quivering she felt every single time he touched her or she touched him. It unnerved her more than she wanted to admit, but she couldn't seem to help inviting the feeling.

Once they were on their way she turned on the radio, which was already tuned to a classical station. She automatically punched the seek button until it landed on Garth Brooks. Good ol' Garth was always playing somewhere.

Besides, it wouldn't hurt to give Damien another clue as to how different they really were. Just in case he still thought they were from the same planet or something.

He merely shot her a look of amusement and began softly tapping out the beat of the song with the forefinger resting on top of the steering wheel.

"Where does your mother live?" Damien asked as they left her subdivision.

"About six miles from here. Turn left at the next light and hit the Loop."

Damien asked for the specific address and exit number off the freeway, then deliberately took a roundabout course to make certain no one tailed them.

Finally they reached a group of modest-looking condominiums and Molly pointed to the second set of buildings. "You can park in that space beside her Taurus."

Molly had the car door open and was out before he shifted into Park. He knew she was eager to get her mother and the baby out of town.

"Get Syd out for me, would you?" Without waiting for him to answer, she slammed the door and dashed up the front walk.

Damien exited a little more slowly, figured out the intricacies of releasing the sleeping baby from her upright bed, and gently lifted her out. She burrowed against him and then went boneless. He followed Molly's path to the door.

The women were standing just inside the doorway, hugging. He could see where Molly had gotten her height and coloring. These were two very attractive women, Damien thought. Striking, rather than classically beautiful. They were somehow very…real.

If he'd met the mother when he shared a hospital room with her son, Damien didn't recall it. But he had been under sedation until the day before Ford Devereaux was released.

The woman must be at least fifty. She appeared much younger than that, though her short red hair was lightened with gray and he could see fine laugh lines around her eyes.

Damien closed the door behind him. The living room possessed the same comfortable, lived-in quality as Molly's place. Quirky accents—pillows, paintings and such—in bright colors, somehow fit beautifully and gave the heavy, antique furniture a decidedly feminine touch.

Mrs. Devereaux disentangled herself from her daughter and looked at him quizzically. Molly reached out and clutched his arm. She did that so naturally, so familiarly, as though they'd known each other forever. Damien found himself wishing they had.

"Mama, this is Damien Perry, Ford's friend."

"How do you do, Mrs. Devereaux?"

"Call me Brenda, please. I remember you from the hospital, though you were asleep when I saw you."

At the moment Damien could think of no good reason to disabuse either woman of the notion that he knew Devereaux well. They might send him packing if he admitted that he had no right to be here in the middle of all this. And Damien definitely didn't intend to leave.

"Molly told me Jack's threatening her. Surely the FBI's not getting in on it," she said, frowning.

"No, I'm not here to help officially, only as a friend," he admitted. "Molly and I have been in touch before tonight." Let her think what she would of that.

"Aha, now I see." She smiled cryptically.

She took the baby from Damien and cuddled her close.

"We're going on a little trip, Syd!" she whispered, swaying, obviously enjoying the feel of the child against her. "Just you and Mommy and Gran."

Damien watched as the grandmother took the baby back toward what he assumed were the bedrooms.

"Oh, God, how will I stand being away from her?" Molly groaned, and turned to him. "I've never left Syd with anyone longer than one night, even with Mom. I'll miss her so much."

Without even thinking about it, he enfolded her in his arms as naturally as she had squeezed his arm earlier. She allowed it, and rested there, her face buried in the curve of his neck, just where the baby's had been a few moments before. This felt right, Damien thought. Very right.

"What will she think if I leave her?" Molly murmured against his neck.

"She'll be fine," he murmured. "They both will be. It shouldn't be for long." Damien liked being her refuge, he decided. She slid her arms beneath his jacket and encircled his waist so that her breasts pressed comfortably against his chest. He liked that, too.

Damien could have held her that way all night, but her mother returned. He gently grasped Molly's shoulders and moved her away from him.

"I put Sydney down to sleep so we can talk about this," Mrs. Devereaux said softly. "Where are we going?"

"Clarkston," Damien told her. "I arranged for a house there."

"Are you sure it's necessary for us to leave town? We could go to a motel or something for a couple of days until you or the police can talk to Jack and calm him down."

"That won't do it, Mom. They can't arrest him unless he does something to us. And I really am afraid Jack might. I want you and Sydney where he can't find you."

Brenda Devereaux rolled her eyes and puffed out a

breath. "Molly, I don't like the man any better than you do, but surely after what Jack's just been through, he wouldn't dare—"

"Ma'am?" Damien interrupted. "For whatever it's worth, I believe she's right."

Her eyes narrowed in thought. "Surely you're exaggerating, Molly. Jack wouldn't risk arrest again!"

Molly dropped to the sofa and crossed her arms over her chest. "I told you he's been following me, Mama. Making phone calls and laughing at me. He got me fired. Or, at least, his daddy did it for him. Worse than that, I think Jack killed Joe Malia."

Brenda met Damien's gaze over Molly's head. She looked even more frightened than Molly.

When she spoke, her voice was hushed with horror. "Oh, my God. Jack?"

"You know he's abusive, Mama. He hit me. Hard. He threatened to kill me that night and he meant it. The only reason he stopped was because he thought he'd succeeded. It's a small step from that to this, don't you think?"

Damien tensed. Molly had tried to soft-peddle her description of that fight when she'd told him about it. "What about the other episodes, Molly?"

"There were only three, counting the last one. I fought back. I tried to leave him several times, but he said he would find me and destroy me. As soon as I found out I was pregnant, I knew I had to get away from him, no matter what. He caught me packing that night."

"And before?" he asked.

"The first two times weren't all that bad." She shrugged. "Just slaps, a few bruises. It wouldn't have gone that far if I hadn't stood up to him. He hated it when I defended myself. Both times, he cooled off and apologized, promised it would never happen again. I warned him if it did, I would leave him for good no matter what he said."

Damien ground his teeth so hard it hurt. She went on. "Neighbors heard the row the last time. By the time they got there, I was conscious and told them what happened. They called the police who caught Jack and arrested him.

"My lawyer showed the judge medical records from the other times. Jack pled guilty. He knew if it came to a jury trial, everything would be public."

"I still say we should have told Ford everything," Brenda said.

"Ford would have killed him. It was all I could do to keep him from it when he thought the fight was partly my fault. I didn't want my own brother arrested for murder. Jack had counted on that before. He told me so and joked about it. Why do you think he didn't post bail? Think the Jensens couldn't afford it? The jerk was scared to get out, afraid Ford would come after him."

"He doesn't seem worried about that now?" Damien asked.

Molly sighed. "No. That's why I think Jack's really lost it."

"I certainly understand your brother's probable reaction," Damien admitted. He flexed his fists. "I have an urge to kill Jensen myself."

"Oh, great!" Molly groaned. "I break my neck trying to keep Ford out of it, and now *you* want to kill him."

She shrugged, a helpless little gesture he'd not seen her make before. Then she settled that teary green gaze on him and blinked. Her voice was softer than he'd heard it yet. "Damien? All I want is for him to leave me alone. Promise me you won't do anything stupid. I figured you wouldn't act as rashly as Ford would. That's why I asked you to help."

He sucked in a deep breath and released it slowly. So, Molly did have regard for him, after all, just as she did for her brother. She didn't want either of them to risk a murder charge because of what her ex had done and might yet do.

But Molly was depending on his finding some way to stop the madness and make certain she, her daughter and mother were safe from Jensen.

Damien knew killing Jack Jensen would be a simple matter. He could, and get away with it, too. God knew he wanted to right now. Jensen deserved death probably more than some men Damien had killed in the line of duty. But Damien always tried to work within the law. He hated to turn rogue this late in the game. Not as long as there were other options.

"I won't do anything stupid, Molly," he said with a half smile he had to force. "I promise you that."

Molly had faced the shame she felt pretty well, she thought. She lifted her chin and dared both Damien and her mother to feel sorry for her.

Jack was a bully, or worse, and she'd been his victim for nearly a year. Degrading as that was, she figured she might as well lay it all out and be done with it. She would *not* be a victim again.

Damien seemed almost as likely to get himself into trouble over this as Ford was. Molly felt torn between talking him out of it and spurring him on. *Something* had to be done.

"Clarkston's not that far away, but you and the child should be safe there," Damien told her mother, neatly changing the subject back to their trip.

Her mom nodded. "After Molly and I talked on the phone, I told Josie she would need to take over the shop for a while. As far as she knows, I'm going on a buying trip up to New England. No point in letting everybody and his brother know where we're going, right?"

"Right," Damien agreed, smiling his approval. "We'll

try to get this straightened out soon so you won't be away for too long.''

Molly agreed. "We'll have to get things rolling right away. Damien can't afford to hang around here forever.''

Those azure eyes seemed to ask, *Why not?* She quickly looked away.

Her mother smiled. "This is really good of you, Damien. I guess Ford will owe you one, won't he?''

"He won't owe me anything,'' Damien said truthfully. "I'm doing this for Molly and Sydney. And now you, of course.''

Uh-oh, that went over like a helium balloon, Molly thought. Sent all kinds of hopes soaring. Her mother's glance darted from one to other of them, that calculating gleam in her eye.

Molly decided she'd better head this off before Mama rented the church and started sewing Syd's flower girl dress.

"C'mon, Mama, let's get your things, so we can go,'' she suggested.

Soon afterward, Damien loaded Brenda's two suitcases into the trunk of his rental car while Molly strapped the baby into her car seat. Much to his disappointment, Molly climbed into the back and offered her mother the front passenger seat.

As he drove, Damien executed a number of unnecessary detours and kept a close eye out for anyone following them.

He only half listened while Brenda Devereaux enumerated Molly's long list of accomplishments and threw in a few incidental brags about her grandchild.

He smiled to himself, suspecting there was a bit of matchmaking going on here. While that should have made him nervous as hell, Damien felt flattered by the attempt.

A moment later he checked the rearview mirror again and his lingering smile died a swift death. "Check your seat belts, ladies,'' he warned, "we have company.''

Chapter 4

The Lexus careered around the curves of the county road and flew headlong into the darkness. Molly surrounded Sydney with one arm and braced her other hand against the back of the front seat.

She glanced out the back window and saw the headlights behind them fade into the distance. A few moments later she couldn't see them at all.

"For a rental, this thing really...moves," she gasped. Damien slowed down a little, but her heart was still traveling at least ninety miles an hour.

She and her mother gave a little scream in unison as Damien cut the lights and bumped off the main road onto one that was unpaved. How he could see where they were going mystified Molly. She closed her eyes and held on, one arm braced across Syd's car seat.

Only a few minutes later, he suddenly braked and shut off the motor.

"Lock the doors and stay where you are," Damien instructed. Then he exited the car, closed the door and disappeared into the night.

"Not one to dawdle, is he?" Brenda whispered with a nervous laugh. "Wonder if he's that quick about everything."

"Hush, Mama!"

"How's Sydney?"

"Out like a light," Molly answered absently, craning around to look out the back window, seeing only the dense blackness surrounding them. She felt claustrophobic.

"Can you see anything, Mama? I wonder what he's doing."

"Don't you trust him to look after us? He seems very capable to me."

"It's not that," Molly answered. "I just wonder where he went."

"I wouldn't worry about *that* boy getting lost."

Molly huffed. "'Boy'?"

Brenda laughed again. "I like him."

So do I, Molly thought. Entirely too much. She stared out into the night, seeing and hearing absolutely nothing. "He must have eyes like a cat!"

They sat silently for a few minutes listening to Sydney's light snoring. That's when Molly noticed the faint light flickering indirectly against the foliage on either side of the car.

Something began bumping and scraping underneath, a sound that continued for some time. "What in the world is he *doing?*" she whispered.

In the stillness, the sound grew louder, making its way around the entire vehicle. Then the beam of light reappeared, illuminating Damien's face as he rapped on the glass with his knuckle.

Her mother popped the locks and Damien got in. He

handed her the penlight. "Hold this. Shine it on my hands."

"What are you doing?" Molly asked when she saw him open the pocket knife on his key chain.

"Deactivating this," he muttered. "Tracking device."

Seconds later he calmly fastened his seat belt. "All clear now."

He cranked up and slowly began backing out of the woods and onto the dirt road. Expertly, he maneuvered the car to the main highway, switched on the lights and continued as though nothing had happened. In the opposite direction.

"What did you do to the car?" she asked.

"I was looking for this," he said, holding up a small black object he had been working on. "It was attached underneath the bumper. I knew Jensen wasn't following us as we left the city. Not closely enough for me to detect, at any rate."

Brenda clicked her tongue against her teeth. "Now where the devil would Jack get a thing like that?"

Damien shrugged. "It's just a simple device, nothing sophisticated that he would need any real connections to obtain. Only a cut above a radar detector."

Molly scoffed. "I can't believe he did this!"

"First bit of evidence," Damien said, dropping the gadget into his jacket pocket.

Molly suddenly realized that Jack would have had to approach her house this very night to put the tracker in place. He would have been right there in her driveway, fiddling with Damien's car while they sat in her house waiting to leave. He could have done worse. What if he had tampered with the brakes? Or put a bomb under the car?

"But how did he know we were going anywhere? Could my house be bugged? Did he hear everything we said?"

"No, I checked all the rooms for listening devices. Your

phones, as well. Best guess is that he's watching your place or has hired someone else to do it. I think he just wants to track you wherever you go and then turn up unexpectedly. I'd be willing to bet he's had a tracker on your van for some time now. When I showed up, he probably decided to place one on this car for the same reason.''

Molly pushed back in her seat and covered her face with her hands, willing her anger to overcome the fear. Then she looked up at the rearview mirror. The dash lights provided a dim reflection of Damien's eyes, those wonderful blue eyes.

How in the world could he calm and reassure her with a glance and create such turmoil in her at the same time?

Shortly after one in the morning, Damien drove through Clarkston, the small town where he had rented the house for Brenda Devereaux and the baby. He swung into the parking lot of a Texaco station, chose a shadowy corner, and cut the engine.

"They've rolled up the sidewalks, I see," Brenda remarked, propping her elbow on the window and resting her head on her hand. "Don't see a soul."

She sounded and looked exhausted. Hell, they were all fatigued except for the baby. Little Sydney slept on, unaware that her father had caused such a ruckus. Hopefully Jensen would never locate them in this place. Still, one could never be too careful.

No cars cruised the streets. Even the convenience store opposite the gas station was closed for the night. Except for a few lighted windows in a house here and there—late-night readers or late show enthusiasts—it appeared the entire town of Clarkston was asleep.

Satisfied they had not been followed or anticipated, Damien pulled out onto the street, counting the houses north from the first traffic light until he came to the one he sought.

The streetlights illuminated the typical, small, Southern-town cottage, a modest one-story, its fat square columns supporting the roof of a wide front porch. The house sat near the end of Main Street, sandwiched between two others that appeared similar in style. An added benefit was the proximity to a three-man police station situated only two blocks away.

Though everyone knew it was much easier to hide some-one in a large city, Damien figured now was definitely the time to do the unexpected. Jensen probably wouldn't bother looking for Brenda and the baby anyway when he realized Molly hadn't accompanied them into hiding.

He made a mental note to thank the local Bureau office and especially the agent whom he had contacted earlier. When he had explained the situation, and told her about Ford's sister, Agent Kim Avery suggested this place and made the arrangements. It certainly fit all his specifications. The location was perfect.

Even the rent had proved reasonable, though he would never tell Molly this came out of his pocket. As far as she knew, they were making use of a regular safe house.

"Why, this looks lovely, Damien!" Brenda remarked as they pulled into the driveway and the car lights flashed the front of the structure.

"All the comforts of home, I hope." He shut off the car and got out, opened the back door first and lifted the baby out for Molly.

Damien couldn't deny how he looked forward to holding the child again. It wouldn't do to dwell much on just why he felt that way. She was cute, that was all. Cuddly and sweet, like a puppy you could hand back to the owner once you'd admired it sufficiently.

Such trust, to sleep in a stranger's arms, Damien thought

to himself. He could hardly credit it, even in one so young. He had rarely slept in the presence of another person, except in dorms and army barracks when he'd had no choice. Even then, he'd had to be all but comatose with exhaustion to do so.

Under sedation in the hospital, he'd had no problem sleeping. Of course, at that time he had almost hoped someone *would* sneak in and put him out of his misery.

He smiled inwardly, mocking the inborn caution he often carried to extremes. Damien sometimes wondered if he hadn't embarked on professions that made his bogeymen very real, just so he could finally confront them face-to-face.

He held the totally limp child, her tiny bum resting on his forearm and her head on his shoulder, until they reached the front door.

"Better let me go in first," he said. Quickly he shifted Sydney to her mother's arms, knelt to retrieve the key from under the potted geranium where Kim had said she would leave it.

"Wait here in the shadows where you can't be seen from the street," he ordered. The women did exactly as he said without any argument.

He pulled his weapon, released the safety and unlocked the door. His search was not cursory, even though he didn't believe there was any way Jack could have discovered their destination.

When he found the place entirely safe as he'd expected, he clicked on a lamp in the living room, returned to the front door and pushed it open. "Come in, ladies. It's actually much more agreeable than I'd hoped."

"Was that really necessary? Jack couldn't possibly have been hiding out in there," Molly snapped as she brushed past him into the house. He immediately forgave her impatience. She was tired and the child was heavy. Her nerves were probably shot.

He smiled at her. "No, but Jack's not the only bear in the woods, now is he? I was merely being cautious."

"And we thank you, don't we, Molly?" Brenda asked with a meaningful nod and a dark look at her daughter. He had never considered that a mother might reprimand a fully grown child with any effect.

"Sorry," Molly murmured grudgingly. "Thanks."

Damien turned away so she couldn't see his grin. "You're quite welcome. Well, what do you think?" He gestured toward the dimly lit room furnished with Victorian replicas and faded fabrics. Old-fashioned crocheted antimacassars and knickknacks remained where they'd probably been for decades. He rather liked it.

Agent Avery said the owner had died and the heir was delighted to rent until he had time to arrange an auction for the furnishings and the house.

Damien had hired Avery to stock the kitchen, have the beds made up and linens put out. All the comforts of home. This was the agent's hometown, as luck would have it, and she'd even provided a cover story for Brenda so she wouldn't be a stranger in town.

"A little bit prissy, but it looks cozy. It's nice," Molly said, trailing her free hand along the back of a damask-covered chair. She wandered down the wide hall and pushed open a bedroom door.

Brenda followed. Damien left them to explore the house while he brought in the luggage.

He set it down in the hallway, returned to lock the door and turn out the light in the living room. Then he followed their voices to the master bedroom.

They were exclaiming over the crib placed near the large tester bed where Brenda had declared she would sleep.

He must remember to tell Ford Devereaux how fortunate

he was to have such friends as Avery to work with. If he ever saw him again. Like as not, Damien would be gone before Devereaux returned. If not, some tall explanations would be in order when Molly found out they hardly knew each other.

Shrugging off the thought, he interrupted them to proceed with the plan. "Brenda, while you're here, you are supposed to be Kim Avery's aunt, so you'll use her last name. She's an agent who grew up here in Clarkston, but lives in Nashville. She and your son work out of the same office."

Brenda frowned. "I don't believe I know her."

"It doesn't matter. Kim will be your contact if you need to reach us. Whatever you do, don't call us directly. Her number is on the list by the phone in the kitchen."

"Will I get to meet her?" Brenda asked. "It was very nice of her to do this."

"She'll probably check in with you by phone to see if you need anything she didn't provide. You needn't be reclusive, but stay indoors as much as you can. The backyard should suffice as a play area so, hopefully, you won't get cabin fever," Damien assured her.

"We'll be quite comfortable here, I think."

"Get some rest now," he suggested. "Molly and I will wait in the living room for a couple of hours, just to make certain everything's safe. We need to be back in Nashville before dawn, but we'll wake you before we leave and say goodbye."

To his surprise, the woman came toward him and encircled him with her arms. "Thank you so much, Damien. I know you'll keep my baby safe, just like her brother would if he were here."

Then she stood on tiptoe, took his face in her hands and kissed his cheek, a warm, friendly display like none he could ever recall receiving.

"And you be careful yourself, hear?" she added, patting his shoulders firmly before she released him completely and stepped back.

"Of course," he answered, feeling decidedly off center. Nobody ever gave a damn whether he was careful, unless it affected the outcome of a case.

He looked at Molly to see her reaction to her mother's gesture toward him, but she was busy making the baby comfortable in the new crib.

At that moment, she leaned over the side and kissed her daughter's head, much in the same way Brenda had just kissed his face. With caring and worry and affection.

Damien felt something well up inside his chest and throat, a keen ache almost like hunger. He was afraid these little tastes of familial warmth would never be enough if he ever got used to them.

Might as well shake it off, he decided firmly, because he didn't intend to spend more than two weeks dealing with this problem.

What did a man like him know or even care about family interaction, anyway? He must be getting maudlin in his old age.

He gently grasped Molly's arm and guided her toward the door. "Sleep well," he ordered Brenda in a curt whisper. "Molly, you might catch a few winks on the sofa. I'll keep watch."

But Damien couldn't dismiss the feeling that gripped him, the powerful need for human contact these three somehow had awakened. Loneliness overwhelmed him all of a sudden, a bleakness he had accepted as his due for so long that he hadn't even realized it was there.

As soon as he and Molly cleared the hallway and stood in the darkness of the living room, he turned and enfolded her in a fierce hug. Unable to stop himself, he pressed his lips against her temple and simply held her tight. Much to his surprise, she allowed it.

"Try not to be afraid," he whispered. "I *will* keep you safe from him."

"I know," she answered softly. Her voice quavered, but not with fear. Damien wondered if he had made a total fool of himself and it amused her, or if his holding her this way pleased her as much as it did him.

He realized they couldn't stand there all night locked in an embrace. Eventually, he had to let her go. He did so with as much dignity as he could manage to recoup, and led her to the overstuffed sofa.

"Better get some sleep, if you can," he advised, looking down at her, sounding gruff when he hadn't meant to.

"Come sit with me," she offered, patting the cushion next to her.

Damien looked down at her strong, capable hand with its long, flexible artist's fingers. His gaze traveled up her arm, noting the soft fleecy shirt with the brightly colored hearts embroidered just above her left breast. "Not wise," he answered with a self-deprecating laugh.

Molly grabbed his hand and tugged. He sat.

"Do you feel it, too, Damien?" she asked, her voice soft, worried.

He could pretend he didn't understand her, but what was the use? Every time they touched—however lightly, whatever the reason—blood rushed though his veins at warp speed and heated to a boil. Of course he felt it, too. How could he not? And it was certainly more than familial warmth he wanted when he did. "Yes, I'm afraid I do."

"Nothing can come of it," she said. "I know I already warned you once, but I just wanted to make sure you understand that I mean it. I'm not playing games here, Damien."

"Oh, I believe you. No games." He sucked in a deep

breath and released it slowly, trying to draw on his professionalism or anything else that would rein in these impulses that were so new to him.

He couldn't count the people who had accused him of being cold, dispassionate. Never in his life had he been so near to losing control, so close to saying and doing things that would be totally out of character. He wanted this woman more than his next breath.

Molly threaded her fingers through his and squeezed his hand, placing her other palm on top. "Trust me, Damien, this *will* go away. It's probably just the…situation or something causing it. In the meantime, I think…I think we should just ignore it." She took a deep, shuddering breath and looked up at him. "Don't you?"

He shrugged. "If you want." Her face looked so earnest in the faint glow of the streetlight through the sheer-curtained window. "However, if you do want that, my darling, then I have to get up from here and sit somewhere else. If I don't, I am definitely going to kiss you."

Her silence and absolute stillness seemed to imply consent. God, he hoped it meant consent.

Slowly, giving her time to escape, Damien lowered his mouth to hers. A tentative touch of lips, and then all hell broke loose.

He just lost it. His brain reeled with relief at her eager response, the lush texture of her mouth, her tongue, the unique and heady taste of her. A fire broke out within him that consumed them both.

Molly threw herself into the blaze, grasping him as urgently as he was holding her. Her heart thundered against his chest. He stretched out, pulling her entire length parallel to his, half on, half off the sofa.

Dimly, somewhere in the recesses of his mind, he realized he should be holding back, letting her lead the way. But she followed so passionately and with such abandon, he refused to heed the instinct for self-preservation that had protected him for so long.

On and on they kissed, turning this way and angling that, their lips and bodies seeking better purchase, a closer melding, a oneness....

"I guess a pot of coffee's out of the question!"

The lamp came on and Damien and Molly broke apart like teenagers caught by the cops.

Brenda laughed. "I could almost hear the pop! Well, I'll just—" she waved one arm aimlessly "—toddle on back to bed, I guess."

"No! Wait!" Molly gasped. "Mama, I swear this is *not* what you think—"

Her mother flapped a hand in their direction. "Oh, can it, Molly. You're too old to owe me any explanations. Sorry I interrupted."

"Brenda?" Damien was stymied when she actually stopped and turned around to face them, grinning wickedly. In the dim light, she reminded him so much of Molly that he shook his head to dispel the comparison.

"Yes, Agent Perry?" she drawled.

"Uh, coffee would be good."

"Exactly what we need!" Molly proclaimed a little too loudly. She scrambled up off the sofa and dashed toward the hallway, halting suddenly.

"Kitchen's the other way," Brenda advised her drolly. She glanced at Damien, shook her head and winked. "The girl needs a keeper."

Damien bit his lips together and nodded, totally at a loss as to what he should say. He wanted to laugh, but it wasn't exactly funny. Not now, anyway. Molly certainly wasn't amused.

Brenda linked her arm through his and sighed as they followed Molly through the dining room to the kitchen. "You can bypass the red-faced apology, sweetie. It's not like I'm gonna drag out my shotgun and demand that you marry her just because of a little kiss.''

Little kiss? He didn't know what to say to that, either. If she'd been a scant two minutes later, she might have seen a more justifiable reason than a kiss to make her demand. And Brenda knew it, too.

What was the big deal here? Molly was nearly thirty years old, not some witless little innocent he'd been about to deflower. They were free to do whatever they pleased, wherever they wanted to do it, two consenting adults.

His conscience reared up even as he had the defensive thoughts. Molly was not one to take lovemaking as lightly as all that. To tell the truth, he didn't think he could, either. Not with her.

And had she really consented? Or had he sort of forced the issue a little. She *was* depending on him to protect her. Had he given her the idea that a little payment was necessary in lieu of the money she'd offered him at first?

Well, he certainly wasn't about to bring that up for discussion. They hadn't made love and it was highly unlikely that he would find himself in this predicament again with Molly. She had made it quite clear that she did not want a relationship with him other than his extending her protection.

Brenda nudged him with her elbow. "I like you, Damien." She whispered low enough so that Molly couldn't hear. "But if you're just playing, it would be wise to back off."

Damien kept his mouth firmly shut and nodded once. He had not been playing at all.

Brenda was right about one thing, however. Backing off definitely should be his next step, the wisest move all the way around.

Chapter 5

Molly cursed her impulsive nature all the way back to Nashville. She had let him kiss her, for goodness' sake. Not only that, she had encouraged him to, and very nearly got more than she bargained for. What was she thinking?

She hadn't been thinking at all, if she was honest about it. Never mind how many of her fantasies he'd fulfilled with that kiss. Even now, this long after, she could still feel the texture of his lips, still taste him, and shiver with the need for more.

The man had always turned her on like the White House Christmas tree. All he had to do was look at her and it was like plugging her in. Worse yet, she was glowing right now, just thinking about it. About him. Damn!

And hadn't Mama embarrassed the daylights out of both of them, walking in on them that way. Sometimes the woman could still make her feel as though she were thirteen, nothing but knees and elbows and ugly red hair.

Try as she might, however, Molly couldn't lay all the

blame on her mother for tonight's little humiliation. No, she had brought it on herself. And Damien.

She threw him a surreptitious glance. *Mr. Cool* hadn't even blushed once. Only now she knew what he hid behind that mask of his. The man was dynamite disguised as a prayer candle.

"I told you so," she mumbled, half hoping he wouldn't hear her.

"What's that?" he asked, calmly steering the car along as if they were on a Sunday outing. She resented his composure. What *did* it take to rattle him, anyway?

"I warned you we couldn't act on it," Molly answered.

"Apparently we could and did. You want an apology?"

Thank heaven he hadn't smiled. If he had, Molly thought she might have to smack him. "Not necessary. Just see that it doesn't happen again." She knew she sounded grumpy and mean, but she was trying to make a point here. She was not going to have an affair with him.

He shrugged one shoulder. "Your mother told me that I should back off."

"She did *what?*"

He nodded. "Brenda worries about you. Thinks I might be...'playing' was the word I believe she used."

Molly rolled her eyes and pounded her fists on her legs. What was she supposed to do now? If she railed about her mother's ridiculous warning, it might make him think she disagreed with her, that she thought he shouldn't back off and that he wasn't playing at all.

"Are you playing?" she asked before thinking.

Damien looked at her then, raised one brow and then fastened his gaze back on the road. "No."

Well, what did he mean by that? He was serious about her, or serious about sex? She did think this time and kept her mouth shut. For miles they rode in silence so thick she could hardly breathe in it.

Molly couldn't stand it. "I'm sorry I can't give you what you want." She was, but her life was too messed up at the moment to add any more tangles. "I just can't."

"You are that certain you *know* what I want?" he asked. "To be perfectly honest, I'm not sure myself."

Oh, she knew all right. A chuckle escaped before she could contain it.

"No, it's true," he argued. "It's probably not you at all, just what you represent."

"Oh, well, great! That does wonders for my ego. And it was none too healthy to begin with, thank you very much." She ran a hand through her unruly hair and tugged on it. He was enough to make her pull it out by the roots.

The expression on his face was a mixture of embarrassment and contrition, new for him.

He pulled the car over, put it in Park and turned to her. "Look, I didn't mean that the way it sounded. It's just that you are a part of something I've never experienced, a way of life I'm not familiar with. You and the child and your mother have something…"

"A dysfunctional family? And that appeals to you?"

"Don't," he ordered. "Do not make fun of what you have together. You can't know—"

"Oh, yes, I do know! My father left us when I was too young to remember him. Mama had to work and found so little time to spend with us, Ford and I were absolutely wild, the scourges of the neighborhood. And it wasn't a very nice neighborhood, I can tell you! We fought the world and fought each other."

"Sounds wonderful," he said.

Molly shrugged. "Then I up and married the scum of the earth who got me pregnant and beat me silly. They thought that was my fault, and maybe it was. It's a flaming wonder any of us even speak to each other."

The sadness in his eyes stopped her ranting. "But you love one another," he said quietly. "Don't you?"

She scoffed at the question. "Well, yeah, but what's so unusual about that? Your family *has* to love you. It's not like they have a choice."

Damien slowly shook his head. He remained silent as he turned away from her and started the car again.

Traffic was almost nonexistent in the early hours of the morning. It was almost as if another Nashville existed after late-night revelers went home and the workforce hit the roads just before dawn. Molly thought Damien Perry fit this time of day, especially after what he'd just intimated.

She had suspected from the first that he was a loner, but she'd thought it was by choice. Now she felt pretty sure he knew no other way to be. This realization was not going to help her resolve to keep him at a distance.

Damien needed loving more than any person she'd ever known. Molly only wished she could be the one to provide it, but knew she wasn't equipped to handle that. Sex wouldn't be enough and would only complicate matters between them.

She was already infatuated with him and had been since she'd met him in the hospital in Memphis. Those feelings he'd awakened in her had a lot to do with her calling him here to help her, though she hadn't admitted it to herself at the time.

Infatuation, she could handle. She knew that would play out, like a teenage crush on a teacher or a rock star. But to be responsible for a man's well-being and happiness, to put his before her own and care about him above anything or anybody. That, she could never do again.

A simple affair was out of the question. Anything she started with Damien could never be that uncomplicated. Not for her, anyway.

She would be taking a terrible risk if she let herself love

him. Damien was too perfect, too self-contained, and way too sophisticated for a woman like herself. Maybe she had piqued his interest because she was so different from the other women he knew. But when the new wore off their relationship—and that probably wouldn't take long—she could just picture what would happen.

Damien would never raise a hand to her, she knew that without a doubt. He wouldn't hurt her intentionally in any way. However, Molly also realized that his leaving her while she loved him would destroy her more completely than the worst kind of violence.

"All I want to do is get on with my life without being afraid," she said to herself, not even realizing she had spoken aloud until he answered.

"I'll see to it," he promised quietly. "I won't leave until you have nothing left to worry about."

Molly turned her face to the window so he wouldn't see the tears. Would there ever come a day when she wouldn't worry about *him?*

Well before dawn, Damien pulled into Molly's driveway and parked. Streetlights shone over the sleeping neighborhood. Peaceful suburbia, an alien land he had seldom observed.

He leaned back and released his seat belt, but made no move to leave the car. "Why don't you wait here while I go in and make a quick sweep? He thinks we're out of town, so I don't believe you have anything to worry about. This is just a precaution."

She didn't look at him, just nodded.

Damien got out, flipped the lock button and gently closed the car door. With expertise that had become automatic over the years, he did a thorough check of the yard and then the house itself.

There was no indication that anything had been disturbed

since they'd left. Gun holstered, he turned on the living room light, opened the front door and beckoned Molly inside.

He watched her get out of the car and admired her athletic grace as she closed the distance between them. Molly's body looked very feminine, but also exhibited a certain quality of boldness in the way she moved. A confidence he would not have expected in someone who had suffered what she had.

When she reached him, he took her hand and pulled her inside the house. "You need sleep," he told her as he closed the door and locked it. There were circles beneath her eyes and she looked pale.

"What about you?" she asked. "You haven't slept, either."

That warm feeling again. She cared that he was tired. "I'm fine. Go to bed, Molly."

Apparently, she was too tired to argue with him.

Damien kept watch, dozing occasionally, rousing at every sound, until she awoke five hours later, around nine o'clock in the morning.

He listened to the distant sound of the shower, heard dresser drawers open and close and realized how much he looked forward to seeing her, spending the day with her.

Suddenly, she was there in the doorway, a tentative smile on her face, the shadows of fatigue either faded or concealed with light makeup.

She wore a rather fluid ensemble consisting of a cream silk top, long unstructured jacket and drawstring slacks the shade of dark toast.

Her long auburn curls, artfully disarranged, were caught up on one side with a tortoiseshell clip. Gold loops and herringbone chain enhanced her ears and throat. She could have graced a runway for the best of designers.

Had she dressed this way for him? "Are we going somewhere?" he asked. "You look wonderful, by the way."

Her cheeks reddened beneath the blush she'd applied and she wrecked her graceful pose by wringing her hands and shifting from one foot to the other. He thought it endearing.

"This is…just in case we do decide to go out. Should we?" she asked.

Damien smiled, unable to resist making her pinken again. "Oh, absolutely. It would be selfish to keep you all to myself. Everyone in Nashville should see you looking like that. I have to say, you are a vision."

She made a comical grimace. "And I have to get some coffee in you. Sleep deprivation's making you hallucinate."

Damien laughed and shook his head. "Go make it then, while I shower and shave. Ten minutes, okay?"

He'd just reached the guest room and unzipped his suitcase when he heard her cry out. Tearing down the hallway, he met her running through the kitchen door. She threw herself into his arms.

Damien grasped her tightly and shifted her to one side, out of the way of his weapon. "What is it? What's happened?" he asked when he could see no apparent cause for her terror.

"Poison!" she gasped in a desperate whisper. "Rat poison!"

"In what? Where?" he demanded, lowering the pistol.

Molly pushed away from him, breaking his hold, and grabbed his hand. She drew him into the kitchen and pointed to the open cabinet over the coffee maker.

"There!" she said, pointing to a black and yellow box, open at one corner, sitting among the boxes of foodstuffs. "That shouldn't be there!"

"Where did you have it before?"

"I didn't!" she exclaimed. "At least I don't think we ever bought any. If it was anywhere on the premises, it would have been secured in the storage room at the back of the garage. *He* brought it in and put it here, I know he did.''

''When, do you think?'' Damien asked.

She threw up her arms and sighed. ''Last night, I guess. It wasn't there yesterday.''

''Are you certain?'' he asked, and watched as she thought back.

''No!'' she admitted finally, her eyes round with surprise. For a moment, she pressed the fingertips of one hand to her lips.

''The coffee canister was empty this morning and that's why I opened the cabinet. For a fresh package. Yesterday I don't think I looked in there at all. But it had to be last night. Before that, I was here every single night. If he had come in during the day, he would have risked being seen.''

Her worried gaze flew to the strange box, an obvious taunt, and maybe an outright threat. ''It's open, Damien. You don't think...''

Damien exhaled in disgust and frustration. ''I don't think we'll be eating or drinking anything with a seal broken. Question is, how did he get in? I saw no sign of tampering with the locks. Who else has a key?''

''Only Mama and Ford. I saw hers on her key ring. But Ford and Mary might have...''

''Left his car keys at home when they flew to Europe?'' he guessed. ''Makes sense they would take a taxi or arrange a ride to the airport to avoid the parking charges.''

Molly looked up at him. ''They live in an old colonial way out in the county. The place has scads of windows and would be easy to break into. Ford's no slouch when it comes to security systems, but nothing's foolproof. Jack could have picked up a few tricks the last couple of years, considering where he spent them.''

Damien nodded. ''I would bet he's learned a few things.

And you can be sure he covered his tracks, wore gloves, made an impression of the key and then left it where he found it. Must have figured a way to deactivate your security alarm. Unfortunately, it's not all that difficult if you know what you're doing.''

"Can you do that?''

Damien nodded as he glanced up at the box of rat poison and frowned. "I doubt there'll be any prints to tie him to this, but let's report it, just for the record.'' He picked up the phone.

Half an hour later, a squad car pulled in and parked behind the Lexus. Damien dropped the curtain back into place and turned to Molly. "Let's not reveal who I work for.''

"Why can't we tell him?'' she asked, glancing from him to the front door and back again. "Wouldn't that help?''

He shook his head. "The locals might get a bit antsy if they think a Fed's encroaching on their territory. Can't blame them, really. Aside from that, word does get around. If Jensen finds out who I am, he might simply back off until I leave and then begin again,'' he explained, then nodded toward the entry. "Let's get on with this.''

Molly opened the door. "Thank you for responding so soon, Officer Sharps.''

"Ms. Jensen. Always a pleasure, ma'am. Got *another* problem, I see.''

"Isn't your partner coming inside?'' Molly asked, glancing toward the squad car. Through the window Damien could see the other officer sitting in the vehicle, thumbing the pages of a paperback.

"No ma'am. I don't think we'll need him.''

His tone was pure condescension. Molly must have dealt with this guy before.

The young policeman squinted down at the clipboard he carried and then raked Molly with an appreciative gaze.

Damien didn't much blame him for that, but neither did he like it.

"You called about a possible break-in," Sharps said. "Just what did you mean by *possible?*"

She backed up and gestured for him to come inside, which he did, removing his cap and sticking it under his arm.

"It wasn't precisely a break-in," Molly admitted. "I think it was my ex-husband who probably used a key he's not supposed to have."

"Uh-huh," the cop mumbled, smiling and tapping his pen on the clipboard. "Stole the key?"

"I don't know," Molly admitted. "All I know is that he's still harassing me, and that he was here while I was out. He left something in my kitchen cabinet."

"I see. And did he phone you and tell you where to find it?" The cop wore a look of amusement now. "Or has he stopped calling and started leaving you groceries?"

Molly glared. If looks could kill, Sharps would have died on the spot. "He called three times the day before yesterday," she informed him.

"Sure it was him?" The pen tapped again. "He spoke to you this time?"

"No, but who else would it be?" she asked through gritted teeth.

"We suggested before that you get an unlisted number," he reminded her a little impatiently.

"I can't," Molly argued. "It's on all my business cards. Prospective clients couldn't reach me if I changed it."

"Mmm-hmm, so you said. And just how are you involved with all this, sir?" he asked as if noticing Damien for the first time.

"D. J. Perry," Damien said by way of introducing himself. "I was here when Ms. Jensen discovered the threat."

"And just what is this alleged threat, ma'am?" Sharps asked her. "You want to show me?"

Molly strode to the kitchen. Damien could see her exasperation building on itself by the second.

Sharps followed her at a leisurely pace and Damien brought up the rear, interested in exactly how she would handle the situation. He hoped she kept a lid on her temper, but that didn't look too likely if Sharps kept pushing her buttons.

"There!" she exclaimed, pointing to the box of poison. "He left that right there, *opened!*"

The cop shook his head and probably would have scratched his buzz cut if his hands hadn't been occupied with the clipboard and pen. "Did he actually put poison in anything?" he asked.

Molly took a tortured breath, crossed her arms over her chest, and began tapping her fingers. "Well, we don't *know* yet until we *eat* something," she answered sweetly.

Sharps laughed and pointed at her with his pen. "Good one!"

Damien decided he'd better step in before she brained the fool. It shouldn't be difficult to use Sharps's obvious youth and inexperience to their advantage. This was no jaded cop with years on the street, he only liked pretending he was.

Damien figured the attitude toward Molly was one the rookie had picked up from one of the veterans on the force. The young ones were usually too gung-ho in a situation like this.

"Officer, we realize you can't make an arrest based on this. Ms. Jensen only wants the complaint listed in your files."

"At the very least!" Molly added, shifting with impatience.

Damien shot her a warning look the cop couldn't see and

quickly continued his appeal. "And maybe you could investigate a little while you're at it." He shrugged slightly. "If you want to help, that is. If you don't, we'd like you to write that down on your report for later reference, as well, that you responded to the call, but found an inquiry unnecessary."

"What for?"

"So her family can sue if they happen to have cause."

"What do you mean, *sue?*" the cop asked warily.

Damien explained patiently. "In the event her ex-husband—who abused her when they were married and has been harassing her since he served time for it—follows through with his threats and is successful in doing her harm. You could be charged with failure to assess the threat properly."

"But there's no B and E here. No threat as far as I can see, and no proof at all her ex had anything to do with it. She could have put that box there herself and accused him to cause trouble. Or you could have done it, for that matter! What do you expect me to do?" Sharps demanded.

Damien inclined his head and blew his breath out slowly, as though considering. "Cover your ass, maybe?" he suggested amiably. "That's what I would do if I were you. Check for prints and test some of the open containers in the kitchen to see whether he used any of the poison? How does that sound?"

The cop's eyes narrowed, obviously a belated attempt to intimidate. "Just who the hell do you think you are, telling me how to do my job?"

"A lawyer," Damien said, smiling his friendliest smile. "And a witness, if need be."

He could see Sharps mentally backpedaling. "You're *her* lawyer?"

Damien shook his head. "Only her *significant other* right

now, but all she has to do is hand me a buck and I'm hired.''

He looked at Molly and saw her roll her eyes heavenward, probably imagining the police running him through their computers, checking his occupation and getting the shock of their lives. Not that he cared. Or thought that any of them would go to that much trouble for an incident such as this. Molly would be lucky if they didn't dismiss it altogether.

"You believe her complaints are on the level, then?" Sharps asked, sounding terribly professional and a great deal more interested in getting the facts.

Stepping closer to the policeman, Damien adopted a man-to-man tone. "Absolutely. You cannot imagine what this lady's been through, Sharps. Well, maybe you can, at that. I'm sure you see a number of cases of spouse abuse out there that you can't rectify no matter how much you'd like to, am I right? Makes you feel helpless sometimes, doesn't it?"

Sharps nodded, his mouth drawn down at some memory that must have come to mind. "Yes, sir, sometimes. We can arrest the offenders now, however, even if the woman refuses to bring charges. We have a very aggressive attitude toward spouse abuse here in Nashville." He quickly added, "But we can't just haul a man in without good reason."

"Do you know Jack Jensen?" Damien asked.

The cop hesitated, then cleared his throat. His voice was low when he answered, "Not personally, no."

"But you know *of* him. You've heard that he did two in County for what some guys think was a natural reaction combined with an accident. Am I close?" Damien knew he was.

Sharps said nothing, so he continued, "You want to be held *personally* accountable if anything bad happens to this woman? If you ignore her pleas for help, if you don't get it in writing that you did all you could within the law, then you will be held responsible." Damien shook his head and looked sad.

Then he placed a hand on the cop's shoulder and leaned toward him as though to impart something confidential. "It won't cost you a dime to write this up and collect what evidence you can. How could anyone—even someone in the department who might sympathize with Jensen—object without seeming to protect a possible suspect?"

To his credit, Officer Sharps did drop his attitude of annoyance and expressed some regret. "Nobody would object to it. That's not how we work! I can write it up, no problem. See, I've already started." He angled the clipboard so Damien got only a brief glimpse.

There was Molly's name and address and a scribble that looked like *frequent questionable complaints*. At least someone had noted the others, however briefly.

"That's a start," Damien said. "I can see you care about the people in your precinct."

"But Lab won't send anybody over here for something like this," Sharps said. "No harm done, no sign of forced entry, no indication that anyone broke in and put the box there. I'm sorry as I can be, but they just won't go to the trouble to come out and take prints and samples without better cause than that. I will bag that box of poison, though, and take it in."

Damien sympathized. "I can certainly understand your dilemma. However, just make a note that Ms. Jensen asked that they come, will you do that much? And you might phone in the request. Just for the record. You've got to think of your own liability here," he reasoned.

"Gotcha! I'll call," Officer Sharps agreed, stabbing the air with his pen. "I'll do what I can, ma'am."

To prove it, he quickly jotted down Molly's complaint

and held out the form for her to sign. He took his pen back when she'd finished. "Excuse me while I make that call."

"Sure, and I do appreciate it," Molly said to Sharps. She looked at Damien with an awe that made his chest swell.

Sharps laid his clipboard on the kitchen counter, pulled the cell phone off his belt and began making his useless requests for fingerprints and test slides of foodstuffs.

Molly drifted over to Damien, looping her arm through his. "Thanks," she whispered in his ear. "If you hadn't stepped in, I think he might have arrested *me!*"

"That's what lawyers are for," he said, and dropped a brief kiss on her cheek. It surprised her, but she didn't object.

They both smiled at the cop who grinned back at them while he argued their cause into the phone. He looked so righteous, Damien wanted to laugh.

The young officer slipped on rubber gloves and bagged the box of poison. Damien knew full well it would sit forgotten on a shelf in an evidence room, but that didn't matter. The existence of it was official. Damien thought about giving him the tracking device, but figured it would probably end up on that same shelf.

Instinctively, he knew there were no prints on either. The important thing was that the poison was noted. The more incidents in the files, the better it would be when Jensen showed his hand and they got proof that he was stalking Molly.

"Now you call us if you have any more trouble, ma'am," Sharps said as he took his leave.

When the door closed behind him, Molly turned and propped against it with a sigh. "That's amazing. They never believed me before."

She pushed away from the door and started back toward the kitchen. "But now I think I might have at least one of Nashville's finest on my side, thanks to you. I'd love to be a fly on the wall when he discovers who you really are instead of an attorney.''

''No lie. I passed the bar exam. Licensed in Pennsylvania. A bonafide Philadelphia lawyer.''

Molly whirled around, mouth open, eyes wide and hands on her hips. ''Are you *serious?*''

He shrugged and grinned. ''Unless you start telling lawyer jokes.''

Chapter 6

She had called the cops. Jack pounded the steering wheel and cursed. "Stupid, brainless idiot!" Couldn't she see how useless that was? Didn't she know there was nothing there to link him to the poison? What did she take him for?

He'd thought surely she would run as soon as she found it, scared out of her mind now that she knew he could get inside the house, kill her anytime he wanted without any warning.

Where had they gone last night? he wondered. He'd hung back when they left, then followed the signal. Damned tracker had failed and he'd lost them not long after they'd left town. Anyway, that had given him the opportunity to come back, get in the house and plant the poison for Molly to find when she came home.

Now he couldn't delay another day with this next maneuver. This was the ultimate masterpiece. Molly's worst nightmare come true, next to death itself. Or maybe it would be death, after all. That was the beauty of it. A little risky maybe, to do it here, but he would just have to take the chance.

His stomach growled. Jack figured he might as well go and get some breakfast and come back later. It looked as though she meant to stay home. There was not much else he could do today as long as she was in the house. He sniffed righteously.

But tonight...

As grateful as she was for it, Molly didn't delude herself about what Damien had accomplished. Winning over one cop did not constitute support of the local police force.

In a way, she could understand their attitude. Most believed she had picked a fight with Jack and then had him jailed when she didn't win it. If only she had refuted all the lies Jack had told about that night, things might be different. But she had kept silent to protect Ford, and she still wasn't sorry.

She sighed with sheer weariness. "This is *such* a small town. Sometimes I long for a place like New York where nobody knows anybody."

Damien shook his head slowly. "No, you don't. Nashville is a great place. Small town flavor with big city perks."

"Has its drawbacks at times. Where did you grow up?" she asked him, curious about the kind of community that would turn out a man like Damien.

He inclined his head, thinking about it for a minute. "I grew up at schools for the most part. Stowe." Then he smiled proudly. "They call the alumni *Old Stoics.*"

Molly laughed. "I'd hardly call you that! I meant, your home, where your family lived. Surely you went home on weekends."

He shrugged. "Not any more often than I could help. At Christmas and for a week or so in summer. Haysleigh Hall always seemed very isolated, a bit spooky and as cold as the Arctic. There was only my uncle and the staff. I upset their rigid routine.''

"Not exactly merry, huh,'' she guessed. "What happened to your parents, if you don't mind my asking?''

"They died when I was very young. I don't remember them. My mother was English, married to an American from Pennsylvania. That's where I was born. My mother's brother came over and took me home with him after the accident. He saw to my education there. I decided to come back to the States for college and then attended law school.''

"Did your uncle mind when you left England?'' she asked, already hating a man cold enough to toss his own nephew into a boarding school after the poor boy was orphaned.

"He died when I was sixteen, just before I completed my upper levels. As soon as his funeral was over, I left. I've sold the house and property, so there are no ties for me there now.''

Or anywhere, Molly thought. He sounded glad of it. Small wonder. She couldn't help her reaction. She crossed the few feet between them and slid her arms around his waist, patting his back. Beneath his lightweight jacket, she felt the impression of the holstered gun.

His genuine laugh surprised her. With his hands on her shoulders, he moved her away from him. With one finger, he brushed a curl off her temple. "Did my life story sound that sad to you? It really wasn't so bad. I had everything I asked for, and I've usually been fortunate enough to do exactly as I please.''

He gave her shoulder a quick squeeze and turned away from her, avoiding her eyes. "Enough reminiscing. I'm hungry, aren't you?''

"Going crazy for a cup of coffee," she admitted, adopting the same light tone he was using.

"Give me ten minutes to wash up and change," he said, already heading down the hallway toward the guest room. "Meanwhile, stay out of that kitchen. I'll help you toss all the questionable food when we get back."

Obviously, talking about his background disturbed Damien, so she wouldn't pry any further. From what he'd told her, there wasn't much more to say, anyway.

Molly had the picture of a quiet, lonely boy who kept to himself and threw his energy into his studies, a boy who had learned from an early age to fend for himself among strangers. To depend entirely on himself. It made her heart ache to think about it.

She sank onto the living room sofa and waited for him, unable to help comparing Damien's upbringing to her ex-husband's. Jack had enjoyed every advantage, parents who doted on him, popularity, scads of buddies, girls falling all over him. And look how he'd turned out.

Damien might have been just as privileged when it came to wealth. It sure sounded as though his uncle had had a bundle. But family-wise, it seemed he'd been sadly deprived. He might as well not have had a home at all.

Yet one man had grown up to be a wife-beating braggart who had no thought for anybody but himself. And the other had turned out to be a man of principle, loyal, brave and a champion of women.

Molly slowly shook her head at the irony of it. Life made little sense sometimes.

"Time to make our debut as a couple," Damien suggested when he returned to the living room dressed in a casual shirt, sport jacket and slacks. An outfit that looked well-cut and wildly expensive.

She knew very well what FBI agents made since her brother was one. Ford certainly couldn't buy clothes like that. Not and still make his car payment. He griped at the cost of a new pair of jeans. He and Mary had sweated the expense of her round-trip ticket to Europe and the added cost of a vacation in Switzerland.

It made her wonder why a man who had sold an English estate and likely inherited the family fortune was working for the government, doing such dangerous work.

Molly had promised herself she wouldn't pry anymore, but he certainly did arouse her curiosity. Among other things.

She picked up her purse. "Fine, let's go. There's this great place called DiPinto's only a few blocks from here. After we eat, I'll give you a nickel tour of Nashville."

Damien nodded. He set the security alarm, which seemed to be in perfect order, and then opened the door for her. On the way to the car, he reached into his pocket. "I think I'll reactivate the tracker. We might as well make it easy for him to find us now that we want him to."

She winced. "I'm not altogether sure that's what I want. You'd better remember, Jack is crazy."

"Molly, my darling, I never doubted his insanity for a minute." He reached over and took her hand, brought it to his lips and playfully kissed it before he released her. "Look what the fool gave up."

Darling? Molly cherished the sound of the word, even though Damien was definitely joking when he said it. *Sugar, babe, hon* and *sweetie,* but nobody had ever called her *darling.* At least not with the *g* on the end. Sounded kind of uptown, she thought with a happy sigh. She tingled from that brief kiss to her knuckles. Who kissed hands anymore? She'd never had her hand kissed.

Lord, she had it bad, didn't she? She was going to have to get over this crush she had on him. And her feelings of sympathy for his early neglect. And the loneliness she sensed in him now.

Good grief, she didn't need this on top of everything else. Damien was a grown man, perfectly capable of taking care of himself. He didn't need *her,* of all people.

The smart thing would be to keep her mind on the pressing problem of her ex-husband. Once they had that solved, Damien would go on his way and she would probably never see him again. That's what she wanted him to do. What he *had* to do.

If she had any sense at all, she would quit hugging and touching him every chance she got. And she would definitely not encourage any more kisses, on hands or otherwise. That one last night in Clarkston, earth-moving as it had been, had almost gotten away from them.

Honorable and good as he was, Damien was a man and would surely take what was offered if she was foolish enough to offer it. She'd soon be picking up the pieces of her heart if she didn't put on the brakes.

Damien punched on the CD player. He had learned to appreciate even isolated moments of pleasure in the midst of chaos, and this one was especially nice. He had a beautiful woman beside him, Rachmaninoff in the background, and the anticipation of a good meal. If only he had a firm and foolproof plan to make things right for Molly, life would be damn near perfect.

"Turn here," Molly directed. He obediently pulled into the parking lot of a small family restaurant.

"Damien! I think that's Jack's car!" she exclaimed, pointing to a dark blue Mercedes across the parking lot. "He's already here! How did he do that? How did he *know?*"

Damien scanned the front windows of the restaurant. "Maybe he just got hungry while he was watching the house. This is the closest restaurant, right?"

"Only one around here, except for fast food. He hates

fast food. Maybe you're right.'' Molly was practically wringing her hands. She looked as upset as when she'd found the poison. ''I'm not sure an open confrontation's such a good idea,'' she admitted. ''Jack can get real mean.''

Damien laid his hand on her arm. ''The place looks fairly busy. He would have to be an idiot to start anything in a restaurant full of witnesses, but let's hope he does. That's exactly what we want him to do. Try not to worry. I can handle him, and I promise I won't let him hurt you.''

''I know that.'' She looked at him and tried to smile. ''Anyway, unless he loses his temper the minute we walk in, he'll probably play the good ol' boy. I doubt Jack will mess with anybody as big as he is.''

Maybe Jensen wouldn't be that smart, Damien hoped. He took her hand and threaded his fingers through hers. They felt cold.

''I would like to see him, face-to-face,'' he explained. ''The better I know him, the easier it will be to decide our course of action. But if this frightens you too much, Molly, we can go somewhere else. We don't *have* to do this right now.''

She took a deep breath and let it out in a rush. ''No, I'm just being silly. What can he do in a public place? Let's go.''

Damien opened the glove compartment, took out his tape recorder and stuck it in his pocket. Then they exited the car and entered the restaurant.

''Over there,'' Molly whispered as they waited for the hostess to seat them. ''By the front window with his back to us. He probably saw us when we drove up.''

Damien followed her gaze to the man sitting alone, his windbreaker stretched tight across wide back and shoulders. ''Be interesting to see what he does. If this is a coincidence and he wasn't expecting us, he might simply get up and leave without a word.''

"Knowing Jack, I wouldn't bet on that," Molly said.

They followed the hostess to a table on the opposite side of the room, took their seats and opened the menus. Both sat with their backs to the wall, where they could see Jensen.

Under her breath, she whispered from behind her menu, "He's coming over here."

"Stay calm," Damien suggested, reaching for his jacket pocket. "And be nice. I'm recording."

She smiled at him and nodded her approval.

"Well, well, well. Here you are again. And I thought you were serious about that restraining order," Jensen said, sounding amused. "Staying a hundred yards away from you is gonna be impossible, Moll, if you keep turning up everywhere I go."

"I wonder how that happens," she replied wryly, and went right on to the introduction. "Damien Perry, Jack Jensen."

"Jensen," Damien acknowledged as he folded his menu and stood. He quickly assessed the immediate threat. The man's clothing was too fitted to conceal a weapon, unless it was a blade. "Molly has mentioned how you keep running into each other in public places. Almost as if by design?"

Jensen was a large man, shorter but stockier than Damien. A jock type with dark hair and eyes, and a kick-butt attitude. He would have been handsome if not for the permanent I-can-take-you-anytime smirk he wore. Damien didn't think it was a result of Jack's time behind bars. It looked inborn.

"You're a Brit," Jensen said.

"You're observant," Damien replied.

Jensen ignored him and turned his attention back to Molly. "Not working today?"

Molly glared. "You know I'm not. And you know why."

"Oh, that's right," Jensen said, drawing out the last word. "Too bad about the job, but it wasn't much, anyway. Wasting your talents there, honey." He made a face, like a grimace of sympathy.

"Go away, Jack," she said, her voice gruff with irritation, "before I have you arrested. You're not supposed to communicate, remember?"

"Uh-oh, I bet we haven't had our morning coffee yet, have we?" he remarked. "I've never known you to leave home without a cup. And eating out this morning, too! Guess home cooking's lost its appeal?"

The cretin was actually taunting Molly with a veiled reminder of the poison. Damien stepped in to diffuse her temper. It would be preferable if Jensen lost his.

"We were just about to order. Are you planning to join us or just stand there and try to ruin her breakfast?" Damien smiled for effect, glanced pointedly at Molly and then regarded Jensen again. "I can promise you, nothing you can say—or do—is going to affect *my*…appetite."

Jensen's expression grew dark at the obvious sexual connotation Damien gave the word, but he managed to recover. "Just visiting the States?" he demanded, barely concealing the note of outright hostility. He wasn't trying all that efficiently to hide it, but he was still in command of himself. One more shot might do it.

"Oh, no, I live here now," Damien assured him. Then he cast Molly a provocative look. "I adore this city. Beautiful, don't you think?" He raised a brow at Jensen, grinned and winked. "And so…accommodating, as well."

The man ground his teeth. You could actually hear it. His hands were fisted and his face was turning red. A vein on his forehead pulsed. However, after a couple of seconds of that, Damien realized Jensen was not going to give them the display he'd hoped for. Might as well retire to their corners until the next round.

"Well, it has been quite an experience meeting you," Damien said with false cheer. "One I hope to repeat under…more opportune circumstances, shall we say?" He stuck out his hand, giving Jensen no choice but to shake it.

Jensen's palm was dry and the handshake bruising. Challenging. Damien squeezed back. Harder. Damien was quite confident of the outcome. Apparently Jensen soon realized it, too, and let go.

Like the bully he was, Jensen backed away from Damien and turned on Molly. "You take care now, Moll," he said softly, menacingly. "You take *real* good care."

To her credit, Molly put on a supremely confident smile of warning and replied, "You'd better do the same, Jackie Boy."

Damien wanted to hug her for the brave front. Not once had she revealed her fear when he knew it must be considerable. "Ciao, Jack," he added pointedly. "That's Italian for goodbye or face arrest."

Jensen said nothing. He merely shot Damien a get-stuffed look, turned away and left. Neither of them spoke until Jensen had slapped down his check and a few bills by the cash register and left the building.

Molly heaved a sigh of relief and closed her eyes for a moment. "Well, what do you think now that you've met him?"

Damien shrugged and sat, picking up his menu. "I doubt he'll invite me to lunch."

"Not unless he's got some of that rat poison in his pocket," she replied with a droll laugh. Then she grew all too serious. "He was just livid, Damien. I really hate to think what he'll do now."

"Whatever it is, we'll be ready," he reassured her, beckoning to the waitress who was circulating with the coffee-pot.

Hours later, Molly felt ready to give up on the city tour. How in the world had she ever thought she could entertain a man like Damien? Oh, he acted interested enough, but she knew he must be bored silly.

After their ride out to visit The Hermitage, Andrew Jackson's home, she'd realized the place must seem relatively new to him, given the ancient castles near where he'd grown up. Heck, his own home had probably been older than the White House. Dumb move on her part.

The art museum here at Creekwood must seem tame when he compared it to, say, the National Gallery in Trafalgar Square. Of course, she'd never seen it except in photos, but she could just imagine how great it was, how majestic and chock-full of centuries' old artworks.

But he marched on, pretending eagerness, all but dragging her into the Pineapple Room Restaurant adjacent to the museum for sandwiches. They sat there now, finishing their iced tea while Damien shuffled through the brochures they had picked up of other Nashville attractions. Molly almost groaned.

"Here!" he said, tossing one beside her plate. "We can't miss this."

"The toy museum?" she asked with a huff of disbelief. "All right, that's enough. Let's go home and watch a video or something. You're off the hook."

"No, no!" he argued, laughing and snatching up the pamphlet. "I mean it. C'mon, I love trains. Indulge me."

She shook her head and set down her tea glass. "You're being nice, Damien, but give it up. I know your eyes must be glazing over by now."

He lay his hand on her arm and smiled that wonderful,

gracious smile of his. "Molly, I can't tell you when I've had more fun."

"Right. You can't tell me because the truth would hurt my feelings! I love Nashville with all my heart, but you—"

"Love it, too," he assured her. Then he pinched her wrist playfully. "But I'd love it even more if I could see those trains. Be a sport?"

Gone was all his savoir faire. He sounded like a little boy, which, she realized, he still might be in one respect. Had he ever had many toys around? Boarding schools probably didn't allow much room for those. And he'd spent so little time at the home that wasn't a home.

She slung her purse strap over her shoulder and got up. "Trains it is, then. C'mon, kid, let's make tracks."

He groaned at the pun and pulled her free arm through his to escort her out. Molly almost groaned, too. His touch made her a little dizzy.

In the next couple of hours she met a whole new Damien. While she stood by in amazement, he carried on about track widths and steam versus electric locomotives until she wanted to scream. The man was in heaven.

They examined every exhibit at least twice, and then checked out the gift shop. He came out of there with a boxed set he swore was appropriate for a child Sydney's age. Molly knew better. Syd would never get her chubby little hands on that prize, she thought with a grin.

As the day wore on Damien periodically assured her that they were not being followed. He had turned off the tracker before they'd left the restaurant and kept close watch everywhere they went.

She supposed it didn't matter all that much whether Jack followed them during the day. He wouldn't approach them again the way he had at breakfast. She had a feeling his next move would not be out in the open at all. Damien agreed.

She was surprised when he wanted to see where Jack lived, but she gave him directions to the Jensens' house after they left the toy shop.

"Pretentious, huh?" she asked as they drove by the gates to the high brick wall surrounding the mansion and property.

"Gives him the illusion of safety," Damien remarked cryptically.

"I think you'd better leave him that illusion," Molly warned. "If you have any wild ideas, you ought to know there are two Dobermans prowling that fence who might like the taste of you."

Damien laughed. After their day on the town, Molly thought he seemed to have loosened up somehow. She knew he had to be tired. He hadn't had much sleep last night, if any. Maybe he was punchy from exhaustion.

At the moment he reminded her of Ford. Not in looks— they were as different as night and day there—but Damien wore the same expectancy, the same eager-for-trouble expression her brother was famous for. Could be an agent thing, she supposed.

"Dogs love me. What else ought I to know?" he asked, nodding toward the Jensen property.

"Are you just idly questioning, or about to get busted for trespassing?"

"Oh, Molly, darling, I am never idle," he said with an engaging grin. "And I have never, *ever* been busted for anything."

Chapter 7

Damien toyed with the idea of checking out the Jensens on their home ground, but figured he could glean all the pertinent information about them from Molly. The main thing he was interested in was getting a better handle on Jack, a profile.

Harassing Molly with phone calls and embarrassing her in public were bad enough, but obtaining a key to her house and placing that poison was something else again. So was buying a tracking device and tailing her everywhere she went. Those things indicated a great deal of thought and preplanning. Actions a true stalker, not just an irate ex-husband, might take.

He watched Molly dish up the take-out steak dinners they had picked up on the way home. The way she had groused about throwing out all the food that Jensen might have tainted with the rat poison, Damien wondered just how tight her funds really were.

"Does Jensen pay you child support or alimony?" he asked, handing her a couple of glasses from the dishwasher.

She shook her head and concentrated on filling the glasses with ice.

"Nothing?" he asked.

"I never wanted anything from him," she explained. "Jack insisted Sydney was not his. His mom and dad believe him, I guess. They've never even asked to see Syd. Like it would convince them if they did! Syd doesn't have a single Jensen trait, looks or otherwise. And I'm glad of that. It's fine with me if he thinks she's not his. Can you see me granting him visitation rights?"

"Good point," he granted.

When she handed him his glass of tea, he saw the anger in her eyes. "They think Jack got himself saddled with lowlife, poor white trash. That I tricked him."

Damien snorted at the description. "You *are* joking?"

She smiled wryly, her natural good humor taking over. "Nope. You see before you a disadvantaged, junior college dropout. I'm sure they imagine Jack finding me in some rundown dump with a sofa on the front porch and a junker in my yard up on cement blocks. I was out to trap my sorry self a guy with money."

"Trap? You weren't pregnant when you married him," Damien stated.

Molly laughed as she set his plate of food in front of him and then sat. "No, actually they think I used my lush and wicked body. That's a laugh, huh? Like, I'm so-o-o enticing."

She was, Damien thought. Enticing as hell, but she didn't seem to know it.

"He must have loved you to go against his parents' wishes and marry you, anyway," Damien said. "He probably still does love you, but it's turned pathological. The hate he feels is just as strong. Did he suffer abuse as a boy, do you think?"

"Possibly," she answered, and then qualified it. "Or

maybe he just observed it. Mildred can be irritating, no doubt about it. And when the old man's not around, she acts haughty as hell, but I think she's probably more scared of John than I ever was of Jack.''

"You believe he mistreats her?" Damien asked, taking a bite of the tasteless beef.

"I can't say for sure. I never saw it happen or noticed any bruises, but it makes sense, doesn't it? Learned behavior? Like father, like son?''

"Could be." He nodded, satisfied that he'd gained at least one piece of the puzzle. Jack had probably been battered, too, not that *that* was any excuse for what he'd done to Molly.

Damien certainly had seen and endured his share of beatings growing up and it wasn't as though he went around pounding on schoolteachers because of it.

Question was, how deep did Jensen's rage go? Would he kill? He certainly thought he had when Molly had fallen and hit her head.

"He feels jealousy, even now," Damien told her. "That was obvious in the restaurant. Yet he wants to hurt you, either psychologically or physically. The man is definitely sick."

"Well, thank you, Dr. Perry," she said with an engaging grin. "That is so profound! Will you be billing me for that diagnosis?"

He laughed with her. "Never mind me. I'm just thinking out loud."

"Uneducated as I am, I had figured all that out by myself. At least the part about Jack. I know he loved me once, and I thought I loved him, too."

Damien said nothing. Of course, she had loved the man. A woman like Molly would never marry where she didn't love. Jensen had betrayed her in the very worst way. For that alone, he ought to be shot.

She pointed at him with her fork. "But his parents could be right about one thing. His wealth might have played some part in my selection process." She shrugged. "Could be, that's another reason I didn't ask for any support. Maybe I felt a little guilty."

"You would never have married for money, Molly," Damien argued.

"Spoken like a man who has never lived without it," she countered with a wry smile. "How do you know what I would or wouldn't do?"

Damien knew, but he wondered if she really doubted herself that much.

"If I promised you a fortune, told you that you and Sydney would have everything your hearts desired, you wouldn't marry *me*, would you?"

She giggled, wrinkling her beautiful nose with its sprinkle of freckles. "Hey, you call the preacher, honey! I'll bake the cake."

He laughed, too, but at himself. Why the devil had he asked her such a thing? Obvious answer, if he was honest enough to face it. The thought of marriage to someone such as Molly had somehow taken root in his mind these past two days. Maybe that's why he'd put the example to her, to diffuse what should have sounded like a ridiculous idea, though it seemed to have the opposite effect on him to say it out loud.

It wasn't as though he could love a woman he'd only known for a few days, could he? He doubted he knew how to love if he'd known her for a lifetime. But the notion of someone loving him certainly had appeal.

Now he had no clue what to say, so he said nothing.

She was still chuckling softly and making whirls in her mashed potatoes with her fork. She looked up at him. "Do you like chocolate?"

"What?"

"Chocolate. I truly need a fix. Let's go to Dixie Freeze and get a shake." Then she snapped her fingers. "No, wait! We don't have to. I've got a bag of candy bars in the van."

He shoved back his chair to get up. "I'll get it for you." Damien was relieved she had remembered the candy. Just thinking about going out again exhausted him even more than he already was. If he didn't get a few hours' sleep, he'd soon be of no use to her whatsoever.

She waved him back down and hopped up. "It's okay. I know right where they are."

With a practiced motion, she deactivated the security alarm and flipped on the light in the garage.

Unwilling to let her go out there alone, Damien followed her and stood in the doorway. She was already at the van, so he waited there, propped against the door frame.

"What in the world is this?" he heard Molly mutter to herself.

Over the van he could see her move toward a white box sitting on the workbench. His first thought was *bomb*. "Molly! No!"

She screamed. Before he could reach her, she'd scrambled backward and huddled into the far corner of the garage, her hands over her head.

Bees swarmed everywhere, filling the garage with a loud angry hum.

"Freeze, Molly! Don't move!" he shouted.

Several stung him on the arms as he dashed for the garage door and shoved it open. Damien carefully stood out of the way until most of the swarm had flown outside. Some remained, angrily circling the white box. A few hit the walls of the garage as they sought escape.

As soon as the hum subsided and the air became fairly clear, he went to collect Molly from the corner so he could get her inside. She hadn't moved.

"Most of them are gone," he said. "The rest are finding

their way back to the hive where the queen is. It's all right now.''

She uttered a keening sound of pure terror as he tried to pull her stiffened body out of its crouched position. He spoke softly to her. "Molly! Listen to me, darling, it's fine now. They're gone. Come on, uncover your head and look around. See? Were you stung? Let me see."

Jerkily, she held up her arms. "Help me," she cried, her voice high-pitched terror. One hand was already swelling and not just at the site of the sting. Her arm, as well. Damien glanced at her face and saw her struggling for breath.

"Oh, my God!" He grabbed her up and ran out to the Lexus, setting her down only long enough to fish out his keys and unlock the door. He shoved her inside and ran around to the driver's side.

Damien remembered passing the hospital on their afternoon tour and judged it would take about ten minutes to get there. He meant to make it in five. The worst thoughts imaginable ran through his mind.

Lack of oxygen could cause brain damage if she couldn't breathe. What if he didn't get her there in time? She might stop breathing altogether. They might not save her at all if he didn't hurry.

Damien pressed the accelerator to the floorboard and flew, running red lights, horn blaring. He cursed when an ambulance blocked the access to the emergency doors. Screeching to a halt, half on the sidewalk, he leaped out and ran around to get her out of the car.

By the time he got her in his arms, she could barely draw a breath and her eyes were swollen shut.

"Hang on, Molly. Almost there!" She was totally stiff in his arms. And shaking. He struggled through the automatic doors, trying not to bang her head or feet, and carried her toward the desk at a run.

"Anaphylactic shock!" he shouted. "Hurry! *Do* something! She can't breathe!"

No paperwork. No delay. Green coats surrounded them and yanked Molly out of his arms.

A hypodermic seemed to come out of nowhere and plunge into her arm. Then another. Someone shoved him aside and he stumbled backward.

They virtually threw her onto a gurney and wheeled her behind a curtain. Damien followed.

"Cuff her! More epi, five cc's! Stat! Get a trach kit ready!" Shouts, demands for meds and equipment rang out, interspersed with curt reports on her respiration, blood pressure and pulse.

Damien remained as close as he could get to the circle of bodies working to save her.

"Get him out of here!" Someone shoved him again.

Damien shifted back a few feet, his heart in his throat, and watched the haste and purpose with which they moved, grateful as hell for it, hoping against hope it made the difference and kept Molly alive.

"Don't die," he whispered rapidly, over and over. Prayer, mantra or whatever it was, finally worked.

"Almost gotcha back." Short pause. Another voice. "C'mon, girl, suck in that oxygen! Oops, mask off… Off, *now!*"

Molly threw up. "Good *girl!*" the doctor crowed, high-fiving one of the nurses without touching. "She's back. Hook her up and stand by."

Back. Back from death. Damien almost retched himself as he listened to Molly gasp and heave. He leaned against the wall of the cubicle and slowly slid to the floor, his head in his hands, his own breathing labored.

God, he'd almost lost her. To *bees,* for God's sake!

One of the nurses squatted beside him. "How 'bout you? You okay?"

Damien uncovered his face and found it wet. Then he brushed his fingers over his hands and wrists, feeling three painful mounds. "I'm fine. How…how is she?"

The woman looked over her shoulder at the three still attending Molly. "Close shave, but she'll be fine now. Did you know she was allergic?"

"She was swelling. I saw someone die from it once. How many stings?" he asked, imagining that the devils had practically eaten her alive.

"Just a few, but sometimes one's enough," the nurse said, giving him her hand and indicating that he should get up now. Damien wasn't certain his legs would work.

He'd been shot a couple of times and held up better than this. But this was Molly. Sweet Jesus, he was shaking. In shock. And it wasn't from the stings. At least not *his* stings. Why was he affected this way? He'd seen people he liked near death before. He'd seen them die. But *like* didn't quite cover what he felt for Molly, did it? Her vulnerability touched him, of course. And he did feel responsible for her. Even those things did not explain his reaction to nearly losing her, however.

The nurse pushed him into a plastic chair and gave him juice.

A half hour passed. Only when he saw the steady rise and fall of Molly's chest, only when the edema in her limbs and features decreased, did his heart stop pounding and his own breathing regulate.

He took care of the bill with his credit card and then impatiently cooled his heels in the waiting room. They were keeping her around for a few hours to make certain there were no secondary reactions to the venom or the antidote.

Without asking permission, Damien reentered the cubicle, stood next to her and kept close watch himself. He couldn't stand to think of her lying there all alone with only periodic checks by the nurses.

Monitors beeped. Machines hummed. And Damien kept a close eye on the digital readouts as if he were the only one aware of them.

He wished he could call Brenda. It would be a comfort for Molly to have her mother here. Yet Brenda had no way to get from Clarkston to Nashville tonight and Damien was not about to leave Molly to go get her.

Probably best not to call her, he thought, imagining how a mother would worry when there was nothing she could do for her child.

Gently, he held Molly's hand, the one she'd offered him in her terror, measuring it with his eyes every few seconds to check for further swelling. He watched her face, hating the puffiness, willing it away.

He'd had no idea whether Molly had medical insurance when they'd asked him. He knew nothing about her medical history other than that she had borne a child and that she was allergic to bee stings. How could he care so damned much about someone and know so little about her?

He shouldn't be caring this way. Instead he ought to be treating her as he would anyone else who was under his protection. Yet Molly was different in so many ways. Maybe because she was not part of an official assignment. Maybe because this was personal. He could not force himself to disassociate if he tried. The bad thing was, he didn't even want to try.

She appeared to be asleep, likely a result of shock. He turned to the nurse who had spoken with him earlier and was now adjusting the machine near Molly's head. "Why not settle her into a regular room for the night?"

"No need. We aren't too busy down here right now and she's already hooked up to the monitors. She can go home in a little while if her vitals remain stable."

"Thank God," he muttered, raking a hand through his hair as he clenched his eyes shut. "You're sure?"

"Yes, but somebody ought to keep a close eye on her for the next twenty-four hours. Just be with her in case."

"I will. I'll be the one," he informed her. "She won't be alone."

"Great. If the swelling starts again, or she gets to feeling tingly, you bring her on back."

Damien nodded. And waited.

What he really wished he could do was get back to her house and determine how that damned beehive had wound up in her garage. However, if Molly had already known she was allergic and Jensen knew it, too, the incident didn't need that much investigation. This would be attempted murder.

Besides, he couldn't take her there, not after what had just happened. She might never want to go there again, and he could hardly blame her.

Damien looked down at Molly's face again. The light freckles that he found so endearing were even more prominent in contrast to her paleness, but at least the dreadful swelling had subsided. Her colorless lips were devoid of their rosy fullness and mobility. "My sweet girl," he whispered.

"Not sweet, not a girl," she rasped, the corners of her mouth turning up slightly.

"Molly? How do you feel? God, I was so worried! I still am," he admitted, then thought how that sounded. "But you'll be fine. They said you'd be all right very soon now."

"Get a grip, Perry." Her eyes didn't open. "Break me out of this place and take me to Clarkston, will you?"

"As soon as I'm sure. We can't have you relapsing. We'll go as soon as they tell us you've recovered," he promised.

"I'm okay now, just exhausted from tossing my cookies," she assured him, looking up at him now. "Attractive, huh?" Her lashes were wet and her eyes were bloodshot, making the green irises seem even greener, if that were possible.

"Beautiful," he declared, meaning it with all his heart. "And beautifully alive." The strength of his relief stunned him. It made him wonder what kind of devastation he would have suffered if Molly hadn't lived. Damien quickly dismissed the thought as too dangerous to consider at the moment.

"I need to see Syd," she murmured. "And Mama."

"Of course you do, but we'd better wait a few more hours," he said gently. "Then we'll go. This time you're staying there with your mother and the baby, no argument."

He held up a finger to silence her protest. "Sleep a bit longer, the time will pass faster that way."

She did. Damien left the cubicle, consulted the doctor, who promised the crisis was over and Molly would definitely survive.

Vastly relieved, Damien found the bank of phones down the hall and made a call to arrange for the delivery of another rental car. He ordered something as totally different from the Lexus as he could get.

Jensen could be watching the Lexus, which Damien had left illegally parked near the emergency entrance with its doors standing open. He hadn't returned to see about it. Maybe they'd towed it away by now, not that it mattered.

"Mr. Perry? She seems to be stable now and in very little distress. If you'd like to take her home, we'll let you sign her out."

Take her home? Not under any circumstances would he take her there. She was eager to leave the hospital and see her mother and daughter. He understood her need to be with her family, so they would go to Clarkston.

Then Damien considered what they would do there if

Molly had a reaction so far away from emergency services. He'd have to convince her to stay in Nashville somehow.

As soon as he had done the necessary paperwork and the nurse had Molly situated in a wheelchair, Damien pushed her through the entire length of the hospital, up one floor and out the main entrance.

The Explorer he'd ordered was waiting. He paid the delivery man an extra hundred to wait two hours before approaching the Lexus parked on the other side of the building to drive it back and turn it in.

Even then, Damien took the most circuitous route he could devise before turning in the direction of the highway toward Clarkston. At least he could have them on the way there when morning came and the danger of Molly having a secondary reaction had passed.

If Jensen planned to follow them this time, he would bloody well need magic, he thought as he made yet another detour.

Molly reclined as far back as the passenger seat of the Explorer would allow. Her lethargy worried him, even though he knew to expect it.

Damien stopped at a gas station to get her a sugary soft drink and some coffee for himself. His current caffeine high was about to crash.

While they were stopped there, he noticed a small motel down the street. ''Molly, would you mind terribly if we stopped to sleep for a few hours? I'm not certain I can make Clarkston in my current condition.''

Exhaustion made it unsafe for him to drive, but the other reasons for not leaving were even more important. He didn't want to be very far from the hospital if her symptoms returned.

Also, if they arrived in the wee hours and woke Brenda, Molly would want to tell her everything about meeting Jensen at breakfast and then what had happened to her with the bees. She needed to rest, not talk the rest of the night.

And, last but far from least, he needed to hold her, just for a little while. He needed that so badly he actually ached from it. The urge felt alien to him. He'd never needed this. It had to be a by-product of burnout or something, this latching on to someone emotionally. He *knew* better than to do that.

She offered him a sip of her soft drink. "I'm sorry, Damien, I didn't think. You must be beat. It would probably scare Mama to death if we rolled in there at this hour, anyway. Morning will be fine with me."

Though he could see her disappointment, he let it go. For her own safety and his peace of mind, they couldn't leave Nashville yet.

Damien returned to the convenience store where he purchased a few toiletry items and an I Love Tennessee T-shirt for Molly to sleep in.

He got them a room on the back side of the hotel and pulled the Explorer around to it.

Only after Molly was in the shower and he was stretched out on one of the queen-size beds did Damien realize that he'd left Molly's house wide open. Not only had he not closed the door from the kitchen into the garage, he'd left the garage door up, as well.

However, Jensen obviously could get in there whenever he wanted to, anyway. And burglars were the least of Molly's problems at the moment.

Useless for him to worry now. He certainly wasn't taking her back there only to lock the house. If anything was stolen in the meantime, he would be more than happy to replace it.

Just then she emerged from the bathroom wearing the shirt he'd bought her. The bright orange of it barely skimmed the tops of her thighs.

Instant arousal. "My God, what legs!"

"Thanks, I think," she replied, laughing as she raked her hair around to one side of her neck.

Damien hadn't realized he'd spoken out loud. "Sorry. It's only that I haven't seen them before." He puffed out a little breath. "Spectacular."

"Are you a leg man, Perry?" she asked, teasing him.

No, he never had been, he thought. Not until now. He took a deep breath and hoped she wasn't looking at his lap.

He'd always been a breast man, if she really wanted to know. He didn't think she would.

With difficulty, he resisted settling his gaze on his favorite female parts and jerked his attention away from her altogether before he said something even more stupid. "How do you feel?" he asked.

"Pretty good, actually, considering I almost died. Thanks for saving me, by the way. I didn't have sense enough left to tell you where to find my kit."

"Kit? Syringe kit for the allergy?"

"Yep. It was in the house, in my purse. Lot of good it did me there, huh?"

He sat up on the edge of the bed and clasped his hands together between his knees. Molly was on the bed opposite him, wielding the hairbrush he'd purchased.

"Jensen knows about your allergy?" Damien asked.

"He knows," she affirmed. Her eyes met his in perfect understanding. He didn't need to tell her anything. She had already guessed.

It wasn't hard to see why, when she added, "Jack's grandfather kept beehives as a hobby. Jack worked with them as a 4-H project when he was a kid. He mentioned it once soon after we married, when a honeybee zapped me in the yard."

"Did you have the same reaction then?"

"Not really. I nearly died once several years before that,

so I had the kit with me. I was all right by the time I got to the hospital, just a little shaky. They just observed me for a while, warned me again never to be without the epinephrine and let me go.'' She laid the hairbrush on the nightstand between the beds.

"This time he's gone too far," Damien said, moving across to the other bed. Molly held out her arms and he pulled her close, burying his face in the curve of her neck, pressing his lips to the pulse there.

"I almost lost you," he whispered, sliding his hands over the softness of her curves, relishing the reassuring warmth of her body. It could have grown cold by now.

She could have been cold. *Dead.* He shuddered.

Why did he feel this insurmountable rage? Training and experience had taught him the importance of retaining objectivity, keeping a cool head. *You feel this way because you've allowed a personal involvement to cloud your reason, fool.* Damien nodded in response to the inner voice he always heeded, the one that had kept him alive so many times. It spoke to him again. Words he didn't want to hear. *You love her.* "Yes," he whispered.

"It's a strange way to threaten me, don't you think? The stings could have killed me, but he knew I had a way to prevent that. He went to an awful lot of trouble to do this, and took a big chance of getting caught, when he couldn't even be sure it would work."

"A damned near thing," Damien said darkly. "Too bloody close for comfort."

"Jack's daring us, Damien. Daring us to prove he did this," she said. "Maybe we can."

"If not, then I have to kill him. I can't let him hurt you again," Damien said, meaning every word.

He had never killed a man before without the reason of self-defense. But he could kill in defense of her, and of little Sydney, who was part of Molly. If that's what it took to protect them, he would terminate Jack Jensen and never feel a second's remorse.

He tightened his hold on Molly and closed his eyes to savor her escape from death.

It troubled Damien that he felt so strongly, especially in so short a time. What if Molly were meant for him right from the first? Suppose his parents' accidental death had thrown some cosmic plan out of kilter. A fanciful thought, that, and he wasn't usually given to those. However, if he had remained in the States, they might have met sooner, somehow.

He would have been different, Damien was certain, had he not been torn out place and plunked down in a different country. If his mother and father had lived, if they had been able to show him a normal sort of existence, he would have the knowledge and skills he needed to make Molly happy.

About the best he could do for her now was to keep her alive so that her daughter would not have to grow up without her. What a tragedy if little Sydney had no opportunity to learn mothering skills from the best teacher available. And perhaps Molly would remarry someday and provide a two-parent home for her.

Damien didn't like to think of another man assuming that place in Molly's or Sydney's life. It was a place he would love to have himself, yet it was one he wouldn't seek because he wasn't qualified.

Sleep deprivation must be affecting him more than usual, he decided. At the moment he should be dwelling on the threat to Molly, determining how to ensure that she had a future for him to worry about.

His fingers sought Molly's wrist and pressed gently as he felt her pulse. Her respiration seemed a bit unsteady, yet not really erratic or labored. They probably shouldn't be discussing Jensen at all since it must be upsetting her.

"You are not going to kill him!" she announced.

Damien could not bring himself to promise he wouldn't. But he had to say something to calm her down.

"Only if it becomes necessary."

Chapter 8

Molly could tell that Damien meant every word of what he said. He held her tighter, his hands on her sensitized skin driving her wild.

She pushed him away. "Will you listen to me?"

"I heard you," Damien said, looking her straight in the eyes. "But all we have is the fact that he knows something about bee-keeping. That's not enough to tie him to this, to prove he intended to kill you. You know as well as I do he would have worn gloves to handle that wooden hive. And if he has any sense at all, he stole the thing."

Molly threw up her hands and fell backward onto the pillow. "Leave, then," she said, furious at his hardheadedness. "Go back to Florida or wherever you came from and forget about it." She knew he wouldn't, but wished he would. "I don't want you in trouble over this, Damien."

"And if I do go? What will do you do?"

"Hide," she said, deciding that was the best option, anyway, whether Damien left or not. "I'll hide until Ford comes home."

But there would still be the problem of convincing Ford that he shouldn't kill Jack. Reasoning with him would be impossible. Maybe she still stood a better chance with Damien. She sat up, reached over and took one of his hands in hers. "Look, I just don't want you going off the deep end, huh?"

"You're right, of course." Damien ran a hand through his tousled hair and nodded. Then he gently pushed her back against the pillows again, pulled the covers from beneath her body and settled them over her.

"This has gone beyond phone calls and scary tricks, Molly. The police need to kick in some help. Tomorrow I'll see that they do. Meanwhile, put it out of your mind. I plan to do the same for tonight."

For a moment he just looked at her lying there, his expression unreadable. "Don't say no, Molly. I have to do this," he told her softly. Then he lifted the covers, got in bed and stretched out full-length beside her.

She didn't move a muscle.

If he kissed her now, she wouldn't have the least bit of will to say no to anything he wanted. But Damien merely snuggled her against him, wrapped his arms around her and closed his eyes. He found sleep a lot more quickly than she did.

The next morning Damien took Molly on to Clarkston, intending to stay only long enough to help her explain the past day's happenings to her mother. He hadn't counted on their combined effort to make him stay for lunch. It was almost as if they were afraid for him to return to Nashville.

For no other reason than to set Molly's mind at ease, he agreed. While the women put together sandwiches and salad, Damien kept an eye on the baby. She toddled around the old-fashioned living room, picking up objects one by one and bringing them to him like gifts. "Dere," she would say with that wide, foolish grin, and go for another prize.

After a while, he sat on the sofa surrounded by knick-knacks, crocheted dresser scarves, and several small toys. Then she proceeded to climb up his legs and into his lap.

"Proud of yourself?" he asked.

She patted his chest with her open palms. "Dammit," she announced.

Damien glanced through the dining room into the kitchen. "Best not broadcast that word," he advised her. "Mom and Granny will *not* be happy, Sydney."

She curled her hands to her stomach. "Chiddy."

"Oh, I see. Names. You're Chiddy and I'm Dammit. We need to work on your pronunciation, don't you think?" He tickled her neck with one finger. She giggled and threw herself against him.

Damien laughed with her. One by one, he picked up each find she had brought to the sofa and said the name for it, chuckling with delight when she gave him a garbled approximation of each word. "You're a sharp cookie, aren't you, my girl?"

He heard a sound and looked up to see Molly standing in the doorway of the dining room, frowning. "What's wrong?" he asked, lifting Sydney down from his lap, standing her on her feet.

For a moment Molly didn't answer, then she came into the room and took the baby. "Time for her nap," she said, and whisked her away.

Damien wondered why his getting better acquainted with Sydney troubled Molly. Was it because he had admitted he knew nothing about babies? Did she fear he would hurt her?

When she returned, headed back toward the kitchen, he stopped her. "What did I do?"

"Nothing," she answered, avoiding his eyes. "It's just not a great idea for her to get attached to you, that's all."

"Why not?"

She did look at him then, a faintly accusing expression on her face. "Because you'll soon be leaving, Damien. If she gets used to having you around, she'll miss you."

They went in to lunch without discussing it any further. He was in no position to promise he would stay, and had no idea whether Molly would want him to, even if he could. It might be best if he left the child alone, and not just for her sake. If he grew any more fond of her, he would probably miss her, as well. He would have problems enough leaving Molly.

As soon as they finished the meal, he left with a promise to call them as soon as there were any further developments. Police headquarters was his first destination.

When Damien arrived at the main precinct, he identified himself properly. He also stated that his request for help was not official, thereby avoiding the usual suspicion of jurisdictional encroachment. This was not a case for the FBI. Yet.

Fortunately, he drew a young detective called Mitch Winton, a fairly recent addition to the force. Consequently, Winton knew nothing at all about the Jensens or Jack's prior arrest until he obtained the file.

After he read it and heard about Jack's antics since his release, Damien had little trouble convincing him to investigate. He followed Damien to Molly's house to gather what evidence they could on the previous night's attempt on her life.

The minute they turned into the driveway, Damien saw that the garage door was closed.

Winton pulled in behind Damien and got out of his unmarked car. "Do you have a key?"

"It shouldn't be locked." He walked up the garage door

and it opened easily. One of the neighbors might have closed it, but he didn't think so.

Together, he and the detective entered. "Both the garage and the kitchen doors were open when we left," Damien declared. "And the hive is missing. He's been here."

"I'll ask around," Winton said. "See if anybody saw anything. No bees left," he noted unnecessarily.

Damien searched along the baseboards in the corner where Molly had crouched after she'd been stung. Finally, a little luck. "Here are two dead ones."

Winton pulled an envelope out of his pocket and scooped them up on it. "Regular ol' honeybees, looks like. Can't prove anything from these, I'm afraid. I will certainly question Mr. Jensen about it. You can be sure of that. He'll deny any knowledge of it, y'know."

"Will you put a tail on him?" Damien asked.

The detective shook his head. "Wish I could. It's not that I don't believe your concerns are valid, Agent Perry, but we just don't have enough on the man to justify surveillance. He'd holler harassment."

"Great," Damien growled, shoving his hands into his pockets. "What do you suggest?"

"Frankly, I can't help you much. He comes within a hundred yards of Mrs. Jensen or tries to communicate with her in any way, then we can arrest him."

"And he'd be out within a couple of hours," Damien said.

"That's the way it works," Winton verified. "He's got a free run until he does something to break the law." He looked around the garage and clicked his tongue against his teeth. "Something worse than this."

"Worse than attempted murder," Damien said with disgust.

"Attempted murder that leaves some kind of cluc he's

guilty,'' Winton added, glaring down at the insects he held. ''Something besides two dead bees.''

Well, he would have to take matters into his own hands, Damien decided.

''Call me immediately if he gives you any more trouble,'' Winton said. ''I promise I'll do whatever I can.'' After offering sincere apologies about the restrictions of the law they were both so familiar with, Detective Winton left.

Damien feared if he brought Molly back home, Jensen might be successful next time. God only knew the man possessed a wicked imagination when it came to this kind of thing. He had probably been dreaming up creative things to do to Molly for two long years.

She couldn't stay hidden in Clarkston forever. Even if Molly were willing to do that, she would have to get a job. Social security numbers were too easy to trace. Jensen would find her. This situation needed settling now, while he was here to help her.

Damien went back into the house, showered, changed, packed clothing for Molly and collected his own things. Then he locked up when he left. It appeared that he and Molly were on their own when it came to stopping Jensen, and she should have a say in what Damien intended to do next.

''I think it's brilliant!'' Molly exclaimed and clapped her hands. ''I just wonder why we didn't think of it before!''

''I'm doing this alone,'' Damien declared.

''No, you're not. If you don't take me with you, I'll be right behind you. You know that's no bluff. I *need* to do this, Damien.''

''Why? You asked me to help you. Now trust me to handle it.''

She lifted that determined chin. ''Because I'm sick of being a victim and acting like one, that's why. I'm ready to take the offensive.'' She paused, looked from him to her mother and back again. "Offense is better than defense, right?"

Her mother objected. No surprise there. "It's crazy, is what it is," she said. "Dangerous, too. Molly, you're going to stay right here with me. If Damien wants to tweak Jack's tail and make him even madder, you let him do it by himself."

Molly leaned forward over the kitchen table and squeezed her mother's arm. "But, Mama, don't you see the beauty of it? Stalking the stalker! Give him a taste of his own medicine. I can help Damien, and I *need* to do this. Jack's either going to get rattled, make a wrong move and get busted, or leave town for good."

"Or kill you both!"

Damien interceded. "Look, Brenda, if you have a better idea, I'm perfectly willing to listen. I've run dry of alternatives." He sighed. "And as much as I dislike taking her along, the plan might be more effective if Molly's there to advise me on Jensen's vulnerabilities."

He didn't seem very happy about having her go with him, but to his credit, he had realized she was right about her input.

They both looked at her. "Hey, I'm in this all the way. I think Jack's already done his worst with the bees. He knew that was my biggest fear in the world and that's why he put them there. Nothing he could ever do would terrify me more. Last night's the last time he'll catch us by surprise. We'll keep him so busy, he won't have time to arrange anything else."

"I can't talk you out of this, can I?"

"No, Mama, you can't, and neither can Damien." She shot him a pointed look. "So when do we begin?"

"Now is as good a time as any. The earlier we get started, the sooner we'll see if this works."

Molly found it much more difficult to say goodbye to Sydney this time. Her Syd, sleeping peacefully on her tummy with her fingers in her mouth, trusting everyone she knew and loved to look after her. Best to make it quick. Molly leaned over and brushed her lips across the feather-soft red curls. "'Bye, love," she whispered. "Be sweet for Maw Maw."

She grinned when she heard her mother's whispered response to Damien. "If the kid actually ever calls me that, I'm going to spank her mother."

"Maw Maw's not that bad," he replied softly. "Sydney calls me Dammit."

Molly breezed through the bedroom door, stopping for a hug and swift farewell to her mother. "Thanks for looking after Syd, Mama. I owe you."

"Like I expect anything for keeping my own grandchild!" She scoffed. "You just keep yourselves safe, both of you."

Damien escorted Molly out and into the Explorer. When he got in, he buckled up and sat there for a minute, one arm propped against the window, looking impatient. "You're determined?"

"Absolutely. Let's do it."

"All right, but there are ground rules. Do exactly what I tell you, when I tell you. No protests or questions. Agreed?"

"Aye, aye, sir," she promised with a salute.

He cranked the car, backed out onto the deserted street and they were on their way. "We're not staying at your house," he told her. "It's too dangerous. We'll be moving around."

"Okay. What do we do?"

"Find and follow him, see what kind of mischief we can make. Basically rattle his cage. It won't be as easy as it sounds, Molly. We need to be there, right behind him, consistently, while maintaining that hundred yards distance. We take turns at watch, so you'll have to sleep when I tell you, and keep your eyes open and stay alert when it's your turn."

"What about bathroom breaks?" she asked.

Damien smiled his approval. "A practical question. I won't bother to tell you what male agents do when we team up on surveillance. That wouldn't help you much. All I can advise is to drink very little coffee and thank your stars the vegetation's plentiful in Nashville."

"Behind the bushes," Molly guessed with a grimace. "Okay. What about meals?"

"Junk food works. We'll stock up."

Molly remained silent for a long time, almost unwilling to make her next, even more practical inquiry. Finally she heaved a sigh and voiced it. "What if he turns on us, Damien? What do we do then?"

"Deal with it," he replied with a nod. "If he pulls a weapon, he's done for, but I don't believe he will. Any other kind of confrontation won't be a problem for us, but it certainly will be for him."

Molly almost hoped Jack would be so foolish. "I don't know exactly how he'll react, but he won't put up with this for long."

"I'm counting on that. All we have to do is find him and stay behind him until he cracks," Damien affirmed as he pulled into an all-night grocery. "Jerky, Squeezit-Juice and Twinkies will do for me. How about you?"

Molly sighed and unbuckled her seat belt. "My all-time favorite meal. Double that order while I find the ladies' room."

They staked out the Jensen estate just before dawn. Even Jack had to sleep. Even if he were on the other side of town watching the house, waiting for her to come back there, he would have to return home eventually.

Molly had kicked back in the front passenger seat and was nibbling the last of the doughnuts Damien had bought for their breakfast. "What if he's in there and decides to sleep all day?" she asked. She had to admit her patience could use some work. They'd been here only two hours and already she'd grown tired of the game. "Do you do this much?" she asked.

"Surveillance?" he asked, looking amused. "Yes. It's one of the most boring aspects of the job, but sometimes necessary."

She nodded, taking in the high shrubbery and trees that surrounded the Explorer. Through a break in the foliage, she could see the gates to the Jensen property. One of the dogs was poking his nose through the spaces in the wrought-iron gate.

"Ah, opportunity knocks," Damien said. He reached over the seat and pulled a package of jerky out of the food sack. Molly watched him rub the food between his hands and then get out of the car.

Sprinting across and down the street, he slowed as he approached the stone wall. Casually, he strolled past the gates and tossed the dried meat through to the dogs. He was humming when he returned and got in.

"Making friends?" she asked. "It won't work. They're killers."

He only smiled. Molly got the distinct feeling he had done this before. "Do they have names?" he asked.

She laughed and popped open a soft drink. "Prissy and Minx." Damien nodded, but didn't answer. The hour dragged on as the sun rose and began to dispel the morning chill.

Suddenly, a high-pitched whistle sounded and the dogs flew away from the gate. Moments later, it opened and Jack's car pulled through.

"This is Control. Subject is on the move, heading North," Damien said in a mock serious monotone as though he spoke over a radio. He was poking fun at her,

Molly realized. This was a new side to Damien. She decided she liked it.

"Backup in place," she replied in kind. "Let's roll."

She marveled at the way Damien operated. He managed to keep Jack's car in sight without getting close enough to be spotted. "Don't we want him to see us?" she finally asked.

"He got a glimpse," he replied. "But he's not sure yet. Watch."

Jack's Mercedes made a swift left turn and sped down a side street. Damien continued straight, turned left at the next opportunity and fell in several cars behind Jack as he pulled onto the Loop. After a mile or so, it was obvious they'd been made again. Molly laughed and slapped her knee. "I *love* it!"

For nearly an hour they played cat and mouse. Damien would drop back out of sight and then turn up again. Jack narrowly missed hitting another car, he was so busy looking in his rearview mirror.

"Enough for now," Damien declared. "Time to let him rest."

"Why?" Molly complained. "This was just getting good!"

"You want it to be over," Damien accused as he wheeled into a Gulf station and pulled up to the tank. "If we're planning to twist him into knots, this has to last awhile. Besides, I know where he's going."

"You were joking about my having to use the bushes, right?"

He grinned. While Damien pumped gas, Molly took advantage of the facilities and bought hot coffee. It was going to be a great day. Best she'd had in weeks. She could tell already.

Chapter 9

This couldn't be happening. Jack maneuvered his way through the downtown traffic, glaring angrily at one mirror then the other. That damned black SUV again! It was the same one, wasn't it?

He squinted, trying to see who was in the car, but the windows were tinted too dark. It would be just like Molly to set a detective on his ass. Nah. She couldn't afford it.

Was it the new boyfriend, Perry, maybe? That wasn't the Lexus he'd been driving.

Cops? Couldn't be. They had nothing on him. Nothing! He'd been too careful for that. No prints, no calls from any of his own phones. He'd even stolen the hive. They couldn't trace a damn thing he'd done. No earthly reason for them to tail him.

His next guess was Ford, but he quickly rejected that idea. The school where Ford's wife worked had said she wouldn't be back for at least two more weeks. Besides, he knew if Ford Devereaux had come after him, he wouldn't be hanging back following the car. Jack wasn't scared of the jerk, he told himself. He was just smart enough to not underestimate him.

But by the time Molly's brother returned, he wouldn't have a sister to worry about anymore. And Jack would be gone.

So, who was it back there? Every time he got ready to stop, get out and confront whoever it was, the SUV disappeared. Until he found out who was trailing him, he'd have to put off doing anything else to Molly.

Spitting out the foulest curse he knew, Jack headed home, seething with fury and frustration. At least the bastard couldn't follow him inside his own gates!

Once Jensen's car entered the grounds and was out of sight, Damien parked on the side of the street so that the Explorer was hidden from the house by the stone wall. Molly was dozing, obviously weary. It had been a tiring day, but he thought Jensen was running scared now, wondering who was after him.

When he heard the dogs, Damien got out, walked past where the animals waited and fed them. Two additional times today, when Jensen had been holed up in his father's office building, Damien had quickly swung by and tossed jerky to the animals.

This time, he held the back of his hand just close enough so they could sniff, but not bite it. He crooned nonsense, calling their names. Both dogs whined, straining between the bars of the gate, begging for more treats. He offered them one each.

"Sit," he commanded. They sat. He rewarded them with praise and another tasty tidbit and then returned to the Explorer where Molly waited.

"This is ridiculous," Molly told him. "You're not going

in there!'' She'd said exactly that every time he'd done this. ''You're *not!*''

''Let's have dinner,'' he suggested, ignoring her words. ''Your choice of restaurant.'' He shrugged when she named one they had passed only minutes before, and proceeded to backtrack and find it.

''Well, the proximity's convenient,'' he said. ''And there is a motel attached. I would imagine you're tired of all our driving around, being cooped up in the car, aren't you?''

He knew *he* was. Having Molly alone in a motel room— again—wouldn't do a blessed thing to relieve this ache for her that was driving him mad, but at least he could stretch out. ''We'll get a room.''

''Rooms,'' she corrected, giving him a level look that said she was thinking straight, if he was not. ''*Two* rooms this time.''

''Connecting,'' he compromised, surprised when she didn't argue.

To Molly's disappointment, the motel restaurant served tasteless prime rib and wine that was little more than sweetened grape juice. The rooms proved as tasteless as the food, but were clean at least. Damien was probably appalled.

''Sorry about picking this one,'' she said as he glanced around her room, frowning. ''It's not exactly the Ritz, is it?''

''It's not safe, either,'' he commented, visually measuring the distance between the plate-glass window and the door lock. ''An amateur with a glass cutter could be in here in seconds.''

He ambled across the room, stopped directly in front of her and settled his hand in the curve of her neck. His thumb caressed the underside of her chin. ''We'd best stay together.''

''Now, just wait a minute, Damien,'' she began to protest, wishing she could tear her gaze away from the desire in his eyes. "We can't—"

He silenced her with that determined look she could never say no to. "We can."

She pulled away sharply then and turned her back to him. "Okay, stay, if you insist! But it's not necessary and you know it as well as I do." She flopped down onto the edge of the king-size bed, turned on her side away from him and closed her eyes. "Good night."

"Good night, Molly," he replied, a hint of amusement in his voice. "Sleep well."

There was less chance of Jack looking for them here than there was of the roof caving in while they slept, Molly thought. *If* they slept, that is. The security of the room—or lack of it—had nothing at all to do with Damien's staying in here.

She knew exactly why he insisted. He wanted to share the bed with her. But they were not going to have sex and that was that, because that's *all* it would be. If it turned out to be more, that would be even worse.

She listened as he moved restlessly around the room, clicked the locks shut on the outer and inner doors, fiddled with the drapes a moment and finally went into the bathroom.

The shower ran for a while, causing her to visualize what a glorious sight he must be, all those deliciously wet muscles rippling beneath the stinging jets of water. *Cold* water? she wondered wickedly. He'd been aroused and hadn't even bothered to hide it.

Later, Molly felt the mattress give as he lay down on the opposite side of the bed. Was he fully clothed again? No doubt he was, but she couldn't dismiss the memory of him half naked in that thin hospital gown all those months ago when they'd first met. Her pulse skipped just thinking about it.

Maybe she should be taking the cold shower, Molly thought with a sigh of frustration. She got up, visited the bathroom herself, drew a little frowny on the steamed-up mirror and then washed her face. There was nowhere to go, nothing to do but return to bed and try to sleep.

Never had a king-size bed seemed so narrow to her, the gulf between her and Damien a magnetic field that tried relentlessly to tug them together, toward the ultimate pleasure, and toward a risk she dared not take. She fought temptation with all her might for the longest time, adamantly feigning sleep, until she heard his breathing even out.

Would it have hurt, to give in to what she felt for him? Not tonight, she told herself. It certainly wouldn't hurt tonight. But eventually, it would make her miserable. Once she'd given herself to Damien, Molly was afraid there would be no getting herself back, even when he was ready to move on.

That he might want to stay should never have occurred to her. She could not allow herself to build any pipe dreams. It was merely her hormones kicking up a fuss. And look where that had gotten her the last time she'd wanted a man.

She had wanted Jack once, Molly admitted, but that had been an insignificant little twitch of hunger compared to the way she craved Damien Perry. All she could do was clasp her hands together to keep them off him, and curl closer to her edge of the bed. That pull was that damned strong.

Damien woke Molly very early, offering no comment on the fact that she was not a morning person. He merely pointed her toward the bathroom while he went out to find coffee for her. Then he guided her out to the Explorer and ushered her inside.

She muttered her thanks, finally, when the caffeine

kicked in. He sort of liked that she wasn't all that chatty on awakening. It was a good quality in a woman, he decided.

This time, it was much more difficult to ignore how sexy she looked while still half asleep. How great that pouty mouth of hers would feel when he kissed her fully awake. Or maybe he wouldn't wake her completely at first. With a firm snap of his head, he dismissed what he was thinking. Not yet, he told himself. Maybe someday, but definitely not now.

Just before dawn, they were situated so that they could see the Jensens' gates again. In the weak illumination of the streetlights, he watched her yawn widely, covering her mouth and issuing a groan. He should have bought her two cups.

She still looked a bit tousled from sleep. Incredibly desirable. Driving him *crazy*.

Damien turned his head and stared out into the darkness, knowing full well Molly hadn't slept any more than he had. When she'd finally drifted off, he had closed the distance between them and held her the way he wanted to. Well, almost the way he wanted. He treasured the feeling of her absolute trust, much as it had discomforted him at the time.

He could have had her then with very little effort or persuasion, but instinct told him that to do so would have been a grave mistake. An error Molly might have enjoyed, but probably wouldn't forgive.

Damien was not certain, even now, how he could stand to let her go when the time came. But along with intimacy, he would have to offer Molly a commitment. She was simply that kind of woman. And Damien didn't believe he had it in him to become what she needed. Marriage had occurred to him more than once, but he'd rejected that possibility.

What did he know of loving or being loved, of giving

more than taking, of sharing himself the way a husband and father should? Such things must be taught from an early age and by example, for them to be real.

Curse his luck, he'd had no teachers available for those lessons. Now it was too late for him. Too late for *them,* even before they'd begun. Before he'd met her. A unique and intriguing woman who moved him more than any person he'd ever known, and he couldn't have her because he simply didn't know how.

He turned on the radio to distract his thoughts. The sky lightened gradually to the eloquent voice of Mirella Freni pouring out her sensitive aria from *Madama Butterfly.*

Damien couldn't resist reaching for Molly's hand, feeling it tense as his closed around it. He caressed her palm with his thumb as he listened to the heart-rending sound of the music. The painful notes of absolute loss with no help for it. He could identify. The sun rose on a particularly poignant passage and streetlights automatically flickered off.

Molly leaned forward and defiantly punched at the radio. Suddenly fiddles blared and a cocky female group declared they were "Ready to Run." He shot her a questioning look.

"Dixie Chicks," she declared, tugging her hand from his. "What's the matter, sport? Don't you like 'em?"

"Oh, *like* can't begin to describe what they make me feel," he admitted, hiding a smile. "Puccini doesn't hold a candle, does he?"

She cleared her throat and crossed her arms over her breasts. "I know changing stations was rude. I apologize."

"Mmm-hmm, but you've done that before," he commented.

"Well, after that hand-holding business and all, I was trying to make a point."

Damien nodded. "Point taken. When I'm behind the wheel, you have control of the radio."

Her laughter was fleet and self-conscious. "No, silly! That our tastes are wildly different. In music, and just about everything else, I bet. You go for Grand Opera, I go for the Grand Ol' Opry. Nothing in common. Not a single thing. So there's no use getting too chummy...in other areas, if you know what I mean."

"You might convert me," he suggested offhandedly, appreciating her embarrassed attempt to ward off disaster, wondering why on earth he was arguing when he agreed with her completely. "Or we could meet on some middle ground. Jazz? I like that. Some rock."

She shook her head, smiling a sad little smile. "Music's only the tip of the iceberg, Damien. We are who we are, and never the twain shall meet."

"Never the twain? Aha, you're a poet at heart! I do like poetry," he said, cocking his head to one side to see what she would try next.

"I nearly flunked English lit," she said, almost proudly. "Poetry always made me giggle."

"'Like a high-born maiden in a palace tower, Soothing her love-laden soul in secret hour,'" Damien quoted to the strains of classic Bluegrass banjos, "'With music sweet as love, which overflows her bower.'"

"Now that's rich!" She did giggle, by God, and it didn't sound faked.

"I suppose our old Percy is a bit flowery," he admitted.

Molly was trying so hard to argue him—and probably herself—out of pursuing a relationship. He already knew it was futile, but somehow resented the fact that she'd realized it, as well.

Her reasons for that realization were what angered him most. She made him sound like a snob of the worst kind, one who put cultural differences above anything else. What would she say if he told her the real reason they should give it up had nothing to do with that?

"Mount up and tally ho," she said laconically. "Our fox is leaving the cage."

Damien jerked his attention to the matter at hand and watched Jensen's car pull out onto the street. The gates closed and the chase was on.

He allowed the Mercedes a sizable lead since traffic was sparse and it was too soon for them to be noticed. Jensen should begin feeling a bit smug first before he spotted them.

"I'll bet he's going to the office again," Molly guessed. "That's the direction he's taking, anyway. Old John must be serious about him taking over part of the business. Jack never seemed to care before."

However, three blocks away from the Jensen building, Jack made a sudden left and pulled up to a Waffle House.

"Cook's day off, or is he curious who's behind him?" Molly asked. "Are we hungry, too?"

"Working up an appetite, aren't you?" Fortunately he was able to remain a couple of cars back in the turn lane until Jack went inside the restaurant.

"Now that's what I call luck," Damien said as he scanned the parking lot. "This couldn't be better if I had orchestrated it myself. Look, there's a squad car, down near the end."

"It's showtime, right?" Molly asked.

"Right." He wheeled in then, and parked so that the car window on her side faced the glass front of the restaurant.

"Jack's sitting at the counter, looking out," Molly observed. "See him?"

"The mouse watching for the cats." Damien smiled and pushed the button to open her window. "And he's about to see us, too. Right…about…now!" He leaned forward a bit so that Jensen was certain to glimpse him as well as Molly.

Anger suffused the man's face, turning it dangerously

red. Damien knew the exact instant Jensen realized who had been trailing him around town.

"Let's raise his blood pressure one more notch," Damien suggested. Then he pulled Molly toward him, took her in his arms and kissed her passionately.

Surprised, she struggled for a second before her mouth melded softly to his. God, she tasted fine! He had to struggle a bit himself to keep his mind clear and his eyes open so he could watch for audience reaction.

Anger to pure mindless fury! Perfect!

Shoving off the counter stool, Jensen tore out of the doors of the Waffle House and stomped toward the Explorer.

Damien quickly broke the kiss and grinned while he hit the door lock and pushed the button to close the automatic window. "Come on, you lowlife, make a scene for us," he encouraged in a low voice.

A split second later, fists pounded the glass. Shouted curses and warnings overrode the sounds of traffic.

Molly laughed nervously and clung to his sleeve. He held her tighter. "Steady, love."

Damien tapped the horn several times, as much to stir Jensen's fury as to distract the cops from their breakfast. "Hmm, that worked swell on both counts," he noted, shifting Molly farther away from the window in the event Jensen managed to break the glass. "Here comes the cavalry. Watch this."

They observed with satisfaction as two uniformed policeman approached Jack from behind and grabbed his arms. In seconds they'd secured him with handcuffs and led him away from the car, struggling.

"Wow!" Molly said with a tense chuckle, and pushed away from him so she could see better. "Ask me if I love this!"

One of the cops tapped lightly on the window and Damien obediently opened it, wearing the most innocent expression he owned. "Officer, thank God, you were here."

"Yeah, well..." Suspicion crinkled the weather-beaten face. "That guy says you were kissing his wife right out here in the parking lot, trying to drive him crazy. Now is that true?"

"Like we'd have to *try!*" Molly exclaimed, rolling her eyes. "We were just sitting here minding our own business. I haven't been Jack Jensen's wife for two years. He just got out of jail for assault. Now he's violating a protection order by approaching me. You think I'd actually go *looking* for him?"

"Guess we better haul him in," the officer said with a weary sigh, no doubt thinking about his abandoned breakfast.

"That might be wise," Damien suggested. "He seems...distraught, to say the least. Maybe dangerous?"

"I wouldn't doubt it," the cop said, turning halfway around to glance at Jensen who was busy threatening the other officer with a lawsuit for false arrest. "You coming down to press charges, ma'am?"

"Absolutely," Molly said. "We'll be right behind you."

"He'll probably be out within twenty-four hours," he warned her. "You might want to make yourself scarce about then, at least until he cools off."

"No problem," Damien assured him. "We'll follow you to the station." He hoped Detective Winton was on duty today. This incident might add weight to the complaint about the bees.

Only that was not to be.

"Where is this going?" Molly asked Damien after they left the main precinct where she'd filed charges against Jack.

What a high she had felt, seeing him cuffed and taken

in, knowing she'd been instrumental in having it done. But she'd quickly deflated when she saw that the arrest didn't scare Jack at all. He'd shown no remorse, no fright, and no intention whatsoever of abandoning his quest for revenge.

The glare he shot her before they had shoved him into the back seat of the squad car remained etched in her brain. It had been a promise. A renewed and beefed-up vow, that look.

"Will I ever get my life back?" she asked Damien. "What's it going to take to do that?"

"I know you're worried. So am I. We might have made things worse." He hesitated until they stopped at a red light, then looked at her with an apology in his eyes. "I had hoped an arrest would drive home the fact that he's not immune to the stalking laws. Also, make him realize that the police would come after him if anything else happened to you. Fear of another sentence should have convinced him to leave you alone, but now I honestly don't think it will."

"No, Jack's more than determined. He's obsessed. If looks could kill, we'd both be dead right now. If he'd gotten to us through the car window, he would have tried to murder us on the spot. And he didn't care who saw him, did he?"

Damien watched the stoplight, his lips drawn tight as he shook his head.

"So what do we do?" she demanded. "There has to be something! He won't put up with our following him around anymore. First time he spots us, he'll leap out of his car and do a repeat of what happened today."

She pounded her palm on the dash. "Only we might not be lucky enough to have the cops around next time. And he might be better prepared. What if he gets a gun?"

"He doesn't have one registered, nor is he licensed to carry. I checked," Damien said calmly.

"Ha! You think that'll stop him?"

"Probably not. As soon as he's released, I'm going to have it out with him."

"Have it out?" Molly cried. "What, exactly, does that mean, 'have it out'? Pistols at ten paces?"

Damien nodded. "If he has one and goes for it, yes."

"Oh, jeez!" Molly huffed, running her palms over her face.

He took one hand off the wheel, reached over and rested it on her leg, just above her knee. "I'm not planning to shoot him unless he forces it, Molly. But I do plan to tell him who I am and exactly what I *will* do if he ever bothers you again."

His face was a study in menace that she wished Jack could see right now.

"He won't doubt my sincerity, Molly. I can assure you of that. I plan to make it quite clear, so that even an imbecile can understand. No more playing by the book. If he comes anywhere near you, threatens you in any way at all, he dies. Proof or no proof."

She believed him. She only hoped Jack would.

He gave her leg a pat and returned his hand to the steering wheel. "After we pick up your mail and check on the house, let's go to Clarkston. This time we won't have to watch our backs. You can totally relax for a change since he's in lockup."

"For twenty-four hours," she grumbled. "If I'm lucky."

"Hey, it is great to not have to hurry, isn't it?" Molly said she sank onto her living room sofa and thumbed through the stack of letters she'd just gotten out of her mailbox.

"Got a couple of postcards from bro," she said, chuckling at the message on the back of one. "Ford says he's learning the language. At least how to order beer." She glanced up at Damien. "Can you imagine what Ford sounds like speaking German? Bartenders will be doubled over for months after he's gone. Here, read it."

Damien sat beside her and took the card. "Molly, there's something I should tell you."

He was too close. All she could do was focus on that wonderful mouth of his, his hand on her arm, his thigh brushing hers. What kind of force field surrounded him that could draw her to him like this? "Damien?" she whispered, her lips suddenly tingling with the memory of that kiss Jack had interrupted.

"Molly," he answered just as softly. "Don't look at me that way. I might—"

"Hush." She leaned forward, closing the distance between them, and captured his mouth with hers. *Just for a minute.* Just for the duration of this one kiss, she would forget they couldn't be together, that it would never work out.

"Molly," Damien rasped her name between greedy kisses, adding one on another, delving deeper, increasing the heat until her heart thundered in her chest. Blood rushed through her veins at the speed of light. She wanted him. So *desperately*.

His hands slid over her, seeking, pressing, finding their way beneath her blouse. He enveloped her breasts as he pushed her down onto the sofa and followed, settling his lower body in the cradle of hers. Relentlessly, he moved against her and made her move in response. "Oh, please," she gasped.

"Yes," he hissed, mingling their words as he took her mouth again. He unhooked the catch on her bra.

The doorbell chimed.

"They'll go away," he promised breathlessly, flexing his hips into hers, not pausing for a second in his assault of pleasure.

"Damien," she moaned, pushing at his shoulders. "The window?"

He ignored her, intent on his exploration, while reality washed over her like a bucket of cold water. "The drapes—" He kissed her again. Wildly. "They're open."

With a growl of resignation, he withdrew his hands and said a word so typically English and appropriate to their need, Molly thought it bore repeating.

Chapter 10

Damien waited until Molly disappeared down the hallway before he answered the door. Through the window, he could see the plain, blue sedan parked in the driveway and recognized it as Winton's.

"Sorry I wasn't available when you came to the precinct a while ago," the detective said the moment Damien opened the door. They shook hands. "I was stuck in interrogation until just after you left. Sgt. Garner said you were asking for me, so I thought I'd stop by on my way home."

Damien ran his fingers through his tousled hair and tucked in the portion of his shirttail he'd missed. Winton turned his head and stifled a grin.

"Come in," Damien muttered.

"My timing's a little off, I guess," Winton apologized, glancing at the floor-length window. "I take it Ms. Jensen's all right now?"

"Quite all right," Damien said. "As you probably know by now, we had an altercation with Jensen. He attempted to tear my rental apart to get at us this morning."

"Yeah, so I heard. His lawyer came in just as I was leaving. Raising hell and name dropping."

He hesitated, brushing a hand over his dark mustache, warning Damien with a look that what he had to say next would not be welcome. "Jensen's papa's got friends in high places, Perry. He'll probably be released sometime today. Just thought you should know that."

"Damn!" Damien cursed. He remembered his manners and gestured toward a chair. Mitch Winton wanted to help Molly, too. He gave the impression of a laid-back kind of guy, but Damien sensed the sharp intelligence beneath that laconic wit and lazy voice. Winton was nobody's fool. "Have a seat. I'll get Molly."

"No, that's okay," Winton said. "Had a long night and I need to get home and grab some shut-eye."

He stepped back through the door, but stopped on the threshold. "The bees won't help us, but I'm still working on that hit-and-run. Phone company says the calls were made from pay phones, so we've got nothing there. I hustled up the lab on that box of poison. Might get a print or something."

Damien nodded. "But you doubt that, just as I do. Thanks anyway, we appreciate it."

"I had one sister, Perry," Winton said, his voice low and grating, its slow drawl suddenly laced with menace. "She got tangled up with a cagey bastard like Jensen. Now she's buried over in Forest Lawn and my parents are raising her two kids."

He shook his finger at Damien. "We're not letting that happen with Molly Jensen, okay? Whatever we have to do."

"What happened to the man?" Damien asked.

Winton's lips tightened and his gaze fell away before he answered. "You don't want to know, and I'm not about to tell you. But if you come up with a way to neutralize this problem," he said, emphasizing the last word, "call me. I'll back you."

Before Damien could comment, Winton strode down the steps, across the yard to his car, got in and drove away.

Damien stood there until the blue Chevy was out of sight. The detective knew as well as he did that neutralizing the *problem,* as he'd called Jensen, probably couldn't be achieved by legal means. He had hinted at vigilante justice. Virtually admitted that he'd used it himself in the sister's case.

It was altogether too tempting to resort to that. It was what Damien had considered, and what he had already planned to threaten. And, if the threat didn't work, he might have to carry it out.

Pushing Jensen's buttons had worked in one respect, though in another it had changed nothing. The man was in custody. But instead of waking him up to the reality of what could happen to him, it had only incensed Jensen further. The man was homicidal. Damien had seen it in his eyes. The bees had been put there to terrorize, not kill. What he planned next might very well be intended to do just that.

Molly's arms slid around his waist and her long fingers laced over his stomach. He could feel the rise of her breasts against his back. Would she be holding him this way if she knew what a dark side he possessed? If she realized that he almost looked forward to destroying the mad dog who chased her?

"They will release him sometime today," he said softly, regretting they would have no time to continue what they'd begun before Winton arrived. How could he even contemplate a serious relationship with Molly until he got Jensen out of the way? First thing, he had to get her out of the line of fire. "Get whatever else you need to take with you. We're leaving."

She took her time once she went to the bedroom, as though she thought he might join her there. They didn't speak of what had happened, but the look she'd given him told him she wouldn't refuse. Molly was through fighting what was between them. So, Damien fought for both of them.

They were headed out the door when the phone rang. He stopped her with a hand on her arm. "Wait. Let's see who it is." They listened as the answering machine kicked on. It was the embittered voice of Jack's father.

"Molly? This is John Jensen. Jack made me promise to call you. He said that since you are determined to destroy him completely, he will be leaving Nashville for good as soon as he's released. You'll never hear from him again. His mother and I have lost our son because of you. I only hope you're satisfied with all these lives you've wrecked. Someday you'll suffer for what you've done, and I just hope I'm around to see it happen. This is not a threat, but I believe there is a higher justice that will call you to account for it."

"Well, hell!" Molly tore her gaze from the phone and looked up at Damien. Then she laughed breathlessly, staggered back into the living room and sat. "Ha! Over. Just like that?"

"No, Molly," he warned her. "I don't think so."

"But it is!" she argued. "He said so. John said Jack's leaving for good. Thank God." She buried her face in her palms and gave a brief sob that turned into another laugh. "I can't believe it."

Damien crouched beside her and pulled her hands away, holding them tightly in his. "You'd better *not* believe it. He's not finished with you, Molly. You saw the look on his face. This is a trick to throw you off guard."

For a long moment she stared at him. He could see the doubt attacking the hope in her eyes. Confusion overpowered both. She pulled her hands out of his and stood. "Let's go. I need some time to think about this."

There was little to think about, but Damien humored her. They were already on the way to Clarkston. He'd see she stayed there for a week or so until he could check out Jensen's whereabouts. Damien meant to find him whether he stayed in Nashville or not. He still had a threat to deliver, one that now had teeth in it.

By the time they arrived in Clarkston, Damien knew Molly had convinced herself that the danger was over. Her wanting to believe that so badly had clouded her judgment, of course. He didn't bother to try to convince her he was right. As long as she remained here where she was safe, it didn't matter what she believed.

"Promise me you won't even think about going back for at least a week," he demanded. "Let me make certain he's gone. Will you do that much?"

"Okay," she said, distracted by the sight of Brenda and the baby sitting in the porch swing, as they drove up to the house.

Damien sighed and put the car in Park, watching Molly dash up the steps and grab Sydney, hugging her and laughing like mad. He had to smile at the rambunctious reunion. The baby gurgled and screeched, patting Molly's head and tugging on her hair.

Brenda looked past them to where Damien stood just outside the car. "Well, come on, you big ol' rascal! Don't just stand there. I've got a cherry pie with your name on it!"

Hands in his pockets, Damien ambled up the walkway to join them. She embraced him the instant he stepped onto the porch. "Molly says Jack's gone for good. I don't know how we can ever thank you."

"Don't thank me yet," Damien said, feeling embarrassed and also warmed clear through by Brenda's affection. She paid no attention to what he'd said, but simply grasped one of his hands and dragged him through the front door right behind Molly and Sydney.

He ate his pie, drank his coffee and listened to the excited exchange between mother, daughter and granddaughter. The odd man out, he sat there and relished the brief scraps of attention they threw him, these three beautiful females with their bright green eyes and wide smiles. It was a circle he ached to join and knew they would allow him in. Only he knew he wouldn't fit. The best he could do was to see that circle unbroken, and that he would do, no matter what it took.

Later that evening, Damien excused himself to use the phone. Calling in all the favors he could, he discovered the paper trail that verified Jack Jensen had registered at the Marriot just this side of Atlanta.

Another conversation with Bill Carr, an agent and friend he had attended the academy with, gained him a reliable resource in that city. Duvek would add an official call from Memphis to the office in Atlanta in the event Damien needed more help.

Even though there had been no crime to warrant official intervention by the FBI, Ford Devereaux was one of their agents and his sister was in danger. The Bureau took care of family, especially when an agent was out of pocket, as Ford was now.

Jensen had counted too heavily on Molly's silence about the stalking, obviously assuming she would never risk involving Ford. However, now Damien wondered if Jensen might be past thinking rationally.

If Jack checked out of that hotel, Damien would be one of the first to know he was on the prowl. For the moment, Molly really was as safe as she thought she was.

Brenda sat alone in the kitchen. Damien had seen Molly

take the baby through the living room to put her to bed. "Any of that marvelous pie left?" he asked.

She dished it up and poured him the last of the coffee. The joy she exhibited earlier had vanished. He suspected it had been a pretense all along. "Damien, what's going to happen?"

"I'll take care of him, don't worry," he assured her.

With an exasperated sigh, she dismissed Jensen from the conversation. "That's a given. I meant with you and Molly."

He stalled, squashing the remnant of the pie crust on his plate with the fork. "Nothing will happen," he replied finally. "Soon as things are settled, I'll take off."

She leaned across the table and placed her hand over his. Damien looked down at her short, unpolished nails, at the prominent veins and premature wrinkles that spoke of a life of hard work. How hard it must have been to rear two children with no assistance from anyone. And now one of them was on the edge of another life-altering mistake.

Damien turned his hand over, clasped hers and looked straight into her eyes. "Brenda, I do realize I'm not right for her. You needn't worry."

Her gaze remained steady on his. "It's not Molly I'm worried about. What is it with you? Does she scare you?"

Surprised, he laughed. "Scare me? Hardly!" Then he thought about it for a second. Perhaps Brenda was right.

"You'll get over it," she said gruffly, squeezing his hand and letting it go. "Molly's falling in love with you, you know. I see the signs. And I can read you like a sixty-foot billboard."

He shook his head. "There's nothing between us that a little distance won't cure." He hated to deny what she'd said because he wanted it to be true. More than anything in his life, he wanted that, even if he couldn't take advan tage of it. It was selfish of him to hope Molly felt what he felt, but there it was.

Fortunately, Molly returned to the kitchen then and he didn't have to lie any further. But Brenda's statement hung there in the air between them all the same.

What amazed Damien was that Brenda didn't seem to mind if Molly loved him. Maybe she figured her daughter would need his permanent protection. That must be the case.

"Well," he said, rising quickly from his chair, unwilling to see where the conversation might wander now that Molly was present. He'd already uttered one lie too many and didn't think he could dredge up another. "I'm for bed. Sydney isn't the only one who's had a busy day. Good night, then."

He left them sitting there, Brenda wearing a thoughtful look and Molly silently avoiding his gaze. Had she overheard what he'd said? Might be best if she had.

Once the house was quiet and dark, Damien lay motionless in the strange bed, staring into the dark, wishing with his innermost soul that his life had been different. He had spent it virtually isolated, his feelings so well insulated he hadn't known they were there, but he'd never felt so alone as he did now.

Small wonder Molly frightened him. She had changed him so radically, he would never be the same. Yet the change still wasn't great enough to make him the kind of man she needed. He doubted anything could ever do that.

Molly wished Damien would go ahead and leave. Maybe if she didn't have to see him and be with him, this sharp edge of hunger would dull. There he sat in the middle of the floor, long limbs cross-legged, rolling a ball back and forth to Syd, as if he had nothing better in the world to do. All morning she had waited for him to announce his departure. He'd made it clear he wasn't sticking around because of any interest in her other than saving her hide. Jack was gone and said he wouldn't be back, so why was Damien still hanging around?

She abandoned dusting the furniture that didn't really need it and sat on the sofa, facing his back. "You said Jack's really in Atlanta. Without a doubt."

"For the moment," he said, catching Syd as she launched herself at him, bouncing the ball off his face. As though he'd read Molly's mind, he added, "I'd like to wait and see what he does next. Do the Jensens have any business interests there?"

"Not that I know about, but I guess it's possible. Probable, even. I'm fairly sure John has contacts there, anyway. You're wondering if Jack will find a job and take up permanent residence?"

"It's something to think about. Highly unlikely he'll simply sit around doing nothing, isn't it?" he asked. Knowing Jack, that didn't sound so far-fetched to Molly.

He disentangled himself from Sydney and got up, leaving her there while he went to use the phone.

Molly took the baby out into the backyard to play, distancing herself—and Sydney—from him as much as possible. However, it wasn't long before he joined them.

"Would you like to go and have your hair done when Brenda gets back?"

She reached up and raked through her curls, wincing. "That bad, huh?"

He laughed and scooped Sydney up, tickling her tummy. "Not at all. Wouldn't you like a break, just to get out of the house and away from everything for a while? Brenda got so excited when I told her it was all right to go, I wondered if it might do you some good, as well."

"Nobody touches this mop until I get back home to my regular stylist. It's tough enough if they know how wild it is and have cut it before.'' She made a face. "Curls are a curse.''

He reached out and touched her hair, winding a strand around his finger, capturing her gaze just as securely. "It's beautiful, haven't I told you?''

"No,'' she whispered, looking up at him. "Thank you.'' His face lowered to hers, but at the last second he brushed her cheek with his lips instead of meeting her mouth. She almost reeled with disappointment.

Then he stepped away, even turned his back to her.

Here it came, she thought. He was going to say goodbye now. She braced herself.

He looked over his shoulder. "What will you do if he comes back after I'm gone?''

"Fight him any way I can,'' she said. "Use the gun if I have to.''

"I need to warn you about that, Molly.'' The concern in his eyes told her he didn't like the idea of her using the pistol. "Unless you're very familiar with weapons, trained to use them, they can work against you. Never threaten anyone with a gun unless you intend to use it, unless you're certain you can follow through.''

"Duly noted,'' she said, plunking Sydney down on the grass and tossing the ball for her to chase. "But I can shoot. My aim's pretty good.''

He looked at her, his eyes sad. "You'd hesitate. That's deadly.''

The lack of confidence he had in her made her furious. "Well, what should I do then?''

"Run,'' Damien suggested. "Run like hell. And scream *fire*.'' He continued, his gaze as serious as she had ever seen it. "When he returns, get your brother to choose the best local self-defense class for women. They'll show you things like this,'' he said, approaching her. "Go ahead, attack me.''

Molly pulled back to slug him. Suddenly his palm flew straight at her face and she dodged back. He rounded with his other hand and stopped it just short of her ear, his hand cupped.

"Eardrum. Painful," he said. "Feint and strike. Then run."

"Faint and fall down, more likely," she said with a laugh. "I think I'd prefer the gun!"

He sighed and pointed his finger like a pistol. "And aim between the eyes, am I right?"

"Not right?" she asked, sparing a glance at Syd who had crawled up on the webbed lounge chair.

"The body. The largest target. Don't aim, just point as if using your finger and pull the trigger. Don't wait to see what he'll do first. Got it?"

"Got it," she said, biting her lip, more scared now than she had been before, wondering what else she thought she knew, but didn't, about defending herself.

"Now, then," he said, moving closer and turning his back. "Attack me from behind."

Molly grasped him around the neck and felt his heel gently bump her knee. "That should cripple him temporarily," he said, holding her arm loosely in place where it rested against his shoulder. Without letting her remove it, he turned to face her.

For a long moment he just stared into her eyes. Molly felt her blood heat. His scent held her captive. His touch burned, a welcome fire that spread well beyond the point of contact. No defense for this, she thought. And ceased to care.

"I keep telling myself to let it be," he said softly, "and then you look at me a certain way. That way. It's difficult not to kiss you. But when I do…"

"You want me, but you don't *want* to want me? You think I'll expect more from you than you're ready to offer?'' She tossed her head, withdrew her arms and crossed them over her chest. "I wouldn't."

His eyes contradicted her, but he didn't say a thing.

Molly went on. "It's not as if I don't know the sort of man you are, Damien, the kind of life you live. I understand why you don't want any ties. And, believe me, I have all the ties I can handle right now."

"So you said before. I believed you." He remained quiet for a minute, stewing over it, she supposed, because when he did speak, he sounded angry. "What *do* you want from me, then, straight sex?"

She raised a brow. "As opposed to kinky sex?"

"Don't do that, Molly!" he warned through gritted teeth. "Don't you make a joke about this!"

"All right. I'm sorry. Really," Molly admitted, swinging her arms wide in a gesture of frustration. "Sometimes I clown around when I'm nervous. Bad habit."

Absently, Damien scooped up Sydney who was about to pitch headlong off the lounge into the grass.

Molly clasped her hands together to steady their trembling. And to keep from reaching for him. "You really do make me nervous."

Sydney cuddled in the crook of Damien's arm like a forgotten little football. Her huge green eyes darted from his face to Molly's and back again.

Molly smiled at her, hoping to reassure her before she set up an ear-splitting howl. If nothing else, it reminded Damien of Syd's presence.

He released a pent-up breath and shook his head as if to clear it. "Talking about it only makes it worse."

"So what do we do then?"

Without looking at her, he suggested, "Why don't we get out of here for a few hours and do something normal for a change?"

"As opposed to abnormal?" she asked.

To her relief, he smiled and handed her the baby. "Dinner and a movie? Sensible enough?"

"Oh, well, there's an idea. Maybe if we behave like rational people, have an honest-to-God date, it will cure all our ills, hmm?" She bounced Syd on her hip and looked down at her. "What do you think, fuzzy-top? Will that make us rational, y'think?"

"No," Syd deadpanned, using her new favorite word.

Damien blew out an impatient breath and stared off into the distance, a half smile on his face. "I expect she's right."

"In that case, I guess we should go straight to Plan B," Molly said quietly, giving him a meaningful look.

Brenda had not returned and it was nearly five o'clock. Though Damien hadn't said anything to Molly about it, he'd begun to worry.

On the pretext of buying extra snacks at the convenience store, he walked around town, looking for the car. The local Cut 'n Curl was locked. He jogged back to the house and found the Explorer parked in the driveway.

"Where did you go?" he demanded the minute he saw her. Obviously, she hadn't had her hair done.

She looked up, all innocence. "Oh, the beauty shop was closed, so I thought I'd just run in and see how business was getting along at home. Everything's fine."

"Please tell me you didn't drive to Nashville!"

"No! Well, not all the way into the city, just to the antique shop and straight back here."

"You should have phoned instead," Damien told her.

Brenda shrugged. "Needed to see for myself. You said Jack's in Atlanta, so I didn't see how it could hurt to go. Nobody followed me. I was really careful, just like you were."

Damien couldn't be angry with her. She'd been so wonderful to stay here with the baby when she must be worried about neglecting her shop. Still, he went straight to the phone and called Atlanta.

Jack was still registered at the hotel. His Mercedes remained in the parking garage there and hadn't been out. All reports said he was holed up, ordering room service and watching pay-per-view movies.

Relieved, Damien apologized to Brenda for overreacting.

Molly appeared then, beautifully dressed in a long green flowing skirt and silk blouse that emphasized her height and slenderness.

Her hair gleamed like satin and was perfectly arranged. That suggestion he'd made about her having it done today had prompted that new style, he knew, and felt a bit guilty about it.

"Don't you look lovely!" he said a bit self-consciously, his libido kicking into overdrive.

To distract himself from lecherous thoughts, he turned to Brenda. "How would you and Sydney like to go the local barbecue place for dinner tonight?"

"C'mon, Mom," Molly encouraged. "It'll be fun. Just the four of us." Damien heard a noticeable lack of sincerity in her voice that made him want to smile.

This was the most foolish thing he could remember doing, but he was going to do it, anyway. A few hours, just a few. She wanted that as much as he did.

"No, y'all run along. Syd and I are going to have our mac and cheese while we watch *Cinderella*—yet again."

"Okay," Molly said. "Would you mind if we catch a movie while we're out? Something a little more grown up than bippity-boppity-boo?"

Brenda laughed. "No problem."

"Be sure to lock up," Damien warned Brenda as he slid an arm around Molly's waist and ushered her out the door.

"I'm glad it's safe now. I don't mind leaving them here quite so much," she said, getting into the car.

He nodded, shut her door, went around and settled in the driver's seat.

"You knew she wouldn't come with us," Molly said.

"So did you."

Her voice held a slight edge of accusation. "And you're not hungry."

Damien shot her a wry look. "Not for barbecue."

"Neither am I," she said, raising that defensive chin.

"I noticed you didn't bother checking the movie schedule," he continued, backing out of the drive. He needed her to say she wanted him, to declare it outright so there would be no mistake.

"We aren't going to the movies." There, he thought with relief. She'd left no room for misunderstanding. None at all.

Damien hadn't deluded himself for a moment about where they were going or why, but a part of him—the decent part, most likely—had prompted him to offer her one last chance to change her mind.

But she wanted him. Not forever, not even until he had to leave her. Molly wanted him just for tonight.

Damien agreed they needed to diffuse this powerful urgency that existed between them. At the very least, to take the edge off so they could put it in perspective. If they gave in to it, they might find it was nothing more than simple lust, after all.

Who the hell was he kidding? What he felt was fist-in-the-gut love as far as he was concerned, and it was unlikely to abate even if he had her every night from now till doomsday. He could continue to fight it, but it wouldn't matter. He'd still feel the same way. He would always feel this way about her, no matter what happened or didn't.

Molly had practically suggested it herself. Since this was

all she would allow him to have of her, he would take it. At least he would have held her for a while.

"Any preference?" he asked with surprising calm, considering the desire surging through his veins like a massive shot of adrenaline.

"First one with a vacancy," she answered, a bit breathless.

He had to admire her boldness. It was damned near as entrancing as the rest of her.

Chapter 11

He would get her. Them. Tonight. Jack paid Shorty Simms his little bonus and dismissed him with a gruff word of thanks. Had to keep the riff-raff happy, he thought with a grim smile. He might need him again.

While Shorty's brother Billy lived it up at the Marriot in Atlanta on Jack's credit card, Jack had simply driven back in Billy's truck and waited around for Molly to turn up back at the house. He'd known that either she or the police would check up on him, make sure he'd gone out of town as he said he would.

Good thing he'd thought to hire Shorty to cover Brenda's shop. That antique business was all she had going for her and he'd known she couldn't leave it alone for long. At least Shorty had had the good sense to tail her when she'd left and call him as soon as he found their hidey-hole. Jack had 'em now.

Did Molly think he'd tuck his tail and run just because she and that pretty-boy limey of hers had set him up? Stupid, faithless bitch. He'd fix her and that piece of beefcake she'd teamed up with.

He laughed and finished off the cold beer he'd bought while he'd waited at the all-night service station near Clarkston for Shorty to meet him. With a sniff of satisfaction, he tossed the bottle into the trash by the tanks and lifted the plastic container of gasoline into the back of Billy's clunker. The old pickup might look like hell, but Billy never drove anything that wasn't souped up to race. It ought to get him to Clarkston and then on to Atlanta before morning, easy.

Damien frowned at the Kay-Lee Korner Motel and its blinking sign out front. He drove right past it.

His peripheral vision caught Molly's silent laughter. She was obviously nervous. Suddenly the whole venture seemed too premeditated. Now he wasn't even certain exactly what this was intended to do. Get rid of the tension between them, he'd thought before. Now he didn't know. If anything, it might increase it.

"This was a ridiculous idea," he muttered. "Find the nearest motel, the first vacancy. The very color of that place was loud enough to keep us awake."

"As though you planned to sleep," she said dryly. "Go back."

"Not if you hold a gun to my head!" he declared, speeding up.

"I want to stay there," she persisted, crossing her arms over her chest. It made her cleavage more pronounced, he saw at a glance, but he was certain that was not her intention.

He huffed. "I'm not taking you to a two-bit dump, Molly, so just be quiet. There aren't any four-star accommodations available, but if we're going to do this, let's at least—"

"Turn around and go back," she said, firmly this time. "I liked it."

"Well, I didn't! However..." He braked, floored the accelerator, and with a squeal of tires, reversed direction in the middle of the road. "You want down-and-dirty night games in seedy surroundings, luv, I can oblige."

"There may be hope for you yet," she said, laughing.

He swung into the parking lot and pulled up to the archway in front of the office. "Well, here we are, *Mrs. Smith.* Happy, now?"

She nodded, fixing him with a look of defiance.

Leaving her in the car, he registered, plunked down cash for a room and got the key. An honest-to-God key, not a card. To Number Thirteen. Appropriate, he thought.

"See, it's not bad," Molly said when he'd opened the door and clicked the lamp on dim. "Homey." She trailed her fingers along the bottom of a lampshade.

It had fringe. Gold. He winced. Otherwise, he had to agree the place was better than he'd expected, clean enough, anyway. Homely, however, rather than homey. The low wattage of the bulb through the gold of the shade washed a soft amber cast over modest motel furnishings that might have seemed worse in a harsher light.

He'd certainly stayed in more disagreeable places, but he wanted better for Molly. The best. Especially tonight.

Despite all the rooms he had been in over the years and all the women who had accompanied him to them, Damien knew Molly was unlike any other woman he had ever known. Different, and very special.

She proved that when she opened her arms to him, negating his need to make the first move. Their accommodations forgotten for the moment, he walked into her embrace and held her close, his heart racing with eagerness to make her his, if only for a while.

"Tonight, you're mine," he whispered, threading his fingers through her hair and kissing her as gently as he could manage.

"Yes," she answered softly, teasing his lower lip, sliding her hands from his back to his waist and lower, urging him closer. "Just for tonight."

Damien deepened the next kiss, tasting her more fully than he ever had.

"Certain you won't regret this?" he questioned, just to make her answer, so he could feel her breath on his mouth again.

"Not if I live to be two hundred," she answered in short breathless gasps. He could feel the tentative smile, hear it in her voice. "Will you?"

Damien knew she expected a flip answer. She was trying to keep this glib, uncomplicated, easy to lose. Instead, he stepped back. Carefully he removed her arms from around him, placed them at her sides and reached for the small covered buttons on her silk shirt.

"No regrets, Molly." He caught her apprehensive gaze and held it, lying seriously as he slipped the buttons free. "None whatsoever." For the rest of his life he would regret that he couldn't have her with him this way permanently. But he couldn't, and he had accepted that.

"You are so beautiful," he whispered, peeling back her shirt, allowing the soft slither of silk to caress her shoulders as he removed it. Carefully he draped it over the back of the nearby chair without taking his eyes off of her. She shivered, but otherwise did not move.

Reaching around her, he unfastened the button on her skirt and slid the zipper open. The challis fabric fluttered down to her ankles and settled on the floor. She wore only a lace-trimmed, pale yellow satin teddy. One slender strap fell off her shoulder, half baring the most tempting breast he'd ever seen.

Damien breathed out a low whistle of appreciation that made her blush all over. "My, my," he growled. "There is much to be said for prior planning, after all. How sweetly seductive you are.''

With one finger, he brushed the other strap free and watched the edge of the lacework cling to her distended nipples.

Molly reached out and caught his hand. Her tentative smile had flown. ''This is where I tell you, trite as it sounds, I've never done this kind of thing before,'' she whispered. One creamy shoulder lifted in a small shrug. ''Really.''

Damien felt his heart twist. He surrounded her and held her, burying his face in her hair, taking in the clean innocence of her scent. ''Don't you think I know that? I *know* it as surely as I know how good you are, my darling.''

''No,'' she protested. ''I'm not very good, Damien…at sex,'' she clarified. ''Never was.''

Another reason to kill Jack Jensen, Damien thought darkly. The sorry excuse for a man had tried to destroy Molly's pride, her belief in herself as a woman.

Damien released her, then lifted her in his arms, carried her the few feet to the bed and gently deposited her on it. With his hands on his hips, he looked down at her. Disheveled, all but nude, aroused and sexy beyond belief, Molly peered up at him with uncertainty clouding her eyes. Dispelling that insecurity became his primary goal in life.

Damien shook his head and smiled. ''Nothing I say will convince you how wrong you are about that. I suppose I shall have to show you.''

Again, that small hesitant laugh he loved. One of her long, slender hands rested on her chest, her fingers toying with the delicate gold chain around her neck. ''You *shall,* Damien? How very proper,'' she drawled, her accent pure Scarlett.

His heated looks must be feeding her confidence a bit, Damien thought with satisfaction. He grinned as he tossed his holstered weapon aside and removed his shirt. Then he sat on the edge of the bed with his back to her, removed the rest of his clothing and reached into the pocket of his slacks. "Not very proper at all, my sweet, as you will soon discover."

"Ah, is this my down-and-dirty-in-seedy-surroundings treat?" she asked, her voice teasing and sultry as hell.

"My specialty," he answered, turning to her. He caught her mouth with his as he donned protection. Much as he would love for Molly to have his child, that was never to be—and they both knew it.

He'd intended to keep the kiss light, as she seemed to want, to need, but the taste of her overwhelmed him. The sweet mix of her perfume and desire, the silken feel of her skin beneath and next to the slippery satin of that lacy concoction she wore made him too hot to play, to prolong what they both wanted so desperately.

She met him with an eagerness that matched his, her hands on him everywhere, those long delicate fingers clutching his arms, his shoulders, his back, sliding lower, grasping. Her mouth invited, surrendered, demanded in moves more consummation than kissing.

Her breasts filled his hands, their rose-colored tips begging for his mouth. He blazed kisses down her neck until he reached them and feasted with a greed that astonished him almost as much as it fueled his hunger. She pleaded for more, her voice a soft mix of need and euphoria.

With no further thought of delay, Damien levered himself above her and pressed her full length, insinuating himself against the place he most wanted to be. One hand between them, he impatiently unsnapped the teddy she wore and immediately sank into her.

The ease of entrance and her wordless sound of sheer pleasure reassured him, a bit belatedly, that she was ready. Damien held still and reveled in the ecstatic sensation of being within her, a part of her at last. But when she moved beneath him, restless for completion, Damien gave in to her urgency and his own.

He withdrew, almost mindless with anticipation, and thrust slowly.

Her fingers dug into his hips. "Please," she cried.

With near superhuman effort, he managed one more lengthy and exhilarating foray, then abandoned himself to the rhythm she sought.

Furiously he took her then, with no inkling of finesse or propriety or sweetness. He devoured her hot, willing mouth and claimed every available inch of her softness with his hands as he thrust into her again and again.

Too soon, and not soon enough, she arched against his weight and cried out. Damien exulted in her release even as his own swept over him, through him and into her. She welcomed it with a last rippling shudder that wreaked havoc on his heart.

Breath shallow, mind numb, and body spent, he held her. "How?" he gasped into the softness of the tumbled curls next to her ear. "How can I ever...let you go?"

She neither moved nor answered, but he hadn't expected she would. What more could she say than she had said already? *No ties.* He'd known almost from the beginning, certainly before this happened.

As reason returned, Damien turned onto his side, still holding her close. With one hand, he stroked her slender back down to her smooth, rounded hips and rested there. "Are you all right?"

"This didn't work, did it?" she asked, sounding worried.

He sighed against her damp temple and dropped a kiss there. "Not as we thought it might, no. I can't envision a time when I won't want you, Molly."

"What do we do now?" Her hand rested over his heart.

He covered it with his, lifted it to his mouth and kissed her palm. "Take what we *can* have and worry about the future when it gets here."

"Plan C, huh?" she whispered, nuzzling his neck with her lips. "Live for the moment?"

"Definitely a workable plan." He kissed her soundly, leaving no question about his present intent. Damien wouldn't trade this particular moment for anything, no matter what the future held for them.

At two in the morning, Damien's cell phone chirped. Molly nudged him awake. "Where is it?" she mumbled, then saw he was already feeling the floor beside the bed for his clothes. He straightened his jacket and fished the phone out of the pocket.

"Perry here," he answered, his voice gravelly with sleep. He sat up, dragged the sheet across his lap and scrubbed a hand over his face. "Brenda?"

"What's wrong?" Molly demanded, on her knees beside him, pulling on her teddy. "What's happened? Is it Syd?"

He shushed her with a motion of his hand and frowned as he listened. "Calm down, Brenda, I can't understand you." Then he straightened, frowning, alert and holding the phone with both hands. "We'll be there in ten, fifteen tops."

Molly clung to his arm. "What, Damien? Tell me!"

"Get dressed," he ordered. "The baby's gone."

"Gone?" Molly cried, hysteria threatening to overtake her. "What do you mean, *gone?*"

He steadied her with one hand and scooped up her shirt with the other. "Brenda fell asleep in the living room. She just woke up, went to check on Sydney and found her missing."

"The crib!" Molly guessed, clutching at straws. "She climbed out of it. She's always tried to…"

He threaded her arms through her sleeves and pulled her shirt together in front. "Yes, well, we had better go and find her, right? Here's your skirt. Quickly now!"

While she fumbled with her clothes, Damien hurried into his, not even bothering with his socks. His speed frightened her.

"Damien? What are you thinking? She's there, I know it. Nobody could have taken her! The house was locked. Mama wouldn't go to sleep without locking up—"

"No, of course not," he assured her, his voice steady and soothing. Then he closed his eyes and took a deep breath, scaring her with the obvious effort to calm himself. "Get your shoes, Molly. Let's *go!*"

"It's Jack," Molly said, shaking uncontrollably as Damien put her in the car. "Jack has her! Oh, Damien—"

"We don't know that," he said, yanking her seat belt across her lap and clicking it closed. "She could have climbed out."

He didn't sound convinced. He didn't even sound hopeful. Molly covered her face with her hands and struggled to control herself, to believe Syd was safe, asleep in some corner of the house where her mother hadn't looked. She couldn't. "Oh, God!"

The speed with which Damien drove to Clarkston barely registered in her mind, but it had to be less than a quarter hour—the longest she'd ever spent—before they wheeled up to the curb in front of the house. A police car, lights flashing, sat in the driveway.

Molly released her belt and was out almost before the car stopped. She tore up the walkway and ran straight into her mother's arms. "Where is she? Where's my baby?" she screamed, struggling to pull away, to go inside and search.

Damien grabbed her from behind and held her. "Wait, Molly. Be still! Listen! Brenda, has she been found?"

"No-ooo," her mother cried. "The window," she said, shaking her head. "He cut the screen and broke the glass right over the lock. I didn't hear it." She bent double, clutching her stomach and sank to the top step. "I didn't hear *her!* I was asleep," she sobbed. Molly watched her rock back and forth, already well into the desperate nightmare just beginning to grip Molly.

"Jensen," Damien spat, and uttered a foul curse. His fingers almost bruised her shoulders as he pushed her down beside her mother on the front steps. "Wait here. I'll talk to the police."

"No use," Molly mumbled against her mother's shoulder. Her own heart thundered so loud she couldn't hear her own words. She wanted to die. Syd, her poor little Sydney, probably already had. Jack hated her, hated them both. Wanted them to die. It was her last coherent thought.

Damien rushed back out when Brenda called. Molly had crumpled, her shoulders shaking unmercifully. He quickly lifted her, carried her inside and placed her on the sofa. Her pulse felt rapid. Her face and lips pale with shock.

"Pillows, Brenda!" he instructed. "Let's get her feet higher than her head." He propped them on the arm of the sofa and lifted Molly's hips so her mother could stuff the sofa cushions under her. He dragged the crocheted afghan from the back of the sofa and covered her. "Get her something sweet to drink," he ordered.

The chubby cop ran to the kitchen and was back in a flash with a soft drink. Damien shook Molly. "C'mon, darling. We don't have time for this!"

"She never falls apart!" Brenda exclaimed, wringing her hands as she knelt by Molly. "Molly's usually so strong!"

"Should I call in the FBI?" the cop asked, sounding as distraught as Brenda. Damien wondered if the man had even hit twenty yet. He surely hadn't seen a crime any more devastating than someone jumping a caution light or running a Stop sign.

"I *am* the FBI," Damien growled. "Get on the horn and get me Detective Mitch Winton, Nashville, main precinct." He jerked a card out of his wallet. "Call him at home if you have to. Move it, Officer!"

By the time Molly responded and tried to sit up, Damien was on the phone. "Winton? Perry here. Jensen's snatched the baby... Yes, I *know* that! Just find out where the hell he really is, will you? We'll meet you at Molly's house within the hour."

He punched the button to disconnect and then dialed the Memphis number to reach the agent-in-charge, Michael Duvek. Fortunately, Duvek agreed that Damien should run the investigation since he was already there and familiar with the situation. He promised two more agents would be there no later than six o'clock the next morning.

"He will call Ford," Brenda said hopefully. "Won't he?"

"Yes," Damien assured her. "I'm certain he will." He turned his attention to Molly who hung on his every word. "It will be all right, darling. We'll find Sydney."

She gasped. "What if he's already—"

"Don't say it! Don't even think it, Molly. He has no reason to hurt the baby," Damien said, hoping to sooth her enough to ward off the hysteria he could see reforming. It wasn't working. He shook her, a bit more sharply than he meant to. "Pay attention to me, Molly. Hold it together. Syd's depending on us now."

She nodded, almost frantically, sucked in a deep breath and nodded again. "Fine. I'm okay." Her face twisted into a grimace of the worst pain Damien had ever witnessed before she covered it and sobbed once. A second later she shook it off. Her eyes blazed green fire and her chin lifted. "Okay, I'm ready. Let's go find her."

Damien felt his own eyes sting. Her courage, her love and her determination were something to behold, he thought with pride. He pulled her up from the sofa and then offered Brenda his hand. Desperate to provide whatever bit of hope he could, Damien said, "You know what I think Jack will do? I believe he'll take Sydney to his mother. There's no one else he can trust to hide her for him."

Molly shuddered. "But what if he—"

"He won't hurt her, Molly," Damien declared firmly, trying hard to believe his own words, praying he was right.

"If we catch him, it's only parental kidnapping, you see? He'll get little more than a reprimand and he knows that. He's banking on that." God, he hoped he was right. "The only reason he took Sydney is because he couldn't find you. He wants you to suffer by wondering what happened to her."

He squeezed her hand and Brenda's. "We're not going to allow him to get away with this." He looked from her to her mother and back again, ignoring the cop's rabid fascination and the fact that he was a witness to the threat. "*I'm* not going to allow it, do you hear?"

"Damn!" the young officer exclaimed. "I'd sure like to be in on this."

"You *are* in on it, Peacock," Damien reminded him dryly. "Guard this place with your life. Keep everybody out of the house and the yard until an investigator arrives in the morning to dust for prints and look for tracks outside. Do not disturb the scene. Do not corrupt it, and don't let anyone else in. Got it?"

"Yes, sir!" Peacock affirmed. "That's just in case it wasn't the daddy that snatched her, right?"

Damien prayed for patience. "We already know who took her. It's routine to gather clues, Peacock. Simply routine."

Molly and Brenda hurried out the door. Damien turned his head as he followed them and nodded to the cop to indicate his belated agreement with Peacock's blunt supposition.

Just in case it wasn't the daddy.

Chapter 12

"Why aren't they all out looking for her?" Molly demanded of Damien as she paced the living room.

So far the two agents, Joseph Blancher and Bill Thomas, and Detective Winton had done nothing but hold a gab fest in her kitchen and swill her coffee.

Damien's sympathetic look did little to appease her. She wanted an explanation.

"Nobody's *doing* anything! Why isn't this on TV? Then everybody could be searching. What if Jack just put her out by the road somewhere or gave her to strangers?"

Damien took her hands, led her to the sofa and pulled her down beside him. "They're in there coordinating a private search right now, Molly, but we've decided it's not wise to televise this. We don't want Jack to panic." He smoothed a hand up her arm, and Molly shivered.

She leaned her head forward onto his chest and rested it there, whispering because the thought she had was so unspeakable. "If he does panic, he might…get rid of her?"

Damien didn't answer, and she knew she'd guessed right. She pushed away from him and withdrew her hands, brushing them down the front of her slacks, smoothing out imaginary wrinkles. She had showered and changed when they got home, in hopes of pulling herself together, but she still felt scattered, totally unnerved. And absolutely terrified.

"This is all my fault, Damien. If only I hadn't agreed to go last night—"

He stopped her. "I know. I feel guilty as hell about it, but we can beat ourselves up later. At the moment we have to think about getting Sydney back safely. That's all that matters. Blaming ourselves won't help at this point."

Molly nodded. He was right, but she couldn't help how she felt. Neither could her mother. "Mama's convinced she's the one to blame for everything. She was so upset, I gave her a sleeping pill. They just hype me up." Molly shook her head and cleared her throat, determined not to cry anymore. "You really think Syd's with Jack's mother? Oh, God, I hope she is!"

"Makes sense Jack would take her there," he said.

Winton came to the door and beckoned to Damien. Molly stood. "You can talk in front of me. I won't go to pieces. Not unless you insist on keeping everything secret from me. In that case, you haven't seen a fit like I'm about to pitch. What have you found out?"

He looked at Damien, for permission, she supposed. He nodded and Winton came into the room. He took the chair opposite the sofa and leaned forward, his hands clasped between his knees. He looked as if he'd already spent a full day on the job instead of the three hours he had been here. It was only seven-thirty. The sun was barely up.

"We had someone go to the Marriot to see if Jensen really was there. He was. Sound asleep. Your pal over there swears the car hasn't moved since he checked in."

Winton puffed out a breath of frustration. "We can't

pick him up. There's nothing even halfway solid indicating he had anything to do with this.''

Damien tapped a finger on his lips, a habit Molly noticed he had when he was lost in thought. He spoke almost as if to himself. ''Theory one, he's working with an accomplice and switched vehicles with whoever was impersonating him while he went to Clarkston. Two, he had an accomplice take the baby for him. Three, he's not involved at all and we have to approach this as a non-parental kidnapping. The Jensens have the wealth that makes that a possibility.'' He looked up at Winton then. ''What do you think?''

The detective shrugged. ''Might be he enlisted his father or some friend to pose as himself, bring him another vehicle, throw you off guard. Make you think he was good as his word and was staying out of town. He had plenty of time to get back into the Marriot this morning before we checked the room.''

Damien agreed. ''And he would do that because he had to know he would be suspect number one.''

''If he'd had someone else break in and take the kid,'' Winton questioned, ''how would he have known you and Ms. Jensen wouldn't be there at the time to prevent it? And that Mrs. Devereaux would be sleeping and provide opportunity? Nope. I don't buy that. Your third idea's feasible, of course, but you said no one else knew the Jensen child was there in Clarkston, so how could she be a target for ransom?''

Molly eagerly latched on to Damien's first idea. ''Jack must have switched cars with the man he hired to impersonate him in Atlanta! He broke in, took Sydney, then left her with his mama and went on to Atlanta to switch places with whoever was there in his place. Perfect alibi, right?''

She pounded her fist into her palm. ''That's it! That *has* to be what happened!'' She shifted on the sofa, looking from Damien to Winton, silently pleading with the men to agree. ''And he left her with Mildred. I know he did.'' Any alternative was too unthinkable.

Winton remained silent and thoughtful, his expression carefully noncommittal.

''I'm going in tonight and see if Sydney's at the Jensens,'' Damien said quietly.

''With a warrant, we can go there today,'' Winton said. ''I can get one, but you can bet the Jensens will know about it the minute it's issued. All those friends in high places, you know. If his parents are in on it, there'll be no trace of the child when we get in there. They'll move her. If they're not involved, what's the point?'' He crooked a brow at Damien.

''I'll have to wait and go tonight. Let's not trouble the judge,'' Damien said. ''Today we'll work on the regular search in case we're wrong.''

''You going in there will amount to illegal entry,'' Winton warned. Then he smiled. ''You advising your buddies in the kitchen what you plan to do?'' he inclined his head toward the room where the agents were drinking coffee and making plans.

''Let's not bother them with this, either. They have enough to worry about.''

Molly stared from one to the other, finally voicing her greatest fear of the moment. ''What if Syd's not there?''

Winton hurried to reassure her. ''I hope she is, but we won't take that for granted, by any means. Today, we'll check out all other possibilities. Don't you worry, Ms. Jensen, we're exploring every alternative you can imagine.''

Damien took her hand, giving her his support while all those other alternatives Winton mentioned ran through her mind.

''It's dangerous for you to go in there, Damien,'' she said. ''Don't forget, you'll have to drug the dogs or something.''

"Not if I take enough beef jerky."

She considered the way the Dobermans had reacted to his overtures through the gates. It would work. It had to.

"What will you do if Syd is there?" she asked him, wondering whether he could arrest the Jensens while he was the one breaking and entering their house.

He brushed his hand over her cheek, smiled and caught her braid in his hand, giving it a gentle tug. "I'll bring her home to you, of course."

The day dragged on. Molly jumped each time the phone rang. Reports from Clarkston only advised that whoever had taken Sydney had left no prints and no tracks. No clues at all.

Atlanta agents verified that Jack's Mercedes contained no evidence that Sydney had ever been inside the vehicle. Also, the car itself had not been driven, or even moved from its parking space, not since Damien's friend in Atlanta had checked on it soon after it arrived.

Jack had covered all the bases, she had to give him that much. He had also succeeded in making her suffer like the damned. Her nerves were shot and so were her mother's. Neither of them could so much as mention Sydney's name without lapsing into tears.

She had called her doctor and had a prescription delivered from the pharmacy. The sedative had worked for her mom, but Molly hadn't dared take anything to sedate herself. Syd would need her fully alert.

Damien had remained in the house, offering what comfort and reassurance he could. But Molly could sense his deep concern and she realized it wasn't all directed toward her. She clearly saw fear in his eyes where none had existed since she the day she first met him. He was afraid for Sydney and that increased her own fears tenfold.

Late that afternoon, Agent Thomas stayed, while Blancher and Mitch Winton left for the precinct. They wanted to be there in case anything turned up, she heard them tell Damien.

Molly shuddered, tried to hide from the knowledge while knowing full well what they meant. A body. A small body. Sydney's.

Damien found her huddled in the wing chair in her bedroom where she'd tried to retreat from her terror. "Molly?" He knelt beside her, one hand on her leg and the other on her shoulder. "They've gone to check the computers, that's all. Missing children turn up sometimes. That's why they went. I didn't want you to think—"

She couldn't speak, but she nodded vigorously to make him think she believed it.

"I'm leaving at midnight," he told her. "I'll be back here before two o'clock if all goes well. Can I get you anything? Are you all right?"

"Bring her back," she gasped, straining to hold back her tears. "Bring her to me, Damien."

"Soon," he promised, planting a kiss on top of her hand.

Damien equipped for the break-in as carefully as if he were entering a terrorist stronghold. The utility belt he wore over his black clothing carried cables for scaling walls, his picks for the locks, an electronic device to disable most burglar alarms. In a lightweight leather bag, he'd stowed various other gadgets that had proved useful over the years.

He was no novice at this sort of thing, but everyone had a run of bad luck occasionally. However, the worst that could happen to him was that he'd get caught red-handed and lose his badge. He could deal with it.

Should it come to that, at least he hoped Sydney would be found before he was apprehended. Winton was prepared in the event she wasn't found. If the alarms sounded and the police came to arrest Damien, the detective would see to it that every inch of the house and grounds was searched thoroughly.

He had just stored his gear in the hatch of the Explorer when Molly appeared beside him, wearing a dark turtleneck and jeans. She clutched a pair of leather gloves in her hand. "I'm coming with you," she declared.

Damien slammed the hatch shut and stared at her for a long moment. If he'd ever seen such determination, he couldn't recall it. "You can't. Even if you waited in the car, you'd be an accessory." He used the only reason he thought she'd accept. "If you go to jail, who will look after Sydney?"

Her smile was grim. "You're not getting caught, and neither am I. Let me go and I promise to stay outside the walls." Her beautiful green eyes narrowed in warning. "But if you leave me here, I'll go by myself. I'll shoot the damned dogs and anybody else who gets in my way once I get in the gates."

Damien knew she meant every word of it. He put his arms around her, and sure enough, she had her pistol tucked in the back of her waistband. He removed it, ignoring her struggle, and called the agent who stood at the entrance of the open garage. "Thomas, take Ms. Jensen inside and restrain her if you have to."

The man looked dumbfounded. "What's going on? Where're you going?"

"None of your business, Thomas. She wants to go with me. I want her here," Damien explained. "Keep an eye on her."

Molly didn't offer any further protests, but the look she shot him promised retribution.

He smiled an apology. "Trust me, darling. I'll work better alone. Worrying about you might distract me."

He sympathized with how she felt. Aside from her love and fear for Sydney, Molly felt terribly guilty about leaving the baby in Clarkston last night. She felt if only she'd been there, she might have prevented what happened.

Damien shared her belief, and her guilt, in spades. They never should have gone to the motel. They never should have made love. Giving in to what they felt for each other had been a mistake in more ways than he could begin to count, but they would have to sort all that out later.

"Trust me, Molly," he said softly. "And let me do this alone."

Without another word, she turned curtly and stalked into the house.

Damien shook his head in wonder. Molly had held up surprisingly well today considering what she was going through. He understood her need to act. If this little adventure were not so dicey to begin with, he might have let her come along. It would probably have helped to have her with him to deal with Sydney.

But who knew what he would face once he got inside the gates? The dogs might not be quite as accepting of him as he hoped. The alarms could be beyond his ability to silence. Worse than either of those prospects, Damien hated to think of Molly's reaction if her daughter had been harmed in any way when she was found.

The Jensens might have sedated the baby to keep her quiet. Or Jack could have gotten rough with her if he'd made her angry and she had treated him to those ear-splitting howls of hers. His capacity for violence had certainly been well documented.

Damien didn't imagine for a moment that Jensen would waste any patience or tender feelings on little Sydney. "Smile and be good, little one," he murmured under his breath. "And for God's sake, stay quiet." He would imagine her asleep. Curled up somewhere out of the way with her thumb in her mouth. Ignored and safe.

He drove at a moderate pace to the tune of Pavarotti's

La donna mobile. By the time he arrived at his destination, Damien felt calm, confident and optimistic.

He pulled into the small lane between the trees, the exact spot where he and Molly had parked to watch the Jensen estate two days ago. Instead of backing in this time to facilitate surveillance, he drove straight in, intending to exit on the other side of the large copse onto the road that ran parallel.

With the interior lights disabled, he exited the Explorer and went around back to retrieve the things he might need. The full moon was brighter than he would have liked for this. He could almost see shadows and that wasn't good, but he'd have to make do.

The gunning of a motor barely warned him in time. Molly's van wheeled in, lights off, and almost squashed him between its headlights and the back of the Explorer. *Damn!*

"Just what the hell are you doing here?" he demanded in an angry whisper when Molly climbed out. "Where the devil is Bill Thomas?"

"He's fine," she announced. "I locked him in the storehouse in the back of the garage."

"How did you get him in...never mind!" He raked a hand through his hair and cursed again. "Get yourself back into that van and get out of here. Now!" he ordered, gritting his teeth over the words. "That's an order, Molly!"

"No," she said simply, standing her ground, arms crossed in defiance. "And you can't make me. I plan to be right here when you come out with Sydney."

Damien glanced at his watch. He supposed he could call Winton to come and remove her, or postpone the mission and take her home himself. But he sensed she wouldn't go quietly.

Reluctantly, he threw up his hands and caved. "Oh, all

right, you can stay, but don't you move from this spot, you hear?''

''Scout's honor,'' she promised. Then she rushed toward him and threw her arms around his neck. ''Oh, Damien, please, please be careful!'' Her fervent kiss almost stole his breath.

Then Molly backed off and reached into her back pocket. She pulled out a small, flat, cellophane-wrapped lollipop and handed it to him. ''This should pacify her until you can get her out of there.''

Damien unwrapped it and dropped it into his shirt pocket. ''There. All ready for her. A bit of lint won't matter,'' he said.

''No, she won't care.'' Her voice was whispery. And so hopeful.

The moonlight made her pale, diminished her vibrancy, made her seem vulnerable as hell. It illuminated and heightened the dark circles beneath her eyes. But for the first time in nearly twenty-four hours, Damien saw Molly smile.

Thankfully the dogs cooperated. He fed them through the fence, gave a command for them to sit, and easily scaled the gate. They wriggled, almost breaking the order, eager for another taste. He gave them one and added soft praise. Their lolling-tongued smiles told him he'd succeeded in making friends. With a cautious hand, he offered them his scent and then a gentle scratch apiece. Now he only had to devise a method of getting them to leave him alone. Hard to remain unobtrusive with two Dobermans on his heels.

''Guard!'' he ordered, pointing to the stone wall. They still sat, fidgeting and uttering little whines. He tried again, ''Patrol!'' They promptly fell into the routine and began pacing the perimeter of their property. With a heartfelt sigh of relief, Damien hurried toward the two-story house.

The windows were dark except for one light in the back,

the kitchen. He ventured up to the outer sill and peeked inside. Deserted. It took him a good half hour to check all the windows.

As luck would have it, he didn't even need his tools. Obviously the Jensens trusted the Dobermans too far. Someone had forgotten to lock the French doors that led off the dining room to the terrace. He simply opened one and walked inside. It was so easy, he wondered if it might be a trap.

A rhythmic snore alerted him as he approached the kitchen. He listened at the door of a small room just down the hall from the pantry. Quietly, he twisted the knob and opened the door just wide enough to see the entire space within.

There was a small chest of drawers, a spindly-looking dresser with a mirror, and a narrow single bed. No crib.

A huge, noisy sleeper lay curled beneath a puffy comforter. A live-in maid or cook, he supposed. One thing for certain, whoever it was had not been pressed into temporary service as a baby-sitter for Sydney. He gently closed the door and continued on his exploration.

Damien carefully checked every inch of living space, every enclosure, no matter the size, no matter how unlikely it was to hold the baby.

Finally, he approached the master suite and risked entering. If Sydney were with the Jensens, then this was where she had to be.

The plan was to take her out of here in secret. He couldn't very well arrest the Jensens since he had no business being in their house in the first place without a warrant. Besides, it would be interesting to see how they would react to finding their granddaughter missing when they woke in the morning. Would they call the police? Did they even know that Jack had broken in to steal her? Probably did, but it would be difficult to prove.

His main concern at the moment was how he would get Sydney out of the house and off the grounds without her waking every soul in the neighborhood. Maybe the lollipop Molly had given him would work, but Damien could just envision her squealing with delight when he gave it to her.

The plush carpeting cushioned his steps. Moonlight through the windows offered enough light so that he could see. And be seen, if they happened to wake up. The thought added extra caution to his already careful search.

John Jensen sprawled in his sleep, the covers twisted about his legs, his left arm beneath the neck of his wife. Her long, dark hair covered her face as she lay on her side, curled next to him.

Damien froze when the woman moaned in her sleep and turned over, disturbing both the covers and her bedmate. Both were obviously nude. Though he felt like a voyeur seeing them that way, he dared not take his eyes off the couple. Jensen's snoring stopped until she'd settled down, then began again.

Judging by what Molly had told him about those two, Damien hadn't imagined theirs to be a close relationship. He had expected them to have separate rooms, separate beds, at the very least. Yet these two looked more than chummy.

Shrugging off the thought, he crept to the door opposite the one he'd entered and found himself in a dressing room. He gingerly felt his way through the darkness of it and entered an adjoining bedroom on the other side.

He fully expected to find Sydney in this one. It was the last place in the house left to search. This was definitely a woman's room, unlike the one where he had left the couple sleeping. So they did have separate accommodations, after all, he thought. It made sense that they would put the baby in here if they'd decided to sleep together tonight.

The large bed stood empty, unrumpled and pristine. He

scanned the corners, every nook and cranny as well as the adjoining bathroom.

Damien sighed and his shoulders slumped with the weight of his disappointment. He would almost rather be caught and prosecuted than to go back to that lane and face Molly.

There was no crib here. No cradle. No quilted pallet on the floor. And worst of all, God help him, there was no Sydney.

Chapter 13

"You didn't find her." Though her heart hung like a dead weight in her chest, Molly had adjusted to the fact that Damien was returning alone by the time he reached her.

She had tried so hard not to hope, but now had to admit how heavily she'd counted on his bringing Sydney out of the Jensen estate with him.

He looked almost as dejected as she felt.

"I am so sorry, Molly," he said, enfolding her in his arms the minute he came close enough. "The Jensens and the maid or cook were there. Sydney wasn't."

Molly tried to absorb the warmth and the comfort of his embrace. He held her as if he would banish all her fear by sheer force of will. If only it were that simple.

"Any sign that she's been there?" she asked.

"No." The word, a reluctant admission that he quickly qualified. "But we will find her, Molly. I promise."

He allowed only enough space between them so that he

could see her face. "Will you be all right to drive? I don't like the idea of leaving your van here, but we can get someone to come later and get it if you feel too shaky."

"I'll be okay," she assured him. "This is only the first try to find Syd. It's not as if I've given up." Now if only she could convince herself she meant that, maybe she wouldn't cry all the way home, Molly thought.

"What could Jack have done with her, Damien?" she asked before she could stop herself. "What?"

He hugged her again, pressing his lips to her temple before he answered. "He must have hired someone to look after her."

Molly told herself that Jack would have had to find a person reasonably adept at caring for a child, someone he could trust to keep her well. If anything bad happened to Sydney—with or without proof that he was involved in this—Jack surely realized that neither she nor her family would rest until he paid the price. He must know her and her brother well enough to fully understand that. "Jack wouldn't just take Syd and then…abandon her somewhere, would he?"

"No!" Damien answered a shade too emphatically. "Of course not. There would be no point in that. None at all."

She bit her lips together to keep them from trembling. So abandonment *had* occurred to him as a possibility, just as it had to her. The second worst possibility.

The worst of all, Molly couldn't voice. She wouldn't even say or think the words again, but the dark fear hovered there in the back of her mind, waiting to destroy her sanity if she gave it any credence at all.

"Let's go now," she ordered, knowing that if she didn't get out of there, she was going to fly into so many pieces, not even Damien could put her back together. If she lost Sydney for good, nothing or no one could do that anyway.

"We'll see if maybe Winton or your guys have some

ideas about where we should go from here. I have to be *doing* something if you want me to stay sane.''

''Good thinking,'' Damien said, nodding.

Molly could feel his worried gaze on her as she climbed into her van.

Even after she had followed his Explorer out the other side of the wooded area and they were well on the way to her house, she could sense that he watched his rearview mirror to see whether she was driving erratically.

Molly didn't resent Damien's concern. He had a perfectly good reason to believe she might go haywire. She wouldn't again. Not while there was hope. That hope might be a little frayed around the edges at the moment, but she kept a stranglehold on it, anyway.

Jack obviously did not have Sydney with him in Atlanta. His parents didn't have her at their house. That either meant strangers were keeping her somewhere, or she was alone. Molly might have to face the only other possibility sooner or later, but for now she fiercely held it at bay.

As soon as they pulled into the driveway, Winton appeared, rushing out the front door, down the steps and across the yard to meet them. He must have been watching from the window.

Molly jumped out of the van and hurried toward Damien, reaching him just as the detective did.

''The baby wasn't there,'' Winton guessed, glancing past Damien into the open door of the Explorer and then toward Molly.

''No, she wasn't,'' Damien admitted. ''Something's happened here?''

Something, obviously, Molly thought. Winton wouldn't be so glad to see them that he'd come galloping out of the house the way he had. Maybe he was upset because she had locked Thomas in the storeroom and sneaked out to join Damien. She didn't care.

"There was a phone call about half an hour ago. We got your mother to answer, so if it was a ransom demand, the caller would think it was you," Winton explained to Molly.

She grasped the front lapel of his jacket. "Who has my baby, detective? Who? What do they want?"

Winton stared down at her hand and then glanced at Damien. "We don't know yet. It was a woman on the line. She said to tell you she would call back later. We traced her to a pay phone over by Hillsdale Shopping Center. She was gone before we could get a unit there to check it out."

Damien slid his arm around Molly as though she needed his support. To tell the truth, she did. At the moment she couldn't imagine how dreadful it would be to face all of this without him.

"We'd better get in the house now in case she calls again," Winton said.

Molly practically ran for the front door. Could it be possible that it wasn't Jack who'd taken Sydney, after all? Had some stranger with only greed for the Jensens's money in mind broken in and stolen her child?

She honestly couldn't figure which would be worse for Sydney. Jack might be as dangerous as any unknown threat Molly could imagine.

Bill Thomas, the agent she had tricked into her storeroom stood with her mother on the front steps. Mama was wringing her hands. "Molly, thank God you're back! She wouldn't talk to me—"

Molly hurried past her toward the open door and then stopped and turned, struck by a thought. "Did you tell her who you are, Mama?"

They walked inside together, hand in hand, approaching the phone, both staring at it as though it contained the answers inside it. "No, I just said hello. Then she demanded to speak to you, said it was critical. I told her you weren't home and she said she'd call back. Then she hung up. She just seemed to know I wasn't you.''

"She didn't mention Syd?"

Her mother let go of her and began to pace. "No, not a word. But something told me—''

"Then it's someone who knows my voice," Molly said, turning to Damien and the detective. "Whoever called knows me!"

Winton sighed and shoved his hands into his pockets. "Which eliminates only about half of the women in Nashville, right? How many people did you go to school with? Work with at the museum or meet somewhere else in town over the years?"

Damien shook his head, disagreeing, and looked from her to her mother as though comparing them. "Their voices *are* similar, Winton. If Brenda didn't identify herself when she answered, the caller would have to be well acquainted with both women to know which one was speaking. I think Molly's right. This person probably knows her well. Brenda, too, if she could distinguish between them after only—''

Winton interrupted. "Here, I'll replay the conversation and see whether you can recognize the voice," he said to Molly.

She listened closely, but the woman on the phone spoke in a half whisper and sounded desperate. The accent was local, or at least Southern.

"It sounds a little like Jack's mother, but we know it can't be her. Damien just saw her asleep."

"Does she have any family, sisters maybe?" Winton asked.

Molly shook her head.

It could have been anyone speaking, but something else on the recording had snagged Molly's attention.

She examined the box Winton had attached to her phone,

punched Rewind and Play and listened again. This time she paid closer attention to the background noise.

"Yes!" she cried when it was over. "Did you hear that noise? I think it's Syd!"

Winton sighed and shook his head. "It's only static, Ms. Jensen."

"No! No, it's not. Listen!" Again she rewound the tape and played it. "Hear? She's smacking!"

Molly looked to Damien for confirmation. "She makes that sound when she's eating something she really likes. I know it's her! I know it! She's there with that woman!"

Damien took her hand, his doubt and regret apparent. Winton looked as if he was biting his tongue to keep from protesting again. She glanced at her mother who had her face covered with both hands.

"It's her," Molly insisted, watching their faces as they tried to hide their disbelief. As a result, she was no longer quite so certain herself.

The phone rang.

Molly snatched up the receiver. "Hello! This is Molly. Do you have her?"

"What? Molly? This is Josie McElmore. Please, is your mom there?"

"Did you call here earlier?" Molly demanded.

"What? No," the voice said, sniffling. "Please let me talk to Brenda!"

"Here, Mama," Molly said, handing over the receiver, not attempting to hide her impatience or disappointment. "It's Josie. Sounds like she's got a bad cold. Please hurry, so we can keep the line free."

Her mother nodded as she greeted her friend. "Yes, Josie? What is it, hon?"

Molly watched her mother's face transform from business-like to horror-struck in the space of two seconds as she spoke on the phone to Josie.

"Was it accidental?" she asked. "Okay, I'll be over there as soon as I can." She hung up and clasped a hand to her forehead as she looked at Molly. "A fire," she muttered. "There's been a fire at the shop. Josie just got there and was calling me from her cell phone."

Molly held her arm as she sank down onto the chair.

"Oh, Mama, I'm so sorry! Could they save anything?" Molly asked, and received only a shrug and a look of profound worry in answer.

The shop was the most important thing in her mother's life, other than the family. It was also her only source of income. The building was rented, of course, and she had the antiques insured, but no settlement would begin to compensate her for the travel and time spent acquiring her precious inventory one piece at a time.

Damien crouched, one large hand on her mother's arm. "Brenda, did she say the fire was set? Does it appear to be arson?"

"They don't know yet, Damien, but Josie did say I need to get over there as soon as I can. You'll take care of Molly for me?"

"*I'll* take care of Molly!" Molly told her. "And we'll let you know as soon as that woman phones us back about Syd. I hope you can save some of the things at the shop."

Winton pulled out his radio. "I'll have a car here in a few minutes to take you over there, Mrs. Devereaux," he assured her.

"Why don't you go with her?" Damien suggested to the detective. "There's no need for both of us to stay here. We'll record it if we get another call. The caller ID will tell us where it came from. Thomas can run it down."

He then said what they were all thinking. "This fire's probably related, a diversion. If so, then he definitely has an accomplice. You believe in coincidence, Winton?"

"Nope, never did," Winton said. "I can get more info

out of the firefighters than she can, anyway. I probably need to speak with the fire inspector about this if he's there yet.''

Within minutes, he and her mother were gone.

''Where is the other agent?'' Molly asked, curling up in the chair right beside the phone. ''Will he be back?''

Damien shook his head and relaxed on the sofa. ''Watching that phone booth where the call was made in the event the woman comes back there. There's nothing more we can do at the moment but wait. Or you can listen to the recorder again and try to think who it might be.''

Molly opted for that. Repeatedly she listened. But she couldn't place the voice. However, the more she heard the tape, the more she was convinced that Sydney was there when the call was made, close to the phone, smacking her little lips. There was one little half hum—a small grunt, really—near the end of the call.

''They've given her something she likes,'' Molly muttered, trying to console herself. ''She's being taken care of.''

''Come over here,'' Damien said softly, holding out his arms. ''Come let me hold you.''

Molly went. The haven of his arms simply tempted her too much to say no. This was not a thing she wanted to face alone. ''Am I wrong?'' she asked him as she settled on the sofa and he tucked her head beneath his chin. ''It could be Syd, couldn't it, Damien?''

''Yes, it could be her,'' he granted, sounding a little too encouraging for Molly to believe he meant it.

She changed the subject. ''You think Jack had that fire set, don't you?''

''Yes,'' he said with no equivocation.

Tightening his arms around her, he pressed his lips against the top of her head. ''I think he took Sydney and is paying someone to keep her for him. I also believe he hired the arsonist to burn your mother out.''

He spent a moment smoothing her hair with one hand and caressing her back with the other. When he stopped, he cupped her face in his hands and turned it up so that he could look into her eyes.

While his voice was soft, the determination in it was fierce. "I'll wait with you to see whether this woman calls again. But as soon as Brenda and Winton return in the morning, I'm leaving for Atlanta."

"You're not going to do anything..."

"Yes," he answered seriously. "I am." He raised one brow and sighed, looking down at her with regret. "I might not be back, Molly. But I promise that Sydney will be. And you'll both be safe from him."

Molly didn't know what she could do to dissuade Damien from a direct attack on Jack, or even whether she wanted to talk him out of it. She would like nothing better than to attack him herself. However, she didn't want Damien to endanger himself or his job with the Bureau. She doubted the FBI would sanction what he must have in mind.

"Don't worry," he said, smiling as if he'd read her mind. "I'll take care of everything."

The phone rang again. Molly leaped for it, almost dropping the receiver in her haste. Damien hit the Record button. Thomas appeared out of the kitchen like magic.

"Hello? I'm here! It's Molly! Do you have her?"

"The baby is well," the voice grated.

"Bring her back!" Molly cried. "Oh, please bring her—"

"Tomorrow." It was almost inaudible. Barely a whisper. Then, *click.*

"Wait!" Molly cried, clutching the receiver with both hands. "Don't hang up! No!" She fell against Damien and wept. "She hung up."

Damien held her while he played back the short recording. "Did you recognize her voice this time?"

Molly shook her head, unable to answer verbally. She thought she might choke on the tears and the fear.

"You heard her, Molly," Damien said soothingly. "Sydney is all right." He released her. "Hang on."

He scribbled down the number on the caller ID. Molly watched him punch the buttons on the phone. A distant part of her mind listened to his curt demands and questions as he did what was necessary to determine the location where the call had been placed. Bill Thomas left, she supposed to visit the phone where the call had been made.

But her mind could not focus on anything other than the fact that the woman on the phone had her baby. A woman who cared enough to let her know Sydney was okay.

There could have been no other purpose for that phone call. No ransom had been demanded. No threats had been issued. No taunts made. The voice had held compassion and empathy from one mother to another. Or had she read that into it? No way she could have misinterpreted, Molly thought as she cried with pure relief.

Tomorrow, the woman had said. Had she meant she would bring Syd back tomorrow?

Damien watched Molly sleep, curled on the end of the sofa, one hand resting only inches from the phone that he'd moved there for her convenience.

He glanced at his watch—*10:00 a.m.* She had slept since around five o'clock, and he'd caught a couple of hours himself. Time now to make some kind of move.

Perhaps take off for Atlanta and beat the truth out of Jack Jensen when he got there, or he could wait here for a while and see what happened if the woman called again.

Normally, he was a very patient man, but the past few

days had worn his patience thin. Every muscle in his body clamored for action. He badly needed to act.

However, before he made a decision, Damien knew he needed to speak with Winton. It only made good sense to find out all he could about the fire at Brenda's antique shop last night. He also should get Winton's take on the second phone call from the woman who had Sydney. He'd called him with the information, but they needed to discuss it again, now that they'd both had time to think about it.

The more information Damien had when he confronted Jensen, the better the likelihood of making him crack.

Molly stirred, mumbling something unintelligible before finally opening her eyes. Frantically she looked around as though she had trouble placing herself on awakening. Damien hated this. He wanted Molly back, not this frightened shadow of a girl.

If Jensen had set out to destroy her, he had chosen exactly the right tool this time. With every hour that passed without her child, Molly retreated deeper into the fear. Her natural confidence had eroded to nearly nothing.

Instinctively, Damien knew that she could have met any other crisis with her usual strength and energy. She had done that and he had seen her do it. But not the loss of her baby. Last night she had given it her best shot. His lack of success at the Jensens had thrown her completely off stride and still she had made an effort.

But the phone call, so unexpected, had confused the issue of the kidnapping. Somewhere in the back of her mind, she had been counting on Jensen's mother to provide safety for Sydney.

Now they had no idea who had the child, though Damien was firmly convinced Jack Jensen knew very well who had her. This was no kidnap for ransom. It was meant to instill the worst kind of terror in Molly, and it had certainly done that.

Unless Sydney was returned unharmed—and soon—Damien hated to think what would happen to Molly. She had not eaten or drank anything since they had found out the child was missing.

She reached out and touched the phone. "Did I dream it? Did she call again?"

Damien crouched beside her and ran his palms over her arms, wishing he could soothe away that awful tension he felt in her. "The second message was that she was well. Did you dream she called again?"

She shook her head and ran a hand over her face. "It couldn't have been Mildred, could it? The woman who phoned? The voice sort of sounded like hers, but it couldn't have been. You're sure you did see her last night. She was asleep, right?"

"They were both there in bed," he admitted with a sigh.

Molly's lovely brow furrowed with anxiety. "*Tomorrow,* she said. Something will happen today, won't it?" she whispered, her tone distant. "I wonder what."

She excused herself as politely as if they were strangers and went down the hallway to her bedroom. Damien waited, forming plans in his mind for his meeting later with Jensen. Somehow, he would erase Molly's desolation if he had to erase the man himself. But first he must find Sydney. Only that would make Molly whole again.

When she returned a bit later, she had showered and changed. Her face looked free of makeup, the faint sprinkle of freckles across her nose, endearingly childlike. Damp auburn tendrils clung to her temples while the rest of her curls were caught up in a mass at the nape of her slender neck.

How delicate she looked, wearing a gauzy beige hip-length tunic and loose pants to match. Her narrow feet with their slender toes and unpolished nails were bare, adding to her aura of tragic vulnerability.

Damien wished he could magically wipe away her worry. If only he could hold her, love her and make her forget for a while. Their eyes met. His held the offer, hers a desperate plea. Would this make her guilt worse?

He took her hands in his and pulled her to him, meeting her lips with his. She leaned into the kiss, desperate for the comfort he wanted to give in any way he could.

Damien heard a car pull up in the driveway. It would be Winton, and probably Brenda, returning. Damn their timing.

Reluctantly Damien ended the kiss and cupped her face in one hand. ''Later,'' he promised with a last touch of his lips. ''When everything is as it should be.''

Her weak smile and nod of resignation offered no assurance that she believed anything would ever be *as it should be* again.

Chapter 14

Damien waited until noon to see whether the woman would call a third time. She hadn't. Every hour that passed, Molly grew more despondent, less like herself. He couldn't tolerate this. Something had to be done and he had to do it now.

Winton had sent unmarked cars to keep watch on the phone booths where the calls had been placed. Thomas had gone to stake out the Jensen estate in the event there was any activity there. Agent Blancher had returned. On Damien's order, he was now stationed in the living room with Molly to assist however he could once Damien left.

Brenda had remained near her shop with her assistant and the fire crews. Detective Winton, after arranging for her safety, had come back to see what else he could do to help. Damien had advised him to catch a few hours' sleep in the guest room while he had the chance. They were all exhausted. He was running on pure adrenaline himself.

Molly sat on the sofa, her hand only inches from the phone.

Now that everyone else was occupied, Damien picked up Winton's cell phone and placed his call. "Jensen's still there? You're certain?" he asked the agent who had charge of the surveillance in Atlanta. "Good. If he tries to leave, detain him. I don't care how you do it." With that, he replaced the receiver and reached for his car keys.

Then he realized he wasn't alone after all. Winton had heard it all. "You've still got that junkyard dog look in your eye," Winton said, shaking his head, hands braced on his hips. "You know you ought not to do this, Perry. We don't have an iota of proof Jack Jensen engineered either the kidnapping or the fire. You go over there and lose your cool, he's gonna sue you personally—maybe the Bureau, too—for harassment. Won't do a damned thing to help the situation. Screw you up good, though."

Damien fixed him with a glare that dared Winton to try to stop him. "Jensen's behind this. He knows where Sydney is."

"Well, yeah, but he knows how far you can go legally. You knock him around a little bit and he still won't tell you anything. He'd be stupid to do that, and we all *know* he's not stupid. All you get's a little satisfaction and a lawsuit, right?" Winton raised a brow. "And a reprimand on your record. Maybe even get fired. He'd love it. That what you want?"

"As long as I get him to talk, I don't care," Damien said truthfully. "Nothing's as important as getting Sydney back where she belongs." Again, he started for the kitchen door, intending to leave by the garage so as not to disturb Molly in the living room.

Winton caught his arm. "Hold up now," he cajoled. "Let's get us a plan here so we don't go off half-cocked, okay?"

Damien pulled away, but didn't leave. Winton did have

a point. "Are you saying you're with me on this? You were just trying to talk me out of it!"

"Yeah, I'm in. Just pointing out the drawbacks. But we need to play it just right, keep a cool head. Remember who we're dealing with," he advised. "Beat him up and he's still not gonna confess. He'd welcome the lumps just to get you in trouble."

Damien leaned against the kitchen counter and crossed his arms over his chest. "We'll work on his weakness, then. What is it, do you think? It's not doing more time."

"Nah," Winton said, shaking his head, worrying his chin with his fingers. "His daddy's money might not have saved him from getting sent up, but it sure made his stay there right comfortable, I bet. I doubt Jack liked it much, but judging by what he's done so far, he must not be too scared of going back."

Damien agreed. "I actually think he believes taking revenge on Molly is worth getting caught."

"You're probably right. He wouldn't do more than a couple of years for a parental kidnapping. Nothing for the arson unless we can catch who acted for him and get them to implicate him. And that's not too likely. Daddy John would pay whoever it was to do the time, which wouldn't amount to much since no one was injured in the fire. Hell, the fire might not be related, after all."

"You said you didn't believe in coincidence," Damien reminded him. "Changed your mind?"

Winton ignored that since it was rhetorical. "I can only think of one thing that might make Jensen give up the game," he said with an evil grin. He even twisted one side of his mustache. "Something even dear old dad couldn't make nice for him after the fact. Something real basic." He shrugged and held up his hands. "Everybody's scared to die, right?"

Damien grimaced. "And I would love to kill him."

''Nah, you don't wanna do that,'' Winton said with a laugh. ''Just convince him you will. I'll help you do that. Give him an ultimatum. The kid comes home today or he dies tonight. That you don't care about the law, or justice, or the consequences to yourself. That baby comes back *tout de suite* or he's ready for a dirt nap come sundown.''

''Exactly what I had in mind in the first place,'' Damien said. ''I've got a helicopter on hold. Let's go.''

''Just where do you think you're going?'' Molly demanded, standing in the doorway to the kitchen, one shoulder propped against the frame. From the expression on her face, she didn't really need an answer. ''Come back here and sit down!'' One slender finger pointed to the kitchen table.

Uncertain whether to resent her belligerent attitude or applaud her renewed spirit, Damien started to explain. Winton intervened. ''We're thinking about having a little talk with Jack and see what we can find out,'' he said, his usual smile firmly in place.

Did the man ever get truly worked up about anything? Of course, he must. This facade Winton hid behind had similarities to the one Damien normally employed himself. He almost smiled himself at the comparison. They had much in common, he and Winton, even though they were as different as kippers and cornpone. He had a feeling that if the situation were reversed and Winton's lady were the one caught up in this, Damien would be the one offering cool reason to a hot head. Yes, he thought, nodding, they should work well together today.

''I heard what you're planning,'' she said, pursing her lips in disapproval. ''What happens if you're wrong about this? What if Jack panics and tells whoever has Sydney to get rid of her? They…might.''

The little hitch in her voice struck Damien through the heart. He crossed the room and would have put his arms around her, but she shoved him back, impatient. "I said sit *down!*"

She glared at Winton until he shrugged and complied. "We need to discuss this first," she added, shooting Damien a look of accusation.

He sat. She could be right. They had no idea who Jensen had hired to keep the baby or whether that person had any compunction about simply doing away with the evidence altogether. Which meant doing away with Sydney herself. Cold fear for her gripped Damien and he realized that this fear was likely only a fraction of the terror Molly felt.

Eliminating the child would certainly accomplish Jensen's need for revenge and also leave him in the clear. He might even have a prearranged code to put that in motion if he made a call to the one who had Sydney. Damien blew out a ragged breath of frustration.

Molly took a seat and leaned forward on the table, her hands clasped in front of her. Her eyes looked weak from tears and fatigue. Damien noticed her nails were down to the quick, her fingertips red on the ends. They had not been that way yesterday. He recognized the nervous habit as one he'd had when he was very young.

She looked a child herself at the moment. A very worried child who could not count on her distraught mother for solace. Brenda had lost her livelihood last night in the fire, a gross disaster added to her grave concern for her stolen grandchild.

All the more reason for Damien to resolve this plight as soon as he possibly could. Above all, Molly needed Sydney with her. She needed her harried mother's mind set at ease. And, at the moment, she also needed someone with the authority she didn't possess to make things right for her. He would.

"I've been thinking and thinking about that voice on the phone," Molly told them. "Even though it was only a whisper, there was something familiar about it, a tone that reminded me so much of Jack's mother.''

Damien started to protest, wanting to warn Molly that the mind could play tricks, manufacture theories that might offer hope.

She held up one hand to silence him. ''I know you told me it couldn't be Mildred, Damien, but are you absolutely certain she was there when you searched the place? It had to be dark in that room. Could it have only looked like two people in the bed? Maybe there were a lot of extra pillows bunched up or something?''

He shook his head. ''She was there, Molly. And she definitely would not have had time to get all the way to that phone booth where the call was made, even if she followed me out as soon as I left. And she did not have Sydney in that house with them. That much, I will swear to. I searched it thoroughly.''

''I know you did.'' Molly tapped her fingers against her lips, lost in thought. Then she asked, ''Could it have been someone else in bed with John?''

Damien's brows shot up and he looked at Winton, who wore much the same expression.

She continued. ''I just have trouble picturing John and Mildred all cuddled up like you described, you know? He might demand sex now and then, but I doubt it. Even if they do still have…relations,'' she said, faltering, blushing, ''I doubt they're that lovey-dovey…after.''

She cleared her throat and tossed her head, dismissing her embarrassment. Damien marveled at her modesty, even as he applauded her savvy. Hadn't he wondered the same thing when he saw the couple together?

''So, what do you think? Could it have been somebody other than Mildred?'' Molly persisted now that his and Winton's attention assured her that her theory might be viable.

And it was quite viable, Damien thought. Why the hell hadn't he considered it before? Well, he knew why. "You believe John Jensen would bring in another woman to sleep in the house with him? In their bed?"

In his experience, men of wealth did not give their wives such ammunition. Being discovered in a flagrantly adulterous position could cost them a whale of a lot of grief, not to mention a pile of alimony.

"What did she look like?" Molly asked eagerly.

Damien thought back. "I couldn't see her face. Almost as tall as Jensen. Nicely rounded. About your size." He noted Molly's huff of disgust and added, "I mean that as a compliment. She looked...well proportioned."

He closed his eyes, recalling further details. "Except for rather large feet," he added, remembering the one he'd seen exposed in the tangle of sheets. "Dark hair, I think, though it was hard to tell. Long enough to cover her face and shoulder."

"Long?" Molly clapped her hands and jumped out of the chair. "Not her. That's *not* Mildred!"

"You're sure?" Winton asked, more animated than Damien had seen him get about anything.

"Her hair's blond, almost platinum!" Molly declared with a self-congratulatory grin. "Medium-length and sprayed to a fair-thee-well. A real sixties-type helmet head. Probably sleeps in a net."

Her excitement grew. She flashed a smile and poked the table with her index finger as if to establish her point. "Mildred's keeping Syd somewhere, I know it! John would never bring a woman into the house for sex unless he *knew* Mildred would be occupied somewhere else and unable to come home and catch him at it."

"The maid was there," Damien reminded her. "Or the cook? The one sleeping just off the kitchen."

Molly shrugged. "That would be Ina. She'd never rat on him. John would fire her and she needs that job."

She reached out for his hand. "You know what this means? Mildred has Syd. I might not be crazy about Jack's mom, but she's really not a bad person. I know she'd never do anything to hurt my baby, even if she were dead certain Syd's not her grandchild."

Winton interrupted her, "If she does have your daughter, then she's following Jack's orders."

Molly seemed to wilt. They were at an impasse. Again. Damien still thought their best bet would be putting the screws to Jack. "What do you think they plan to do next, Winton? Your best guess."

The detective looked from one to the other and sighed. "Jack obviously took Sydney to cause Molly here some grief. I'd be willing to bet he did it on impulse. Maybe went to Clarkston to get at you two, found you gone and took the baby. Then he had to decide right quick what to do with her so he could hotfoot it to Atlanta to cover his butt. He enlisted his mama to help him out. If John knows, I bet he sent her away from the house in case we came with a warrant to search."

"What about the other woman?" Molly asked. "You would have found her there."

Winton grinned. "He could say she was a maid. Easy enough to explain unless we caught them in bed together. Right, Perry?"

"Yes, and I agree with your theory," Damien said.

Molly brightened. "I don't think Mildred would consent to take Syd unless Jack gave her a good reason. Right? She wouldn't dare be party to a kidnapping unless Jack told her Sydney was his and he wanted to get her away from me. She'd do it then. Mildred never did approve of our marriage because I was outside their league. Beneath them. I guess she felt sorry, though. She is a mother."

It made perfect sense, Damien decided. "And since Jack didn't have a prayer of ever obtaining custody in court because of the conviction for assault on you, he just took her. That's what he would have told Mildred. She would sympathize. She'd want the baby."

"So you think they plan to keep her?" Winton asked. "For good? But they'd have to hide her to do that."

Damien got up. "I think we need to give Jack a very good reason to have Sydney returned." He pointed at Molly. "You stay right here in case she calls again. At least we know she's sympathetic enough to try to alleviate your worry about Sydney. I'll give you odds Jack has no knowledge of his mother making those calls to you." He smiled at Molly and turned to Winton. "Shall we rattle his cage a bit?"

"You shake the hell out of it," Molly ordered. Her green eyes flashed sparks. "You tell Jack I want my baby back right now or I'll see him roast in hell!"

Damien leaned over to brush a kiss on her heated cheek. "He will get the message, darling. I can promise you that. And you'll get Sydney."

He left her wearing a look of hope that compounded his resolve to make it happen.

Two hours later he pulled alongside Jack's Mercedes in the parking garage. He and Winton had everything worked out, timed to the split second. Damien carefully checked his weapon and Winton followed suit. Without speaking, they exited the Explorer, identified themselves to the agent sent to watch Jensen's car, and marched to the elevator.

They also made brief contact with the agent stationed in the lobby when they reached it. Damien acquired the room key. The men here would be prepared if Jensen made a break for it after they left.

"You feelin' mean enough?" Winton asked when they had reached Jensen's room.

"Let's do it," Damien replied with a feral baring of teeth. His muscles bunched beneath his shirt and jacket, tensing for action.

He stuck the card key into the slot and handed it off to Winton as he pushed down the handle. Quietly he slipped inside the room and let the door close behind him with a loud click.

At the sound, Jensen flew out of the bathroom, a newspaper in his hand. Outraged, he squawked, "What the hell—"

Damien slammed him, face against the wall, a forearm cutting off the air supply. "Open your mouth one more time, you son of a bitch, and I'll off you right here," he warned, his voice low, gritty and bordering on psychotic. He was barely pretending.

Without warning, he snatched up the waistband of Jensen's boxers with his free hand, his other arm still immobilizing the neck, and hauled the jerk across the room. The high, tinny groans of pain and fear fueled Damien's need to increase them.

With effort, he pushed back the thoughts of how this miscreant had snatched a helpless baby out of her safe warm crib, how he had put that look of misery on Molly's sweet face.

You can't kill him. You aren't supposed to kill him. He repeated the phrases in his mind until reason returned.

It came back slowly, only after he had exacted a few more moments of satisfaction at Jensen's mounting terror. Then he tossed him onto the bed.

Jack quickly rolled over onto his back, clutching his throat with one hand, his groin with the other. Wide-eyed and gasping, he wisely said nothing.

"Yes, you *are* going to die," Damien said in a deadly

calm voice. He drew his weapon and switched off the safety.

Jensen held up a hand, palm out, and whispered, "What...what d'you want?" He swallowed a sob. It did Damien's heart good. "Money? I got money."

Damien chuckled, sounding a bit mad, even to himself. Hell, he was mad. "I've got money, too, you bloody wretch. You don't have a damn thing I want except that child."

"Child?" Jack asked, all innocence. "I don't know what you're—"

Damien was on him like a falling rock, one knee in the gut, the barrel of the Sig Sauer firmly placed to Jack's nose.

"Now then. You will phone whoever has the baby and tell them to take her home. Unharmed. Immediately. If you refuse one...more...time, I will empty this weapon into your right nostril. You have two seconds to agree."

Jensen sobbed. "Wait! Wait, I swear I don't know where she is!"

Damien pulled the trigger. At the metallic snick, Jack cringed and issued a high-pitched whine. He wet himself. Damien could smell urine over the strong stench of fear.

"Ha, a misfire? Strange." He shrugged and clicked his tongue. "However, I am certain this is loaded. We'll try it again." He jammed the barrel farther into flesh. "One last chance?"

Then he felt Winton's hand grab his collar from behind, the other hand gripped his wrist as the detective yanked him backward off the bed and dumped him on the floor. "Police!" Winton barked over his shoulder for Jensen's benefit.

With a wink at Damien, he pulled back his fist and clipped him soundly on the jaw. Damien collapsed for the next act, peeking through his lashes to assess Winton's acting skills.

Jensen scrambled off the bed. "He just busted in here and tried to kill me!" he complained. "You witnessed it! I want that bastard arrested!"

"Okay, sure," Winton agreed. "I'll drag him downstairs. Get the locals to take him in." He sighed with regret. "Of course, they won't hold him long. Perry's got a whole bunch of friends here, y'know."

Damien almost laughed. The *whole bunch* Winton spoke of consisted of one, barely an acquaintance, who had extended a bit of professional courtesy. The agent-in-charge in the Memphis office, Michael Duvek, had later requested continued, full surveillance through Atlanta headquarters. Damien couldn't even call Duvek a friend. He acted as control on certain cases, a contact, his liaison with headquarters in Virginia. But Duvck *was* a friend to Ford Devereaux, Molly's brother.

What a discomfiting feeling, Damien thought, to realize he had no real friends, no one to call on just because they might care if he needed help. Not that it had ever bothered him before. In fact, he'd gone out of his way to avoid any lasting friendships. It bothered him now.

At the moment Winton seemed a likely candidate, Damien thought, suppressing a grin.

Jensen was on his feet. Damien continued to watch, feigning unconsciousness, eyes slitted so they appeared closed. Winton clicked the handcuffs onto Damien's wrists, scooped up the weapon he'd dropped and stood to face Jensen. "You know, Jack, if I were you, I think I'd do what I could to get that kid back to her mama. Otherwise, this guy's just gonna come after you again. I won't be riding to the rescue next time."

"You put a tail on him," Jensen ordered. "You watch his every move and if he comes near me again, I want him shot!"

Winton inclined his head and seemed to consider it.

"Nah, I don't think I'll be doing that." He ran a hand through his hair and expelled a weary breath. "I'll just let him kill you."

"You can't!" Jensen protested.

"Oh, yeah, I think I can. See, if I have to write up a shooting, I'd *much* rather have the victim be you than him. He's FBI. Didja know that, Jack?" He nudged Damien's leg with the toe of his boot. "Hard to justify shooting a fellow officer of the law, don'cha see?"

"FBI?" Jensen croaked. "He's an agent?"

"Damn straight," Winton said evenly. "Got all kinds of awards and stuff. Said to be the best they had and never missed a collar. Sorta went rogue on 'em, though. All that undercover stuff just got to 'im. Too many kills, I guess. Had to put him on leave for a while. Let him get himself together a little bit. Still, I wouldn't want to shoot him even if he is nuts." Winton shook his head. "Nah. Internal Affairs would prob'ly have a fit."

"Why would you want me dead? I haven't *done* anything!" Jensen insisted.

"I don't especially want you dead, Jack. I just don't care one way or the other. You took that baby, and we know it." Winton glanced down. "*He* knows it."

He clapped a hand on Jensen's bare shoulder and gave it a rough shake. "You take a word of advice, ol' son, and get your tail outta this crack before you come to grief. Give that little girl back while you got a chance."

Winton nodded once toward Damien. "See, he don't really care what happens to him. He's crazy about that kid. Or maybe he's just crazy, period. Got enough paperwork to back up an insanity plea, that's for sure. I'd testify he was looney when he shot you."

"You can't just let him come after me again!" Jensen whined.

"Hey, if you do the right thing, he'll probably leave you

alone. That way, he's happy, the kid's happy, the mom's happy…and you just might be alive. Right now," Winton said, and shook his head regretfully, "he's just obsessed with getting that kid back home."

Still protesting, Jensen insisted, "Look, whatever your goddamn name is, I tell you I don't—"

"Aw, now, don't talk ugly, Jack. You just do what you gotta do, okay?" Winton said with total calm. "Get that door for me, would ya?" He reached down, grasped Damien's legs and dragged him across the room, past a speechless Jack Jensen and out into the hall.

Jensen must have been standing in the doorway watching. Damien couldn't see behind him as Winton towed him all the way to the elevator, rolled him inside and punched the button for the lobby.

"Good show," Damien said, releasing his pent-up laughter. "Get these damned cuffs off me and I'll applaud."

Winton grunted as he squatted and plied the key. "Bet your ass Jackie's on the phone to mama right about now."

"And they're set up downstairs to monitor calls?"

"Yep. Let's go see what happens." He offered Damien his hand to get up. "You okay? I didn't clip you too hard there, did I?"

Damien slapped him on the back and assumed Winton's plowboy accent. "Now did ol' Andy of Mayberry ever harm a soul you heard tell of?"

"Hey, you do that pretty good," Winton praised. "Ever decide you want to stick around down South, you'd prob'ly fit right in."

"I'll certainly take that under consideration," Damien promised. He'd already had it under consideration for some time now. It had just taken Winton's voicing it to make Damien admit it to himself.

Accents were a surface trick he'd mastered long ago. He could fit in practically anywhere he needed to in that respect. The question was, could he learn all the truly important things required to become what Molly and Sydney needed in their lives?

His experience with family matters was so limited, he wasn't even certain what qualities he lacked or if they could be cultivated once he found out. It might be too late for him, but he knew he couldn't abandon the notion now that it had taken hold in his mind. He wanted Molly. Needed her. And she needed him.

"I bet you never give up, do ya?" Winton asked, shooting him a sidewise glance as the elevator dinged and the doors slid open.

"What?" Damien asked, wondering for a second whether he'd spoken his thoughts out loud.

"On a case like this. Or anything else for that matter," Winton explained. "I bet no matter how long it takes, you just keep right on pickin' to the end of the row, don't ya?"

Damien flashed him a grin. "All this plowboy wisdom of yours must come in awfully handy, Winton."

"Yeah, Perry, I reckon it does," he replied, pushing open the door to the room where an Atlanta agent monitored the phone line from Jensen's room. He gestured politely toward the empty chairs. "Thinking on doing a little plantin' pretty soon, are you?"

Damien shrugged. "I need to get a bit more familiar with the terrain first."

Winton laughed, punched him lightly on the shoulder.

"Call going through," the agent announced, "Nashville number."

"Hi, there, Mama!" Winton said with a lazy chuckle.

Damien frowned at the readout on the call box. "No, actually it's *Hello, Dad.*"

His worried gaze collided with Winton's as they listened to the conversation between Jack and his father.

"Cut her loose," Jack said without so much as a greet

ing. "We don't, then I'm cooked. It's gotta be *very* clear I'm not involved."

The elder Jensen sighed audibly, sounding disgusted. "It'll take a few hours to get rid of her. Show yourself around there and stay put. I'll handle it."

The line went dead.

An icy chill swept through the marrow of Damien's bones. A sympathetic Mildred Jensen would have no say at all in what happened to little Sydney.

"Get the chopper revved. Use the phone in the lobby," he told Winton. "Redial that number," he ordered the agent. "Then I'd like you to leave. You won't need to hear this conversation."

Chapter 15

"Jensen residence," a female voice answered.

Damien figured it was the maid. "Get John Jensen on the line immediately. It *is* a matter of life and death."

Less than a minute lapsed. "Jensen here."

"This is Agent Perry with the Federal Bureau of Investigation. If you do not restore Sydney Jensen to her mother within the next two hours, smiling and unharmed, I will kill your son. And then I will kill you. Do I make myself clear?"

The strangled sound made Damien wonder if the man was suffering an attack of some kind.

"You...you can't do this!" Jensen exclaimed. "The FBI can't—"

"Did I mention that I am acting in an unofficial capacity? This is a very personal matter to me. And to you, I'm sure. You now have one hour, fifty-nine minutes. If you wish to waste a few of those, ring Jack and ask him what he meant by being cooked unless you cut Sydney loose. I would imagine it has to do with his breathing down the barrel of my Sig Sauer a few moments prior to your conversation with him.''

The silence stretched out so long, Damien wondered if Jensen really had put him on hold to make another call.

Following a harsh expulsion of breath, Jensen admitted defeat. ''I'll need longer than two hours.''

''That's your decision to make, of course,'' Damien replied calmly while his heart pounded with relief. His hands shook as he held the phone, but at least his voice remained steady. Deadly. ''You are down to one hour and fifty-eight. At precisely six thirty-five, I will phone Molly Jensen's house. If the child is not there, and in perfect health, my plans proceed as promised. Are we understood?'' Another long silence ensued.

''Understood,'' Jensen finally growled.

Damien broke the connection and dropped into the nearest chair, lowering his face into his palms. ''God,'' he whispered. ''Thank God.'' He couldn't recall the last time he'd had such a case of the sweats.

Winton returned. ''Hey, man, you okay?''

''Fine,'' Damien said, rising. ''Is the chopper ready?''

''Waiting on you. What's the word?'' he asked, nodding toward the phone.

''Jensen's bringing her home in about two hours,'' Damien said. ''I told him I would kill Jack and then him if he didn't.''

''Ha! You bluffed him into it?''

Damien wiped a hand over his face and shook his head. ''To tell you the truth, Win, I wonder if I *was* bluffing.''

''You could get canned over this, y'know? Making death threats and all. But I guess you're safe enough unless they confess everything and mean to take you down with them.''

''I can always take up farming,'' Damien said lightly as he strode to the door. Nothing, not even the loss of his career, could d...

on her way hom...

The weather in ... o'clock. A half hou... flashed. Thunder boon... whipped the trees and tu... yards. Molly watched thro... crossed over a chest that felt ... Damien.

Blancher, the agent who had ... himself to make a sandwich, offering to ma... Molly declined. She couldn't force a mouthful dow... when her poor baby might be hungry. Surely Mildred wouldn't allow that. Would she? Then again, the woman had no idea what Syd would and wouldn't eat.

"But you're not all that picky, are you, sweetie?" she whispered to the rain. More tears escaped when she'd thought them all used up.

A car turned into her driveway. Somebody bringing Mama back over, Molly thought. Then the doors opened and a man and woman got out. It was nearly dark and she couldn't tell who they were through the curtain of rain. Then the woman opened the rear door and leaned inside to get something.

When she emerged, one little white foot stuck out the bottom of the wriggling bundle.

Molly gasped, then cried out with joy. She was barely aware of running to the front door, flinging it wide and dashing out into the storm. "Sydney!" she shouted, all but tackling the woman.

Her feet slipped on the wet grass as she grabbed the baby but she held her ground. Hands on her shoulders steadied her from behind.

baby?'' Agent Blancher de-

ized he was right behind her. ''Oh,
''It's Syd!'' Yanking the top of the blanket
she burst into tears at the sight of the precious
Sydney was grinning up at her, a dark ring of chocolate surrounding her sticky mouth.

''You're really here!'' Molly moaned, planting her lips
on Syd's wet red curls. Rain pelted them both, washing
away all the horrible fear of the past night and day. ''Oh,
baby.''

''Oh, bebe!'' Sydney parroted and squealed.

''Well, for heaven's sake, get the child inside before she
catches pneumonia!'' Mildred Jensen ordered. ''What kind
of mother are you?''

Molly didn't know whether to hug the woman or deck
her. It didn't matter. She had brought Sydney back.

Whirling around, Molly ran for the door. Suddenly it
seemed imperative that she examine every inch of Syd to
make sure she was well. Molly needed to see all of her,
right now. ''How 'bout a bath! Wanna splash, sugar? Play
with ducky?''

''Duckeeee!'' Sydney crowed, straining backward and
waving her arms. ''Ducky, Gammy?''

''Gammy?'' Molly turned and raised a brow at Mildred
as they reached the foyer. ''She calls you Gammy?'' Her
ex-mother-in-law stood there dripping, silent now, eyes
darting anxiously to her husband.

Agent Blancher entered behind them, a smear of mustard
on his mustache, his hand under his jacket. He shut the
door and looked uncertainly from one to the other. Molly
turned the whole business over to him while she knelt and
stood Syd on the floor, unwrapping her and checking her
out.

Barefoot and slightly damp beneath the blanket, Sydney

wore a child's souvenir T-shirt, the kind available almost anywhere tourists might stop, and a disposable diaper a size too small for her. Molly scooped her up, quickly stepped into the living room and wrapped her in the knitted afghan off the chair where Blancher had slept.

Cradling Syd, she moved back to the foyer. Blancher was replacing his badge folder in his pocket and asking John, "You want to tell me what's happening here, sir?"

John wiped a hand over his face and grimaced. "We received a call about an hour ago. I collected and dropped off the ransom money and they told us where to find her. We picked her up and came straight here."

Molly knew that for a lie. Syd hadn't learned that Mildred was her *Gammy* in that short a time. And John Jensen wouldn't part with a nickel to save a baby he'd never thought was Jack's in the first place. But at the moment, Molly simply didn't care. It was hard to think of anything but Sydney and the fact that her baby was right here in her arms where she was supposed to be.

"I'll call this in," Blancher said. "We'll hold the rest of the questions until everyone gets here." Through the long frosted panes on either side of the door, lights flashed as a car turned into the drive. The agent opened the door a crack and looked out. Car doors slammed. Molly heard voices. "Looks like Detective Winton and Agent Perry are back, ma'am," he said over his shoulder to her.

Damien. Well, she hadn't thought she could get any happier than she already was, but her heart rate had bumped up another notch.

Just then she happened to glance up at John and saw him fade to the color of biscuit dough. Oh, this was going to get good in a few minutes, Molly thought with a shiver of anticipation. Damien would get the truth out of him. That ransom tale of John's wouldn't hold any more water than Mildred's soggy rain cap.

She gave Syd another hearty hug and a juicy kiss on her round, damp, chocolate-smeared cheek.

"Ducky, Mama?" her precious asked with that beautiful toothy grin of hers. The little genius remembered about the bath.

"Ducky will have to wait awhile, sweetie pie! Uncle Dammit's home!"

Damien ignored the relentless rain as he crossed the yard and approached the steps to Molly's house. Getting soaked again was nothing compared to what the storm winds had nearly done to the chopper on the way back.

He only hoped he hadn't rushed back here only to find that Jensen had welshed. The extra car in the driveway gave him hope that hadn't happened.

Blancher opened the door to admit him and Winton, then stepped back out of the way without a word. And there she was. That lovely little ditto of Molly.

"Sydney," he said with a satisfied smile. "Welcome home."

Molly beamed at him as if he'd brought the child to her himself. Or maybe she was simply glad to see him, to share her joy at having Sydney back again.

He shrugged out of his coat and let it fall as he crossed the few feet of foyer that separated him from Molly and the baby. The mere sight of them provided a warmth that banished the chill of wet clothing, the storm outside, and the emptiness he had carried inside him for so long.

"Is she all right?" he asked gently, and watched Molly nod. Her face radiated a happiness that transcended words. "Then all is as it should be," he said, wondering if she remembered what he had promised her last night. Her blush told him she did.

He turned toward Jensen, then raised his wrist to look at

his watch. "Two minutes to spare," he noted with a lift of his brows.

"I—I need to speak to you," Jensen muttered. "Privately."

Damien waited a few beats, watching him sweat. "Very well. Molly, darling, you and Sydney should find dry clothes, shouldn't you? Blancher, see to some towels for Mrs. Jensen and Detective Winton. There's a stack in the laundry room off the kitchen, I believe." He stood there, perfectly composed, watching Jensen fidget as the others left the foyer.

When they had gone, he offered the man a cold smile. "Now, what can I do for you, sir?"

Jensen was steamed, but residual fear must have kept him civil. "What do *you* intend to do?" he asked curtly.

"Arrest you for kidnapping, of course," Damien replied. "You, your wife and your pitiful excuse for a son."

"Be reasonable and let it end here," Jensen said, glancing toward the kitchen. "Mildred and I were only trying to help out. Jack wanted his little girl. He thinks Molly's not capable—"

"Careful there," Damien warned pleasantly. "You don't want to incite my rage again today, now do you?" The edge of fury crept into his voice in spite of his resolve to contain it. "I know exactly why he took Sydney, and so do you."

Jensen's eyes grew hard. "I can buy protection from you, Perry. For myself and my son. I can also have your badge if you push this."

"Threatening a federal agent, Jensen? This gets better and better. Charges are stacking up." He took the cuffs out of his pocket and held them out. "You want to come quietly, or do I get to shoot you, after all?"

"Don't be ridiculous. You've got no proof! And you'll never find any. I paid the ransom, got the kid back and delivered her here. That's my story. Check the phone company. There'll be a record of the call by the kidnappers. The bank will verify an emergency withdrawal of fifty thousand cash from my personal account within the last hour. And all three of us have alibis for the night she was snatched.''

Damien calmly replaced the handcuffs in his pocket. ''Money can accomplish wonders in some instances. One thing you should realize, however.''

''And that is?'' Jensen said smoothly, certain he had won the round.

No father, good or bad, would want to hear what he had to say, but Damien hoped he would listen. ''You cannot buy safety for a man who is out of control. Think what your son has done, Jensen. He terrorized a woman and child. His own child!''

''That's debatable,'' Jensen muttered, but his words lacked conviction.

''You know it isn't. Even if that were the case, he still made you and his mother accessories to a crime. And he's not finished unless you do something about it. Jack is headed for destruction like a runaway train. If you're wise, have him committed and get him some help before it's too late.''

Jensen snorted and rolled his eyes. ''This advice, from the man who threatened to blow Jack's head off?''

Damien sighed and shrugged. ''Yes, well, I might yet have to do that if there's no other way to stop him.''

After a staring down that Damien won, Jensen sighed and rubbed his hand over his face. With his bluster gone, he looked tired and old. Sick at heart. ''I'll keep Jack out of town, away from them. He'll listen to me.''

''How can you be sure?'' Damien demanded. ''Has he ever listened before?''

Jensen nodded. ''Money's the key, unfortunately. Jack

has no other means of support. I'll make it a firm condition. He won't come back."

"If he ever does," Damien vowed, pinning Jensen with a glare, "it will be his final trip home. Or anywhere."

Jensen's expensive wingtips squished as he strode to the kitchen, grasped his wife by the arm and marched her back past Damien to the front door. Without another word or look, the couple left, slogging through the dark downpour to reach their car.

Winton had followed them as far as the entry. "Mrs. Jensen repeated that fairy tale about the ransom. The old man covered their butts, didn't he?"

"With solid-gold britches," Damien confirmed. "Right down to the phone call, withdrawal and the drop. He's quick, I will grant him that."

"Will you pursue it?" Winton asked.

Damien wondered if he should. The fact that he hesitated told him more about his own position than he wanted to know. He was sworn to uphold the law and the Jensens were clearly guilty, all three of them.

He also understood how the legal system worked. If he took them in, they would be free on bail within hours of the arrest. The trials—assuming there were arraignments in the first place—probably wouldn't be on the docket for at least a year. With no priors for John and Mildred, they would get probation. Jack might get a few years, but even that was iffy. Juries could be bought and John was in a mood to throw money around. Sydney was Jack's daughter. They might even be sympathetic.

He looked at Winton to gauge his reaction. "If we leave it alone, Jensen has promised to keep Jack at a distance. If we bring him back, he'll be released on bail and be *required* to stay here. Defeat the purpose, wouldn't it."

Winton made a face. "Be a bugger to get any proof when we know the old man's got all the bases covered." He shrugged and sighed. "Win some, lose some. That's the way it goes, but damn, I hate it."

Molly rejoined them, wearing a long fluffy robe. She had slicked her wet curls into an off-center mop on top of her head.

"You shine," Damien said without realizing he'd spoken out loud until he heard his own words.

She laughed full-out, head back and eyes closed. If he'd ever seen anyone look more appealing and delicious, he couldn't recall it.

Winton cleared his throat. "Guess I'll hit the road. Glad you got your little girl back, Ms. Jensen."

"Thank you," Molly said sincerely, still wearing a huge smile as she held out her hand.

Damien opened the door and shook Winton's hand as he left. "I owe you."

"Send me a case of beer," Winton suggested with a wink. "Take care of 'em," he added, inclining his head toward Molly.

Molly slipped into his arms the minute the door was closed. In a low voice, she droned, "Your mission, should you choose to accept it, is to relocate Agent Blancher. He's laid claim to my kitchen and I think he wants me to adopt him."

He laughed and kissed her forehead. It felt like satin and smelled of baby shampoo. Her body moved sinuously against his, suggesting a reward if he undertook the task she'd assigned.

"Give me two minutes and Blancher is history," he murmured. "Is Sydney asleep?"

"Down for the count," she answered, her face now sober, her body motionless in his arms. "It was all I could do to leave her in there by herself, but I know she's fine. This hasn't seemed to upset her at all. Mildred must have been good to her."

"Sydney is her granddaughter," Damien reminded her. "Regardless of what Jack told Mildred about that, I'm sure she knows the truth. That aside, it would be impossible for anyone not to love Sydney even if they were not related."

Molly wore a questioning look as though she wondered if he referred to his own feelings toward Sydney.

Damien took her arms from around his waist and lifted her hands to his lips. "I'll banish Blancher. You call your mother."

"Already called. She's coming by on her way home from Josie's."

"Staying the night here?" he asked.

She shook her head. "Just to see Syd for a minute."

"Great. After that, we'll see about dinner. You must be famished."

Her questioning look stayed with him. He'd said it was impossible not to love Sydney. He could have told her that he loved her baby. It would be true.

He also could have explained that his feelings for the child were a natural extension of the way he felt about the mother.

But now was not the time. Announcing that he loved them would imply a lifetime commitment to Molly. He wasn't quite ready to declare himself yet.

How did one suddenly become a family man after existing as a loner for thirty-five years? It might not be possible. Molly wouldn't understand. She had always had her mother and Ford, and now had her daughter.

He wanted Molly too desperately, too urgently, to judge why. Was it the kind of love that sustained a marriage over the years? Or was it the greatest sex he'd ever experienced combined with the opportunity to get on the other side of that window he'd had his nose pressed against all his life?

No doubt she would embrace him, too, and love him without reservation because Molly was like that. So were

Sydney, Brenda and probably Ford and his wife. Demonstrative, loving and affectionate, and perfectly natural with the interaction.

Could he accept all of that? And if he did so, could he learn how to reciprocate?

He would find out. But for tonight, he would put the question of long-term plans aside and simply hold her, content that he had been instrumental in restoring Molly's greatest treasure.

The satisfaction in that would be quite enough for one day.

Chapter 16

"My appetite's returned," Molly explained, reaching for another helping of the packaged lasagna she had put in the microwave for dinner. Her hunger extended way beyond what was on the table, she thought wryly. A pity Syd's nap had lasted only long enough for her to scrape together a meal from the freezer.

Damien shot her a smile and immediately went back to coaxing Sydney to use a spoon with her SpaghettiOs. Molly sighed. They looked so sweet together. Like father and daughter. She smiled. That is, *if* you disregarded their respective coloring and all their features.

If only Damien were not playing at this family thing temporarily. She imagined the novelty of it would wear off pretty quickly for him now that things had leveled out.

He had explained what John had promised to do if they let the charge of kidnapping slide. Molly agreed that was for the best.

Arresting the Jensens wouldn't help matters. Snobs that

they were, she could understand why they had done what they'd done. In a way, she appreciated that they were concerned enough about Sydney's welfare to do what they believed was best for her. Even if they were dead wrong, at least they cared.

Maybe she was being naive about that. Their concern might have been solely for Jack, but it wouldn't hurt to give them the benefit of the doubt.

They never had liked Molly, never thought her good enough for their son. However, John and Mildred were the ones who were naive, if they believed money mattered when it came to morals and good character.

Molly shrugged off her meandering thoughts and got back to the nitty-gritty. With Jack permanently out of town, Damien had no real reason to stay any longer. That was just as well. A swift, clean break would be better. She would keep things light and happy for his sake, even if it killed her.

"You're pretty good at that," she observed, just as Syd reached under the spoon for a handful of spaghetti and squished it on her tray. "Uh-oh."

Damien patiently wiped up the mess with a paper towel. "Have you considered limiting her diet to finger food?"

Molly chuckled. "Everything *is* finger food for Syd. She'll get the hang of utensils sooner or later. Don't worry."

"I'm not obsessing about this," he explained, and began feeding Syd with the spoon himself.

"No, no, didn't think you were," she assured him.

"She's to learn at her own pace," he said, sounding like a TV authority on child-rearing. "The handling of the spoon is merely to get her accustomed to the feel of it. You expose children to things that are a bit beyond their capabilities now and then. Challenge is good for them."

"My goodness, Dr. Spock! Where did you get all of this

information?'' Molly asked as she buttered a piece of bread.

Was he blushing? She leaned forward so she could see more of his face. He *was!* ''Hey, have you been reading baby books, Damien?''

''A magazine,'' he muttered.

She wiped her mouth with her napkin and held it there for a moment to hide a bittersweet smile. Damien reading *Parents?* How could she not love this man? Such a short time he'd been with her and already she could not imagine life without him. But she would have to get used to it, and soon.

''I'll be leaving tomorrow,'' he said, as if he had read her mind. ''My written reports on the Florida job are past due. I can't delay much longer.''

''I see,'' she said quietly. She got up and went around to wash Syd's hands and face with a cloth.

Damien stroked her arm and settled his fingers around it. ''Molly, it's not that I want to leave.''

But he would go, anyway, she knew. ''That's all right. We'll be fine,'' she said with a smile, letting him off the hook. It was the least she could do after all he'd done for them. ''I doubt Jack will trouble us anymore. John can be pretty forceful when he wants to, and he does control Jack's purse strings. You don't have to worry.''

''It's not that,'' he said, rubbing his forehead with two fingers. ''I'm not quite certain I can explain this.''

''Oh, I can!'' Molly said lightly, tugging Syd free of her high chair and perching her on one hip. She headed across the kitchen, hoping to cut off what might prove to be an awkward confrontation about their relationship. Well, what might have become a relationship, she amended.

''We're a pretty tame bunch when you get right down to it,'' she said offhandedly. ''Now that the trouble's over, you'd probably die of boredom if you stayed another week. No need to explain, Damien.''

''Wait a minute.'' He was getting up, coming after her. She didn't want him to because she wasn't sure how much longer she could keep up the act. ''Molly—''

''Scuse us, Uncle Dammit, we're off to bed! Say goodnight, Syd.''

To her relief, he let her go. Now if she could get Sydney back to sleep for the night, she would go straight to bed herself.

If Damien was as smart as she thought he was, he would leave her alone. She didn't know a man alive who would actually seek out a woman to elaborate on his reasons for dumping her. Especially when that woman made it perfectly obvious she'd figured it all out for herself.

Despite her suppositions, Damien was standing in the doorway of her bedroom when she came out of Sydney's. It had taken a good half hour to rock the little rascal back to sleep. But there he was, propped against the door frame, his arms folded and one foot crossed over the other. Waiting patiently.

She noticed his hair was still damp, but not from the rain. He had showered and changed, now wearing loose, pleated slacks and a half-buttoned tan suede shirt that looked soft to the touch. His leather deck shoes looked sexy with no socks.

His outfit might be pure *GQ*, but anybody with half a brain could see the man beneath was not model material, even if he did possess the body and the face for it.

Those intense blue eyes now regarding her with speculation gave away how dangerous Damien really was. Coiled for action inside that laid-back exterior. Or spoiling for a fight to end everything neatly?

She shook her finger at him. ''You don't really want to dissect what's between us, I can tell.''

"Take it apart? No, never that," he said evenly. "But I refuse to leave in the morning with you thinking that anything about you or the way you live has turned me off."

Molly grinned. "You're not completely turned off, I can tell that, too. That's why you waited where you're waiting, right? Once more, for old times' sake? That what you got in mind?"

She wasn't against the idea herself. If tonight was to be all she'd have of Damien, she would take it. Hadn't she sort of promised him this? "When things are as they should be," he'd said, and she had nodded. A few more memories of the man she loved were certainly better than nothing, even if it would make saying goodbye more painful.

Slowly he shook his head. "You seriously undervalue yourself, Molly. We need to work on that." He pushed away from the door frame and unfolded his arms. They reached for her. "Come here."

"I'll think about it, on one condition," she said, catching his hands before he could embrace her. He laced their fingers together and his were gentle. Not grasping urgently as she would have expected if he were all that hot to have her. She didn't care much for his deliberate restraint, since she could plainly see it was forced.

Molly raised her gaze to his again and held it. "No more talk. That's my one requirement. Just be with me tonight and be gone when I wake up in the morning. No goodbyes, no awkward excuses, no false promises. Okay?"

"No," he whispered. "It's not okay. I have to leave you tomorrow, that much is true. But I will be back as soon as possible. That is a definite promise and one I will keep. As for the excuses you don't want, you've already heard my reasons. I do have work left unfinished."

Molly quirked a brow and gave his hands a squeeze. "You said you weren't sure you could explain about something. Was that job-related? I don't think so."

She shook her head and looked away, unable to endure the intensity any longer. "No, I don't want the explanation. Don't make it. Let tomorrow take care of itself, Damien. It will, you know?"

Damien disentangled their fingers and wrapped his arms around her. "Yes, I know."

His mouth claimed hers in a kiss so tender she could barely contain the tears. She was losing him. Oh, God, how in the world would she bear it? Without meaning to, she deepened the kiss herself, wishing she could take him into her and hold him there forever.

Without pausing, Damien backed them into her bedroom and closed the door behind her. She leaned against it, reveling in the press of his body against hers, as hard and unrelenting as the panel at her back. Molly arched into him, twining her arms around his neck. She raked her fingers through the damp silkiness of his hair while he raised her to her toes so their bodies fit perfectly.

He moved his mouth from hers and grazed her cheek. "Molly," he whispered.

"Hush," she hissed, trying to capture his lips. He evaded, his lips everywhere but on hers. His mouth was hot, seeking, as it blazed down her neck. One hand cradled the back of her head while his other splayed across her lower back, pressing her into the hardness she craved.

His arms shifted. Dizzy with need, she felt him lift her and turn to take the few steps to the bed. When they reached it, Damien came down beside her and raked open the robe she wore. She shimmied out of her panties while he shrugged off his shirt. His shoes thudded on the carpet. Eagerly she tugged the waistband of his pants. His hand covered hers.

"Pocket," he gasped, hurriedly fishing for a foil packet himself.

Molly abandoned herself to the sheer carnality of another

kiss, her fingers plowing through the springy dark curls on his chest while he made ready.

Too soon, not soon enough, he rolled toward her, covered her and slowly, very deliberately sank to the hilt. Her entire body shuddered in profound welcome.

"Don't move," he whispered. "Don't." His hands clasped her behind, holding her immobile while he pulsed rhythmically inside her without thrusting. She came. So violently, he had to follow.

With a wild burst of motion, he took. And gave more than she could ever have asked, bringing her to the edge and over again before he reached it himself. With a deep-throated groan of pure satisfaction, he lay still, holding her.

How he could grip so tightly when her own muscles had turned to butter amazed her. Everything about Damien amazed her. A crooked smile stole over her lips while her eyes closed in total exhaustion.

"Now *there* is a memory," she growled to herself. One to live on forever, she thought sadly even as she slid into sleep.

He was right there when she awoke, despite last night's request that he leave early. Molly was unaccountably glad he had not honored that one. She only wished she hadn't wasted the rest of their time together catching up on the sleep she'd lost while worrying about Syd.

Briefly she entertained the idea of suggesting he stay one more night, but just as quickly discarded the notion. He had done enough, given about all a woman could reasonably ask of a man like him.

Damien was definitely not the type to treasure picket fences, or fences of any other kind, for that matter. If that was what he wanted, he could surely have had it by now. So, she would tack on a grin that looked happy and send him on his way. No point clinging and saddling him with guilt he didn't deserve.

Besides, she wanted Damien to remember their time together as something positive in his life. No tears, she cautioned herself. Not a single one, or he will have regrets.

She wiped her cheeks of the offenders while she watched him sleep. The morning dawned gray, sifting in through the curtains like a cloud of smoke, but she could see his classic features clearly enough, memorize each one separately and in their wonderful entirety.

"I love you, Molly," he whispered, unmoving.

Caught by surprise, she gave a half laugh. "I thought you were asleep!"

He reached out to her, but she backed away and quickly sat up on the edge of the bed, holding the covers to her chest. "How about some coffee? I can make breakfast before you leave. French toast okay?"

Without waiting for his answer, she leaned down and grabbed up the robe that lay puddled on the floor. She sensed him watching her as she shrugged into it, but didn't dare turn around to meet his eyes. Instead, she hopped up and left the room before she did something really stupid such as beg him not to go.

Maybe she should have told him how sweet it was of him to say he loved her, but she couldn't bring herself to do it. He might even mean what he'd said right this minute, but what did that matter when he'd be gone in less than an hour? Well, he wouldn't leave worried that he had left her here with a hole in her heart. She'd see to that.

She peeked in on Sydney, saw she was still asleep, and padded on to the kitchen.

Willing her hands to stop shaking, she put on the coffee and rummaged in the refrigerator. Ten minutes later, she had bacon and French toast ready.

Damien joined her just as she plunked the bottle of syrup

on the table. His frown of concern bothered her. What had she done to cause that? Hadn't she been a good sport?

"Hi! Hungry?" she asked brightly, straightening the silverware just to have something to do.

He shook his head. "No. You go ahead. I just called Winton. He's on duty this morning, so I'm headed down to the precinct to meet with him."

"Why? I thought everything was settled."

"Before I go, I want to make sure you have adequate protection. Winton has a list of guys who moonlight as bodyguards occasionally, and I'm going to check their qualifications. I'll drop by later to pick up my things and say goodbye."

"Take them with you," Molly ordered curtly, dumping two spoons of sugar into her coffee that she always drank straight. Some granules spilled onto the table. Angrily, she brushed them off. Her hand trembled and she clenched it into a fist. "Don't come back. Please."

Silently he watched her, his eyes piercing as always, probing for words she wouldn't give and was certain he wouldn't want to hear if she said them.

"And you can forget the watchdog," she added. "I can't afford it, even if I needed one. Which I don't."

Belatedly remembering her promise to herself, she stretched her lips into a determined smile. "Now get out of here, will you? I'll tell Ford you said hi when he gets back."

She swallowed hard, holding her expression as steady as she could. "And thanks, Damien. Thank you for everything."

Without another word, he turned and left. He must have gone back down the hall and gathered his things because several minutes passed before she heard the front door click shut.

A car's engine revved. He was gone. Molly laid her head

on her arms, heedless of the sticky residue left by the sugar, and cried.

Jack needed a gun. Too bad Shorty was gone now or he might have sold him one of those little Saturday Night Specials. He could just imagine that bullet bouncing around inside Molly's thick skull. That'd fix her.

Tears burned the backs of his eyes. If she were dead, would he be able to forget her then? He shook his head. Why couldn't she really, really love him the way she was supposed to?

A tramp, he thought. Just like all the rest. Every single one he'd ever known, including his mother. She'd never loved him either. Oh, she'd pretended until he got old enough to say what was what and have his own way. Then she acted the same toward him as she did to his father. As though they were scum, as if they were nothing. Scaring her was the only way his dad could keep her in line. Jack had tried that. Hadn't worked with Molly, though. He figured it was her upbringing. Wasn't raised to respect men or herself.

That was the way with women. They all wanted control of a man. Not one of them would do like they should on their own. And if they were like Molly, you couldn't even beat them into behaving. If it didn't work this time…

He glared at the house, his eyes settling on the black Explorer in the driveway. A bomb would be good if he knew how to make one. Wouldn't be hard to find out, he thought. Later, he would take time to learn. Agent Damien Perry was going to regret messing around with Jack Jensen's woman.

And the woman herself was going to learn who called the shots. One more chance was all he was giving her. Just one.

Jack almost jumped out of his skin when the front door

opened and he saw Perry come out with a travel bag. He hadn't expected that. "Well, well," he crooned. "Tired of her already, huh?" Probably Molly's stubbornness, not to mention her alley-cat ways that soon sent them all packing. They couldn't handle her, either.

Jack watched the car until it disappeared around the corner at the end of the block. Longer, he waited, while he psyched himself up for what was necessary. Twice, he sniffed deeply and sighed, feeling more powerful than he ever had.

He'd played around long enough now. It was time to make her pay. Make her mind. Hell, he didn't need a gun to whip her into shape. Or to kill her if that's what he decided to do. It might be the best thing, after all.

Chapter 17

She had to get herself back together before Sydney woke up, Molly decided after a good ten minutes of self-indulgent mourning. But Damien was a man worth shedding a few tears over, wasn't he? Still, there was no use wasting her energy and making herself sick over this.

She pushed up from the table and went to the sink to wash her face.

The door chimes halted her in her tracks. *He'd come back!* She just knew it. Who else could it be this early? It was hardly daybreak!

Molly flew across the kitchen and down the hallway to the front door and peeped through one of the long panes beside it. Through the frosted glass, she saw the tall outline. It was *him!* She flung open the door.

Hands shoved her backward and she lost her balance and breath in the same instant. Her hips hit the floor and her shoulder struck the leg of the foyer table. Stunned, she braced herself on one elbow and looked up, horrified. "Jack!"

With a grunt he kicked, his shoe catching her in the thigh as she curled away from it. "Bitch!" he growled, pulling back his leg again. "I'll fix you good this time."

Molly rolled, avoiding the worst of the blow. She scrambled quickly to her knees and bounced upright. "You stay away from me!" she warned, hands out, balanced on the balls of her feet. He stood between her and the open door. There was nowhere to run without leaving Syd defenseless.

He lunged. She dodged toward the table and grabbed the heavy crystal bud vase that had tipped over. Damien's words rang in her head. *Feint...strike.*

She threw up her left hand, palm open toward his face. When he jerked his head back to avoid it, she swung the vase with her right, connecting with his jaw. Jack staggered and she thought he'd go down. Not waiting for that, she crashed her right foot into his knee. He howled as it buckled.

Molly bolted for the living room, jerked open the drawer to the curio cabinet and found the pistol. Jack staggered after her, almost on her before she could turn around.

"I'll shoot!" she cried, holding the gun with both hands, pointing it directly at his head. Damien's instructions leaped to mind. *Larger target than a head.* She lowered the barrel, aiming for Jack's midsection.

Could she shoot him? Jack had halted, arms outflung, balancing on his uninjured leg.

Hysterically, Molly thought he looked like the little guy in *The Karate Kid,* balanced on that pole. Only not serene. He looked wild. His eyes flared and his mouth fell slack.

"Stay!" she commanded, her voice surprisingly strong while the rest of her quivered like Jell-O.

I have the weapon. He's not even armed. All I have to do is keep him here until I can get help. She lowered one hand from the gun, moved sideways toward the phone and grabbed up the receiver. No dial tone. Angrily, she tossed it aside. Jack must have cut the line outside.

Now where would she get that help? She remembered the security alarm. She hadn't activated it after Damien left. He wouldn't have done it on his way out, would he? Maybe. He was nearly fanatic about keeping the thing set.

It rang a silent alarm at the police station if the code wasn't entered three minutes after the door opened. She would wait fifteen minutes. If the cops hadn't come to check on her by that time, she would think of an alternative.

If all else failed, she could scream bloody murder and maybe the neighbors would come running. Unless they had gone to work. Her mind scrambled for a solution. She'd just have to stand here threatening to shoot him until somebody decided to show up.

Slowly Jack lowered his arms and leg and slumped. His shoulders began to shake and he covered his face with his hands. "I'm sorry," he moaned. "Oh, Molly, I am so sorry. I never meant…" His words trailed off in a fit of piteous sobs.

Molly stared at him in shock. Jack crying? Begging forgiveness? She must be hallucinating. Unthinking, she lowered the weapon slightly.

He struck. Without warning, his long arm shot out, batted her hand to one side and snatched the pistol from her. Before she could react, he had put several feet between them and Molly was staring down the chrome sights of her own gun.

Her heart skipped, felt like it stopped. What would happen to Syd? Would he hurt her, too? Maybe if she got Jack to talk, she could keep him busy in here until the police arrived. *If they arrived.*

"*Why,* Jack? Would you please tell me why?" she said as calmly as she could manage.

He laughed, sounding more than a little mad. The pistol waved unsteadily, but she was too far away to grab for it.

"You know why, Moll. Treatin' me like dirt. Never doin' what I told you. Screwin' around on me!" He sneered. "Thought you could palm off that kid as mine, didn't ya? And then sending me up for it when I reacted like any normal husband would. Low, lady," he snarled. "Very low."

"Oh, Jack," Molly said. "You were rid of me! The divorce was final when you got out. All you had to do was leave me alone, pretend I didn't exist, find somebody else. It was over!"

"Don't you get it yet, you sorry tramp? I never *wanted* anybody else! But you just weren't good enough, and I couldn't *make* you be what—"

He shook his head as if to clear it, then scanned the room as if he expected ghosts. "They all had you, didn't they? Every damn one of them. They came here. I know they did!"

"Who, Jack?" Molly asked, working to keep her voice low, soothing. "Who told you those *lies?*"

The question worked. Made him stop to think. His gaze wandered again and he seemed unaware of her for a second.

Molly quickly sidestepped toward the hallway, dashed down it and out the front door. Her bare feet hardly touched the steps, then hit the ground running just as she heard him shout.

Thank God, he'd chased her. She could lead him away from Sydney and scream for help at the same time. He might still shoot her, but at least it wouldn't be in the house with Syd. Surely he'd forget the baby or be caught before he could go back. She sucked in a breath without slowing down and yelled "Fire! Fire! Help!"

No one came outside. Cars were gone. People at work. She could feel him hot on her heels, heard his curses over her own frightened gasps. Zigzagging, expecting a hand to snatch her to a halt or a bullet to rip into her, Molly ran for all she was worth.

He grabbed her hair and swung her. Molly fell backward and landed in a heap, cornered between the tall hedge of the neighbor's ligustrum and the chain-link fence bordering her own backyard. She pushed up off the ground, struggling to get her breath back.

"Don't you scream," Jack warned. "You just hold it right there!" The harsh invective he spouted grew louder with each word, so venomous, she stopped listening. He gestured wildly, waving the gun around as though he'd forgotten he held it.

Molly clenched her eyes shut, terrified it would discharge. A screech of brakes alerted her and she looked past Jack to the street. Damien's Explorer! He jumped out, weapon in hand. Her knees turned to water and she exhaled with sharp relief.

"Lower the gun, Jensen," Damien ordered. He stood a good six feet behind Jack. "Gently to the ground and kick it away from you."

Instead Jack braced it, aimed directly at Molly's heart. He smiled evilly and his voice quavered as he answered Damien's command. "I can get off a shot! Even if you shoot first. You can't have her!"

"All right, Jack. Take it easy," Damien replied, his tone firm but reasoning. "Now lower the weapon. You don't want to go down for murder, do you, Jack? Don't you think you've hurt your family enough? Your mom? Your dad? And what about Molly? You love Molly, Jack."

"No!" he cried, his hands restless on the pistol grip, finger trembling on the trigger. Molly watched tears break free and trail down Jack's face.

He sniffled once and then spoke, but his words weren't for Damien. "This is…your fault, Moll," he said brokenly.

"All *your* fault! You remember that, long as you live!" Swiftly, he raised the gun to his head and narrowed his eyes. "You did this!"

"Jack, *no!*" she screamed as he pulled the trigger. The sound blocked out everything, her hearing, her sight and her reason. A harsh, silent wail vibrated inside her just before she shut down.

Damien hurriedly removed Molly's pistol from Jack's hand and automatically checked him for a pulse. Not that he expected to find one with a portion of the head gone, but it was standard procedure.

Then he moved quickly to Molly, almost thankful she had fainted. The dark gray of the cloudy morning hid little of the ugliness of Jensen's death. Forgetting all she'd already endured would be impossible. She didn't need to see any more of this than she already had. He gave her a swift check as she lay on the grass. She didn't appear to be hurt, not physically, anyway.

Damien lifted her, carried her into the house and put her on the sofa in the living room.

The phone's receiver lay off the hook. He picked it up and found the line dead. He'd have to go back to the car to get his cell phone. A black-and-white turned in just as he opened the front door.

He walked out to meet the officers as they exited the squad car.

"Ms. Jensen's alarm sounded. Is she all right?" the younger one demanded.

Damien recognized Sharps, the one who had answered Molly's complaint about the poison. "Suicide," he told the officer, inclining his head toward the corpse in the corner of the yard. "It's Jack Jensen."

"Is Ms. Jensen hurt, sir? Will we need two ambulances?"

"I'll take her in if she needs to go," Damien said.

Sharps nodded and pulled the radio off his belt to make the call while the other cop approached the body. Damien left them to it and went back inside.

Molly had come to and was sitting now, leaning over with her face buried in her palms. He joined her on the sofa and pulled her into his arms. "The police are here," he said. "I'd like to take you the emergency room, have them check you out. Are you hurt?"

"No, I'm okay," she murmured against his chest. "You did come back," she added in an even quieter voice, her hands gripping his arms. "I thought he was you when I opened the door."

"It's all right," he assured her. "Everything will be all right now. Why don't you lie down and I'll get you a—"

"I need to see about Syd," she said, pushing away from him and getting up. "I just need to see her."

"You're still shaky." Damien lifted her again, moved swiftly down the hall and stopped at Sydney's room. There he lowered Molly to her feet while he opened the door.

"Ah, look at that," he whispered, smiling down at Molly's chalk-white face with its wide green eyes, hoping to divert her attention from what she'd just experienced. "She's still asleep."

Molly moved with less than her usual grace as she crossed the room. Damien hovered just behind her to catch her if she fell. Her fingers reached out, brushed a wispy curl off the baby's forehead and then retreated.

The word *fragile* came to mind when he looked at her now, though he would never have used it before to describe Molly. How young and vulnerable she seemed in that white terry robe, bare toes peeking out beneath the hem, her hair a soft, wild tangle that begged to be touched.

The truth hit him like a brick. The same brick that had left a dent when it struck him earlier on his way downtown to see Winton. He could never love anyone the way he loved her. Nothing else mattered.

She turned to him as if something had just occurred to her. "Why did you come back, Damien?" she asked, trembling. Frowning.

He cradled her face in his hands, that infinitely precious face with its sprinkle of freckles and generous mouth. "I was nearly halfway to the main precinct when I asked myself why I was leaving Nashville today. It seemed a foolish thing to do when I have unfinished business right here. With you," he added softly.

"Your job," she reminded him. "Those reports?"

"I can fax them to Duvek." He trailed his thumb over her bottom lip. "Would you mind if I stayed for a while?"

Her sigh was heavy and her face looked pained. A tear trailed slowly down one cheek. "Yes. I *would* mind, Damien. I would mind very much."

Clear enough and painful to hear, but Damien could hardly blame her. Molly had just witnessed the self-destruction of a man she'd once thought she loved, the father of her child. Small wonder she wasn't up to discussing a future with someone else right now.

Regardless of what she'd just said, Damien wouldn't leave her, but she didn't need or want a lover right now. Damien understood. What she needed was a friend.

"Let's get you out of here," he suggested. "Why don't you get dressed? You'll have to anyway since the police are waiting for us with all the questions. It shouldn't take long. Then I'll take you and Sydney to your mother's."

Her gaze wandered again to the baby who still slept on. "All right," she said quietly as she looked up at him with a puzzled frown. "I guess I should cry, but I can't. Jack *was* Sydney's daddy."

Damien scoffed. "You know he was never a father to Sydney. And why on earth should you shed any tears over a man who kidnapped your daughter and terrorized you the way he did?''

She shrugged, still watching the baby sleep. ''Maybe I should have tried to get help for him before he got so sick.''

Damien had to force himself not to grab her, hold her and try to banish the guilt he saw in her eyes. Instead, he used the most reasonable tone he could manage. ''You couldn't have helped him, Molly. There was nothing you could have done for Jack. You cannot feel responsible for what he did out there this morning. You *can't.*''

''You're right. I know,'' she agreed a bit too quickly. ''I ought to call Mildred and John,'' she said, sounding numb. ''I hate for them to hear it from the police.''

''I'll take care of that,'' he said, knowing the cops had probably notified John Jensen already. Even if they hadn't, Damien didn't think Jack's parents would want to hear the news from either Molly or himself. She must be in shock to imagine her telling them would make it any easier. If anything, they would resent her even more.

He turned her from the crib and gently ushered her out of Sydney's room and across the hallway to her own. When she simply stood there in the middle of the carpet, he went to her closet and selected a pair of brown slacks and a sweater for her.

Damien laid the clothing on the bed and went back to find shoes to match. He set them on the floor. ''Get dressed, Molly,'' he said firmly. ''We have questions to answer. The police need to do the report.''

She jumped a little, as if she'd been lost in thought. ''Fine. I'll be there in a minute.''

''Will you be all right by yourself?'' he asked, worried about her pallor. ''Do you feel faint again?''

''No, I'm okay,'' she said, shaking her head. ''Go ahead.''

Reluctantly he left her, glancing back again when he

reached the door. She was moving toward the bed, so he trusted she would be able to function.

A half hour later Molly forced herself to leave the bedroom. She looked in again on Syd. After a deep breath to call up her courage, she walked toward the living room. Damien was waiting for her there, just outside the doorway. He took her arm.

Detective Winton had arrived. "Sit down, please," he said gently. "This won't take long. Just tell me what took place this morning."

Repeating all that had happened seemed to lessen the impact of it, reduced it somehow to terms she could face and accept. That didn't seem right to her, but there was nothing she could do about it. Just as there had been nothing to do to save Jack from himself.

"Did you know about his habit?" Winton was asking.

"What?" Molly demanded, her senses snapping to full alert. "What habit?"

Damien, who was standing behind her chair, placed his hands on her shoulders. Grounded her. "Cocaine, Molly."

"Your ex-husband had a pretty good supply on him today," the detective told her. "Must have made a buy this morning. It appears he was a fairly heavy user. I thought you might want to know that."

"Oh." Molly breathed the word. "Would that have caused him to…do all that he did?"

Winton sighed and nodded. "Could and probably did. It sometimes causes paranoia, depression, even violence. Cocaine can also cause people to think they can accomplish just about anything, no matter how ambitious the undertaking. Makes them feel smarter, believe they're able to think circles around everybody else. Can't seem to be rational about any long-term consequences, however." He slapped his little notebook in his palm and got up. "Anyway, I thought you should know."

Molly hung her head, shaking it sadly. The drug had almost surely exaggerated Jack's problem. He had been jealous when they were dating, but not to that extreme. Just enough to flatter her. After hearing about the coke, she could almost pinpoint the month during their marriage in which his personality had begun to change. At least she could stop beating herself up for not realizing what he was before they married. And could also admit that she had loved the man he had been at first.

"Thank you for telling me."

She reached to her shoulders and placed her hands on top of Damien's, thankful he was still here. Wishing he would stay with her. Knowing he would if she asked him to. But she didn't want that. He had his own life to live and she had to get on with hers.

"You are finished, aren't you?" Damien asked. "I'd like to get Molly away from here. We'll be at Brenda Devereaux's if you need anything else for the report."

"That ought to do it until the inquest," Winton said, getting up to follow them out. "You stick around town for that, Perry. Don't want to have to come looking for you."

"I'm not going anywhere," Damien declared. As he said that, his firm grip on Molly's arm felt like a promise meant for her. He couldn't very well leave when the detective had told him to stay for the inquest, but Molly knew the longer he remained with her, the more difficult it would be to say goodbye when the time came.

It would come, she had no doubt of that. Damien hesitated to leave her because he was Ford's friend. Even though Jack was no longer a danger, Damien must think she still needed someone to look after her until her brother returned. Given how she'd been acting since the shooting, she could hardly blame him for thinking that, but she didn't want him to feel responsible for her.

Molly wanted Damien around only if he loved her *and* thought they had a good chance at making a life together. Only she knew Damien didn't do long-term commitments. And she couldn't settle for anything less. She would have to make him leave. Or at least leave her alone.

The funeral had been a large affair, attended by many of Jack's high school classmates and their families, people who had known the Jensens all their lives.

The fact that Jack had served time, definitely done drugs, wrecked his life and then destroyed it, did nothing to discourage attendance at the service.

Damien had remained in the back of the sanctuary and on the fringe of the crowd at the cemetery, present only because he thought Molly might show up and need his support. He'd thought her guilt might compel her to do so, but obviously it had not.

Immediately after he had taken her and Sydney to Brenda's condo, Molly had asked him to leave her there and not to call or come by. Oh, she'd been polite about it. Need for solitude was the reason she gave, but he knew the real reason. Molly was in love with him and didn't want to be. It was right there in her eyes, totally exposed because her emotions had been stripped raw by the horror of that day.

The ridiculous thing was, she had to know he loved her, too. True, he'd only told her the once, but she knew. He figured she didn't think that was enough to hold them together. Damien had also decided she was in no frame of mind to make any decisions at the time, so he'd given her the space she asked for.

The inquest this morning was short and succinct, only held to satisfy the requirement by law for a death not of natural causes. When it was over, Damien was one of the first to leave.

Now he waited beside his car, which he had parked next to Molly's van. She had come alone today, and after a stiff little smile of greeting in the coroner's office, had pointedly ignored him.

He supposed Brenda was keeping Sydney today. A good thing, since he needed to speak with Molly alone.

There she came, that confident long-legged stride of hers grabbing the notice of every male in sight. A tailored yellow blazer molded her figure to perfection. A panel of creamy lace concealed any cleavage. Her slim skirt ended just above her knees, revealing only a modest portion of those long, marvelous legs.

He supposed the upswept hair was meant to make her appear business-like. It was provocative as hell. Several bronze wisps had escaped since she'd pinned it up, making him want to free the other curls that hadn't slipped out of captivity.

If she dressed to attract attention, she seemed totally unaware of it once she received it. But even for men who didn't know her at all, it would be impossible to ignore her. Molly was sensuous innocence personified.

Poor ol' Jack—already saddled with a jealous nature and having it compounded by a mind-altering substance—must have gone through hell a thousand times over. No excuse for his reprehensible actions toward Molly, however.

Damien had to admit to a sharp little sting of rivalry himself when heads turned to watch her walk by. That was an altogether new and unexpected emotion for him, one he would definitely keep concealed. His pride in her ought to cover it well enough.

He trained his hungry gaze on her eyes as she came closer, and saw the exact instant when she noticed him propped against his car. Her stride shortened almost imperceptibly.

"Hello again," he said when she approached.

Her left hand gripped the thin shoulder strap of her purse. Her knuckles turned white. "I thought we'd agreed—"

"To give you your solitude. You've had ten days," he said, unfolding his arms and putting his hands on his hips. He inclined his head and studied her for a minute. "Are you angry about something?"

"No, of course not," she replied with a stiff little smile. She busily fished the keys out of her purse and inserted them into the door of the van.

"Molly, talk with me," he told her. "I'm not going away." His letter of resignation was already in the works and he was reviewing to stand the Tennessee bar. What would she say to that? he wondered.

She turned, sighed, and gave him a considering look. "I hope you won't make this difficult, Damien. I do thank you for all you've done for us, but—"

"But I'm not finished," he said pleasantly. "Could I take you to lunch?"

"No. Thank you," she said, an edge to her voice. "I'm not hungry."

Yes, she was, he thought. He could see her color rising, turning her alabaster cheeks the loveliest shade of rose. Good, he thought, she had her spirit back. Desire was there, too, banked, but definitely present in spite of her denial of it.

"I'm on my way to the house," she told him rather curtly. "It's going on the market in a couple of weeks and I need to sort through some things before the movers come."

He shrugged, turned and unlocked his car. Without another word, he got in and fastened his seat belt. He watched her do the same.

She didn't even glance at him before she cranked the van, backed out of her parking space and drove off into the heavy noon traffic.

Damien pulled out right behind her and followed, whistling along to his favorite passage from the *William Tell* overture. On the last resounding note of the finale, he popped out the CD and switched to the radio. The tickling fiddles of blue grass replaced Rossini.

Molly didn't know it yet but he was home to stay.

Chapter 18

Molly wheeled into the driveway and carefully avoided glancing at the corner of the yard where Jack had died. She'd known it would give her the willies to come back over here. Mama had volunteered to do it for her, but Molly had to face it herself.

Damien would be here in a minute. She glanced in her mirror and saw him pull in behind her even as she thought about it. As much as she knew she should avoid him, she couldn't help being glad he'd decided to be stubborn. Without turning around, she watched him get out of his car and amble toward hers.

He looked different today than he ever had. Though she'd tried to ignore him at the inquest and afterward when he waited for her, he'd made it impossible. He had on worn jeans, his soft leather jacket and new boots.

She bit back a grin. Damien in cowboy boots, something she would never have thought to see. Knowing his tastes, she'd bet they were special order and made of ostrich skin or something just as expensive.

Molly knew exactly what he was doing. But boots or no boots, Damien had no idea what he was trying to let himself in for here. And if he wasn't careful, she was going to take him up on it.

For ten days now she had lectured herself on how imprudent it would be to continue what they'd started. She'd been firm, too.

He would get tired of her. He would have to leave soon anyway. Men like Damien didn't fall in love with women like her. Women like her only idolized men like him. It wasn't so much his worldliness. Not entirely their conflicting tastes. Or that he seemed to have been born a loner. It was all of those things and much more. They were just too wildly different, she told herself.

But no matter how hard she tried, Molly couldn't deny the fact that she loved him, everything about him, totally and without reservation. And she suspected that he did love her in his own way. At any rate, he still wanted her.

When the affair played out, however, she knew she wouldn't be the only one hurt by it. Sydney would surely grow to love him. Already she remembered *Dammit* and had asked for him several times. The eventual breakup would affect his friendship with Ford, too. And her mother would be devastated. She thought the world of Damien.

For their sakes, as well as hers and Damien's, Molly knew she had to convince him to forget about it.

"Hey, Molly" he said, leaning his palms against the door of her van, "you don't want to do this by yourself. Come on, I'll help you." He opened her door and offered his hand.

She took it and got out. "Why?" she asked. "Why are you doing this?"

"I want to be with you," he said. "Simple as that."

Not so simple, Molly thought. Not simple at all, and dangerous to explore. So she changed the subject. "You sound strangely like Detective Winton. Been hanging out down at the main precinct?''

"Some," he admitted. "Ol' Win and I went fishing a couple of times. Bass.'' He kept hold of her hand while they walked toward the front steps, releasing it only when she tugged it away to unlock the door. "Mostly I've been looking around for a place to live," he said.

Molly tamped down her excitement, warning herself again why this wouldn't work. "Really? Where are you staying now?''

"Motel," he replied, punching in the code to turn off her alarm system. "But I think I've found a house.''

"What?" she asked turning all the way around, staring at him as if he'd lost his mind. "Why in the world would you want a house? You're not going to live here!" She hesitated a second. "Are you?''

He motioned toward the den. "Let's go sit down and talk about that, okay? Once we get everything worked out, I'll help you go through your things. Then we can pick up some lunch and I can show you what I found. See what you think about it.''

Hope reared up and she kicked it down. Thinking about a house was a temporary madness on his part. A whim that would surely pass when he stopped and really thought about it.

She halted in the middle of the room and looked up at him, shaking her head. "You don't sound like yourself today. You don't even look like yourself. Is this supposed to impress me? Prove how...adaptable you are, or something?''

He nodded. "Are you convinced yet?''

Molly laughed. This made absolutely no sense. "So you can fit in anywhere, huh?''

"Oh, absolutely," he admitted, drawling as if he were native to Nashville. "It's a gift I use all the time. You want a French businessman? Maybe an Irish poet or a German stockbroker? You name it.'' He grinned. ''Sorry, I can't be a jockey from the Bronx. Even I have limits.'' He raked the backs of his fingers over his denim-clad thigh. ''You like my duds?''

Smiling at his foolishness, she wandered over to the sofa and sat. With a shake of her head, she looked over at him and sighed. ''Oh, Damien, what am I going to do with you? Regardless of what you might have heard, clothes do *not* make the man. Neither do speech patterns.''

He inclined his head with a knowing look. ''My point, exactly. Is it the man inside that you object to?''

Molly thought about it. ''In a way, yes.''

''Explain,'' he demanded, defensive now, clearly not understanding. ''Tell me what it is that you don't like.''

She couldn't be anything but honest with him. ''Come here,'' she said, patting the sofa beside her and waiting until he sat. She took his strong hands in hers. ''Here's what bothers me, Damien,'' she said, wishing he wouldn't caress the backs of her fingers with his thumbs the way he was doing. She cleared her throat and blinked. ''And we've discussed this before. Remember, nothing in common?''

''Love of children. Fondness for coffee. Marvelous sex,'' he reminded her with a wicked leer.

She rolled her eyes. ''Yeah, well, that's not quite enough. What about—''

''Views on marriage,'' he said succinctly, suddenly very serious. ''I firmly believe in it, you're not sure you do. A problem, but not insurmountable.''

Her mouth dropped open and she stared at him. ''I have nothing against marriage, Damien, but you—''

''Want to rush things,'' he said, interrupting. ''My impatience gets the best of me now and then. I'll try to go slowly, but you have to understand—''

"You don't want to get *married!*" she accused. "Not to *me!*"

"If not to you, then you're correct. I would never want to. At the moment, I'd like you to think about an engagement. Take all the time you want."

A laugh escaped her. "Think what you're asking! You show up decked out like a good ol' boy. And sounding like one. You admit you change like a chameleon. Is the Damien I think I know real, or another disguise? How am I supposed to figure out who you really are? Do you even know yourself?"

Those piercing blue eyes caught her gaze and held it fast. "I'm nobody unless I'm with you," he said in a gravelly voice that was sincerity itself. "Until I met you I had no idea what was missing in my life or even that anything was. You make me want a life that's not a succession of shadowy characters. You make me real."

"Oh, Damien," she said, barely breathing the words, unable to look away. She could see need and all the love anybody could ever want. She saw straight through to his soul and knew it was only because he let her. He trusted her that much. If she refused him, he would close up again and go back to that lonely life he hated. "All right," she whispered, almost unaware that she had spoken. "Yes."

He let go one of her hands, reached into his pocket and slid off the sofa to one knee. "Will you wear this until you can deal with making it permanent?"

Molly glanced down at what he held. "My God, Damien!" she exclaimed at the huge emerald cut diamond he held out. "It's so *big!*"

"You don't like it?" He pitched it over his shoulder. It clinked off the front of the television onto the carpet and bounced. "We'll find one that's right."

Molly stared, unable to take her eyes off of it. The stone caught the sunlight from the window and glittered with promise. Damien had chosen that ring especially for her. And that business with the jeans, boots and the accent had convinced her. Outer trappings didn't matter at all. Neither did their differences.

Then Molly looked at him. "I like it just fine," she whispered, raising a hand to his face, loving the feel of him. She brushed a thumb over his lips. "I love big." She sighed. "I love you."

"You'll marry me, then?" he asked, as if he wanted things perfectly clear. "Someday, whenever you're ready?"

"Saturday," she said with a nod.

He laughed and grabbed her, dragging her right off the sofa into his arms. Then he kissed her so thoroughly she could taste the desperate relief. Half of it was hers, she was sure.

His hands tangled in her hair, loosening the pins until it fell around his fingers. "I do love you," he whispered when he finally let her up for air, "so much more than you know."

Molly brushed his lips with hers and traced the lower one with her tongue. "Then you'd better show me," she suggested.

"Here on the floor?" he asked with a devilish smile.

She reached out and yanked two large cushions off the sofa. "Here on the floor."

Damien pulled her into his arms and kissed her so thoroughly, she never knew when he unbuttoned her jacket and brushed it off her shoulders. She hardly felt the slide of silk when he slipped her camisole over her head. Her palms flattened on the hard, hot muscles of his chest as he shrugged out of his shirt.

Then he reached for her bra.

"Molly!" a deep voice called, drawing out the last syllable of her name. "Hey, where are you, kid?"

She shoved Damien away. "Oh, God! It's Ford!"

Before she could locate her camisole, he was standing in the doorway of the den, eyes flared with shock. "Molly?" Then the eyes narrowed. The fists clenched. He started forward. "Perry? What the hell—"

Damien gained his feet before Ford reached him. He caught Ford's fist in one palm, grabbed a wrist with the other and had her brother on his knees before Molly could protest. "Wait!" she squealed. "Damien! Ford! Stop this, you hear me?"

Ford rolled, catching Damien's arm in a scissor lock, one shoe braced against his chin. He broke the hold.

Molly threw herself between them, her back to Damien, her hands against Ford's chest, pushing. She squinted up at him. "Don't make me hurt you, Ford!"

He backed off, breathing like a bellows, his teeth gritted. His chin jutted toward Damien. "What's *he* doing here?"

"You have to ask?" she shouted. "What are *you* doing here?"

"We got home this morning." He threw up his hands and began to pace. "I dropped Mary off at Mama's and came to see if I could give you a hand here."

Ford shot her an accusing look. "And what do I find when I finally get here? You making out with this...this...you don't know this guy, Moll. He's—"

"About to marry your sister," Damien offered without the slightest hint of apology.

Ford's eyebrows shot up. He looked at her. "That's not true?"

"Yes, engaged," Damien answered before she could. He reached down, picked the diamond up off the floor, snatched her left hand and slid the ring onto her finger. "Officially."

"No way," Ford said, his head moving from side to side.

"Not to *my* sister, you're not!" He picked up her jacket and threw it at her. "Put that damn thing on!"

Molly clutched the blazer and gave him a playful shove, but he didn't budge. "Don't be a pill, Ford. He's your friend! What's your objection, anyway?"

"He's not a friend," Ford told her, his menacing gaze pinned on Damien. "If he told you that, he's a damned liar. I hardly know the man. Not well enough for him to be undressing my sister! We got shot together, that's *all!* But I know enough about what he does, Moll. He sheds skins like a snake. You might think you know him, but tomorrow he could be—"

"The French businessman," she declared with a clap of her hands and a suggestive wink. She leaned forward, lowered her voice and poked him in the stomach with her finger. "But nobody spreads the blarney like my Irish bartender. How 'bout a beer, bro? Celebrate with us?"

Ford struggled with his temper, stuffed his hands into his pockets and swung his glare from her to Damien and back. "We'll see what Mama has to say about this."

Molly laughed. "Tattletale! I'll have you know Mama *loves* him. She thinks he's James Bond! Now, it's great you're home, Ford, but don't you have somewhere else to be? Go get Mary, Mama and Syd. We'll be out to your place in an hour, okay?"

With a parting grimace at Damien, Ford turned to leave. Just he reached the door, Damien suggested, "Make that an hour and a half."

Ford halted for a second, then groaned and left.

Molly waited until the door closed, then cut her gaze toward her intended. "You're not friends."

"Obviously," Damien admitted, sucked in a deep breath and released it slowly, his expression hardly changing. "This was what I was most worried about from the begin-

ning, Molly. That I would never fit in with your family,"
he confided.

"Not fit in?" She laughed and plopped down onto one
of the cushions. She tugged on his hand until he joined her
on the floor. "Ford's gonna love having you around once
he gets used to the idea. I bet he likes you a lot already."

"Excuse me for not noticing," Damien said with a snort.
He reached up and rubbed his neck where Ford had
stretched it with his foot. "Are you sure I won't be coming
between you and your family, Molly?"

"You'll be as welcome as Mary was," she promised.
"But I have to ask you this, Damien. If you really didn't
know Ford all that well, why would you come when I asked
you to? Why did you do all you did for us? The only reason
I contacted you was because I thought you might do it for
Ford, because I was his sister."

"It was your laugh, I think. Those freckles on your nose.
The fire in your curls." He shrugged one bare shoulder.
"And perhaps that photo of Sydney with the garter on her
head."

Molly cleared her throat. She tried to look away, to break
the connection. Somehow she couldn't. "That's it?"

He smiled then, surely sensing he was home free. "It
seemed quite enough at the time. I really needed to see you
again."

She pursed her lips and tilted her head, still held fast by
those azure eyes. "You always say the right thing, I'll give
you that."

"Not every time," he admitted wryly. "For instance, I
have no earthly idea what I should say at the moment. But
I'd like to say again that I love you more than anything."

"Well, if you plan to nail down the local pronunciation
on that phrase, hon," Molly said slyly, "then you're not
holding your mouth quite right."

"No?" he asked, apparently waiting for her to make the

first move. "And how would you suggest I hold it, darling?"

She moved closer and slid her arms around his waist. "Against mine would be a real good start."

"I'm an exceptionally quick study," he promised, nipping her lips with his, tasting her, bringing her right back to where they were when Ford interrupted.

Molly shifted sensuously against him. "You don't really have to be all that quick. We have a whole hour and a half."

Epilogue

Damien smiled as Molly lifted her flute of champagne high above her head. The wine matched her dress of Venetian lace over satin. With that mass of coppery hair caught up in pearl clips, she was the picture of elegance. Lifting a fork in her other hand, she tapped an empty glass that sat on a nearby table. The ring of crystal silenced the laughter and conversation around them. What was she up to now?

"Fill your glasses! One more toast!" she called. "To the groom!"

"Bottoms up?" teased Winton, who was slightly tipsy. A round of laughs and applause greeted that. Everyone seemed to be in high spirits, Damien thought. Even the usually dour Michael Duvek spared a few smiles for Agent Kim Avery. That looked promising.

Only Brenda, Sydney, Ford, Mary and Winton had accompanied Molly and him to the courthouse for the brief civil ceremony, but there were nearly a hundred in attendance at the grand reception that Ford and Mary had offered to hold at her ancestral home outside Nashville.

Damien had spared no expense on the food, decorations and orchestra for this affair when he found that Molly only wanted a private wedding. A bride and her family should have fond memories of her special day.

Damien knew almost none of the guests well, other than Mitch Winton, who had agreed to act as best man. For the first time in decades, he felt unaccountably shy. He supposed that was due to the fact that tonight he was not masquerading as anyone else for a change. It seemed strange, just being himself, not hiding behind a fake persona for the purpose of gathering evidence.

To his surprise, most people seemed to like him well enough just as he was. Ford had forgiven him for appropriating Molly, though he still had a few reservations. Mary welcomed him as though he were the brother she'd never had. And, as usual, Brenda alternated between treating him as the only other adult present and chiding him as if he were a child of six. All of them were affectionate, fractious, impulsive and wonderful. Someday he meant to fit into this family. Fortunately, Molly loved him already, and that was more than he'd ever hoped for before.

"To my husband, Damien," Molly said to everyone assembled. "The man I love with all my heart, the future father of my daughter and, God willing, her brothers and sisters!" She grinned at him and pinched his cheek. "Lawyers don't blush, honey. They get in the last word!"

Noisy calls of "Hear! Hear!" echoed around the ballroom as everyone saluted with their champagne and drank the toast to him.

Damien took Molly's glass after she'd sipped and raised it again. "To the elegant and endearing Marian Olivia, who is and always will be my darling Molly. 'If ever any beauty

I did see, which I desired, and got, 'twas but a dream of thee.'''

He watched as she pressed her fingers to her lips and stifled a giggle. Poetry did that to her, he remembered with a grin. But there were tears in her eyes all the same. "I love you, Molly Perry," he said, and drank to her. Then took her hand, kissed it and then her lips.

"Did you mean that?" he asked her a few moments later when the party resumed and they were dancing. "About...other children? We've never discussed it."

"Oh, yes!" she assured him, giving his shoulder a little shake for emphasis. "Don't you want more? I *do* produce beautiful geniuses, you know. Or is that geniui?" She shrugged. "Well, pretty smart kids, anyway. Hey, look at Syd if you doubt it!"

He looked. Brenda was whirling to a waltz with the baby's arms latched around her neck. Damien was amazed at how gorgeous Sydney had grown in the few short weeks he had known her. Pink ruffles became her very well in spite of the red hair. That lovely little girl would be his daughter now, for real when the adoption was complete. A father. Who would have thought it?

Molly had just promised him a whole family of children. At that moment, he knew that despite all she had been through, all the reasons she had to mistrust men for the rest of her life, Molly trusted him completely.

She was smiling up at him when he looked at her again. "You *belong* now, Damien," she said softly.

He was unable to speak for a moment as they danced. Holding her close, feeling her move with him as though they were made for each other. And knew it was true.

* * * * *

If you enjoyed what you just read,
then we've got an offer you can't resist!

Take 2 bestselling
love stories FREE!
Plus get a FREE surprise gift!

Silhouette

INTIMATE MOMENTS™

presents a riveting 12-book continuity series:

A Year of loving dangerously

Where passion rules and nothing is what it seems...

When dishonor threatens a top-secret agency, the brave
men and women of SPEAR are prepared to risk it all as they
put their lives—and their hearts—on the line.

Available February 2001:

SOMEONE TO WATCH OVER HER
by Margaret Watson

When SPEAR agent Marcus Waters discovered Jessica Burke on a
storm-swept beach, bruised, beautiful and in need of his protection,
he never imagined that sharing close quarters with her would lead
to spiraling passion. Or that this young beauty would entrust him
not only with her life—but with her innocence. Now, as they
waited out the danger together, the world-weary agent battled
an even greater enemy to his bachelor heart: love!

*Available only from Silhouette Intimate Moments
at your favorite retail outlet.*

Silhouette®

Where love comes alive™